Triple Crown Publications pr

BO$$

This is a work of fiction. The authors have invented the characters. Any resemblance to actual persons, living or dead, is purely coincidental.

If you have purchased this book with a 'dull' or missing cover—you have possibly purchased an unauthorized or stolen book. Please immediately contact the publisher advising where, when and how you purchased this book.

Compilation and Introduction copyright © 2013 by
Triple Crown Publications
3124 Genevieve Drive
Columbus, Ohio 43219
www.TripleCrownPublications.com
Library of Congress Control Number: 2011937297
ISBN: 978-0-9832095-84

Author: LaKeisha Butler
Photography: Treagen Kier
Editor-in-Chief: Vickie Stringer
Editor: Cassandra Hayden, Jason Harrell, James W. Wiggin

Triple Crown Publications presents ...MR AND MRS BO$$

First Trade Paperback Edition Printing 2013

10 9 8 7 6 5 4 3 2 1

Printed in the United States of America

PROLOGUE

July 6, 2010

Here I was standing in a twenty-thousand-dollar Vera Wang gown on my wedding day. I was supposed to be the happiest girl in the world, because I would soon be Mrs. Boss. But the truth is I was one of the unhappiest women on earth. I wore a mean front-suit and rocked it well.

A million bitches would have loved to be in my size-seven Red Bottoms. I had everything I could possibly imagine in exchange for my pride and dignity. "You look amazing," is all I kept repeating to myself as I stood looking in the mirror. The woman I have become is not the real Maliya—I don't even know her. Although we look just alike, we're totally different. The woman that stood in this expensive, ivory-white Vera Wang loved a man more than she loved herself. This woman degraded herself in so many ways for a man that claimed he loved her, but he really didn't love anyone but himself—selfish bastard.

Now, before I met Don, I had mad-respect for myself. I loved me and couldn't no man get me to do some of the things I've done for Don, my soon-to-be husband.

But love can make a girl do some crazy shit, and when there's money involved, it's a dangerous game. *Should I leave 250 guests out there waiting to see me and Don tie the knot, or should I stay in a miserable marriage pretending to be someone I'm not?*

I scanned the room and looked at all the expensive bottles of champagne and the Neil Lane diamonds draping my neck, which Don borrowed from a jeweler just on the strength of his name. I pondered for a second, and thought about all the bitches that were waiting in line to take my spot and shine. I passed on being happy for worrying about the next bitch. *He won't never floss on me with the next bitch* ... I thought as I signaled for Debra, my make-up artist, to touch up my make-up.

OVERNIGHT CELEBRITY

CHAPTER 1

Most bitches would have called this day the best day of their life. Shit, I did; damn was I dumb. All I saw was a good-looking brotha that was caked up. His whole persona made me think of money, power and respect—which meant a *boss* in the street life. That was the type of shit a little ghetto girl from the hood, like myself, called the best day of her life. Getting approached by a boss, my very own Donnie AKA Don.

"Damn, are you slow, stupid or just deaf? Hello!" the fat greasy nigga yelled. He interrupted me as I day-dreamed about his homeboy who stood beside him and talked business on his iPhone. Boy, did he look good. He was a tall, dark-skinned cutie with nice arms, not too much muscle—just how I liked them. I've never been a fan of a muscle-bound nigga. *Damn, wouldn't I look good on his arm*, I thought, still in awe as I eyed the man of my dreams.

"Okay. Fuck this shit! Look, bitch!" Fat Ass got irri-tated. The smell of his breath brought me back to reality.

"Welcome to McDonald's. How may I help you?" I said with my nose turned up from the stench of his stank-ass breath.

"Damn, how was your vacation? Welcome back. Shit! Where did you go?"

"Sorry about that. What can I get for ya?" I apologized only because my supervisor was standing behind me, and I didn't feel like hearing the *customers are always right* bullshit.

"Give me a number two, super-size my shit, and make the drink a Diet Coke."

Why do fat people do that? Eat a whole bunch of shit, then ask for a diet drink.

"Boss, you want something?" he asked, looking to the side of him at Swagalicious, who had gotten off his phone.

"Nigga, you know I don't eat this shit. Your ass shouldn't be eating it either."

Oooh, sexy and healthy...

"You know what? I changed my mind."

Well, maybe not healthy, but he's still fine....

He gazed in at my nametag. "I want a Maliyah. What number is she?"

"Hmmm!" I was shocked, only somewhat though, because I knew I was the shit. I smiled, and showed off my million-dollar smile that would have made any nigga melt.

"Boy, you crazy." It was the only thing I could think to say. I was so lame, but I was young. I was only eighteen—had just turned eighteen as a matter of fact. I had gotten a part time gig at Micky D's to pay for my car loan, a Honda coupe sitting on some eighteen-inch rims. Yeah, I thought I was doin' it, and was in a car club and all, cruising Crenshaw Boule-vard every Sunday. The Honda was my graduation present from my parents with the agreement that if they paid the down payment, I'd pay the note. So, I was like, *Easy! My own whip!* But, really, I put my foot in my own mouth because the job was for the birds. I hated everything, from my racist-ass super-visor, who hated on me every chance she got, to the black Dickey's that didn't do my nice, round ass any justice. But if I wanted to cruise Crenshaw with my hot-in-the-ass homegirls, Kayla and Tia, I had to get my Ronald McDon-ald on.

"Nigga, are you serious? She's average!" Fat Ass said. He made a huge mistake because I went off.

"Nigga, don't let this uniform fool you, you Big-Mac-Chicken-McNugget-Quarter-Pounder-with-Cheese-eating muthafucka!"

"Bitch, I make yo' paycheck in five minutes. As a matter of fact, my chain is worth more than yo' life!"

Before I could reply and be on top of his head like hair, my supervisor signed me off my cash register and told me to follow her to her office.

Sad to say, I lost my job. But in exchange, I found the love of my life. I walked out of the McDonald's mad as hell as the voice of my supervisor replayed in my head, saying, "You're fired!"

"Fuck her! And fuck that job!" I said as I vented to myself. *Beep! Beep!* I pressed my car alarm to unlock my door. "I can't believe this shit!" I barked and hit the steering wheel. I put my head down for a brief moment. That's when I heard a tap on my window.

"Ay!"

"You sonofabitch!!" I screamed when I saw face of the fat, greasy muthafucka who caused me to lose my job. "I lost my job all because of you!"

"You didn't want to work here; it's not a good look." At this point I just stared at the muthafucka with looks to kill. I was on the verge of losing my goddamn car and here was this muthafucka I'd never seen in my life telling me I didn't want the only income I had.

"Get the fuck away from me before I lose my freedom next for killing yo' ass!"

"Oooh, I'm scared. I didn't know you could kill somebody with a spatula, you burger-flipping ho!"

"Move, Tank. You can't do nothing right. I told you to come get her—not run her off. I got this." There was my dream man again. "Hey lil'mama, I'm sorry about what happened back there. You have to excuse my friend. Did you lose your job?"

"Mmm-hmm, it's all good. Something better is out there waiting for me. Everything happens for a reason."

"Yeah, you're right about that," he said. He looked into my eyes and licked his lips. "I'm Don."

"I'm Ma—"

"Maliyah." He cut me off. "I remember from your name tag."

"You have a good memory."

"Not at all. I'm a smoker, I only remember things that are important, know what I mean? You're too fine to be working at a place like this. You should be working at somebody's office at the front desk, displaying that beautiful smile, or shit, working for me."

This nigga is a pimp. That was the first thing I thought. *And Fat-Ass is his assistant pimp.* "I'm not about to sell my pussy for nobody!" I yelled like a complete ass.

"Who said anything about selling pussy?"

"Oh, well, I..." I stuttered at a loss for words and felt as stupid as I looked.

"It's okay, Ma." He laughed and showed off his sexy-ass smile. He was so damn pretty, and I'm not talking about a pussy pretty; this nigga had pretty-boy swag. He had a low-cut fade with his waves on swim. His line-up was fresh, and his mustache and goatee neatly connected. The only thing that was missing was my pussy on his face. His lips were big and he licked them after almost every word. That day he had on some expensive-ass jeans that I couldn't pronounce, a nice shirt, and some fresh Nike's.

After I agreed to go out with him that night, we met at the W Hotel to have drinks in the lounge. I was out of pocket for meeting this nigga at a hotel for our first date, but I did. He begged for almost thirty minutes. I didn't feel like going out, especially after losing my job, but I figured I might as well have some fun, because after I told my parents about losing my job, I knew they were gonna snatch up my whip faster than the repo man.

When I strolled into the lounge, Don was sitting there looking good, just like I knew he would. Wearing some jeans, a blazer, a button-up shirt, and a fitted NY hat—the Jigga man look. His look let me know I was dealing with a grown-ass man and not the average, white-T nigga.

I wasn't looking too bad myself, for an eighteen-year-old lame. When it came to fashion, I could take some crumbs to the mall and come out with a fit that looked like I spent an end on it. The outfit I wore totaled up to about sixty dollars and some change—forty at Bakers on the stilettos and twenty on the skimpy dress I got from Forever 21.

"Hey, sexy," Don said and greeted me with a hug and kiss on my cheek.

"Hi," I said as I sat at the table.

"I just ordered a bottle of Rosé. What you drinking on, Ma?"

Rosé? I knew about all the expensive champagne from videos I watched on TV, but I had never seen a bottle close up. The girls and I ordered shit like a Long Island or an Adios Muthafucker, and Tia would have to get those, being that she was the only one who was twenty-one. *Damn, what was that drink I always wanted to try?* I thought.

"Ma, what are you drinking on?" Don asked again, as the waitress stood and waited on my slow ass.

I didn't know where it came from, but it just rolled off my tongue so naturally. "I'll have a Nuvo."

"Good choice," the woman said with a pleasant smile.

"Everybody loves that Nuvo shit. I think women just like it because it's pink and the bottle looks like perfume," Don said.

"I guess," I agreed, but the truth was I had never tasted the popular sparkling vodka whose name was ringing in the streets. After two glasses of the pink stuff, I got loose, touchy and feely. That shit snuck up on me something serious. I got so comfortable that I was wearing his NY hat on top of my wavy hair. He loved the tipsy me.

"So, Don, what do you do?"

"I'm a businessman, Ma, know wha' I mean?" Every time he ended a sentence like that, my pussy got a pulse. He sounded so sexy that I wanted to fuck him right in the lounge around all those people.

"A businessman—that must be nice."

"It is," he replied. He gently put his hand on my thigh.

"You got that businessman swag about you."

"Do I? Most people say I got that drug kingpin swag about me."

"Shit, you know every businessman had to start from somewhere." He smiled at my response and took a sip of his drink.

"Damn, you're doin' it. A businessman at your age?" I probed, hoping to learn all the basics about this man that I felt with a passion.

"How old do you think I am, Ma?"

"I'm pretty good with ages. You're about twenty-five."

He smiled before busting my bubble. "I'm thirty-five."

"Thirty-five? Damn! I was way off."

"I guess you're not as good as you thought." He smiled.

Damn, he looks hella good to be almost push-ing forty, I thought as I stared at a man who looked every bit of twenty-one.

"Shit, I guess I'm not."

"Is that gonna be a problem for you, young shawty?"

"Excuse you?" I placed my hand up against my chest, feeling fancy. "Young shawty?"

"Well, you are young; eighteen is not old."

"How did you know I was eighteen? I damn sure don't look it."

"I'm pretty good with ages," he said. He was trying to be funny. "Wait a minute. Let me correct myself—I'm pretty good at everything I do," he said, then licked his lips like LL Cool J.

Damn I can't believe he's thirty-five .... I wonder if he can eat some pussy with those lips, I thought. The man had me speechless. I was officially ready to give the nigga who was damn near my momma's age some of this young snatch.

After chitchatting for a while, he invited me up to his suite. He touched on my thigh one too many times down at the lounge. I knew what he wanted, and I wanted it, too. From the moment we stepped foot in the suite, we couldn't keep our hands off each other. He picked me up and carried me over to the bed. He then slid my thong off and spread my legs apart.

"Wait, we shouldn't be doing this," I said, a straight dummy. A nigga was about to give me some head, and I stopped him.

"Why? Don't you want to, Ma?"

"I —."

"I what?"

As I looked at him, I couldn't resist. "I want to." Once I gave him the green light, he dove face-first into my soakin' wet pussy. That was what got my young ass wide open, that fire-ass head, because he did his thing. He slurped, sucked and finger-fucked my pussy for hours. He ate my pussy until it was numb, and we didn't even fuck that night.

I stayed the night with Don and he didn't even attempt to push dick in me. We lay in bed and held each other. All I could think about was the good head that he gave me. I knew if the head was fire, the dick was gonna be blazin'. But that night, I didn't get a chance to find out.

Early the next morning, I woke up lying in bed alone. "Don!" I called his name as I scanned the room but got no answer. When I glanced at the alarm clock, I saw it was eight o'clock in the morning. Next to the clock, there was a note and a wad of cash. I grabbed the note and began to read:

Maliyah,

I had to run and handle some business. You were sleeping too good, so I didn't want to

*bother you. But now I know how you got to be
so beautiful – beauty sleep.*

*I left you a little change. Go buy yourself
something nice, and it's more where that
came from. I'll meet you back at the hotel at
eight tonight.*

Don

(Call me when you wake up: 555-5455)

I smiled, grabbed the wad of cash and counted it. My mouth dropped—it was three grand. "Oh no, he made a mistake," I said, grabbed the hotel phone, and dialed his number.

"I see you got my note," he answered.

"Yeah, I did. I'm calling about the money. You know it's three thousand, right?"

He laughed before replying, "Yeah, I know."

"Well, I was making sure."

"I like that, but one thing about me, I'll never make a mistake when it comes to my money. Now go buy something nice and meet me back there at eight."

"Okay." We both hung up. I had to call the girls and tell them about this Julia Roberts, *Pretty Woman* shit.

"Damn, what?" Kayla answered with a morning voice. She hated to get awoken from her sleep.

"Girl, guess what happened!"

"Damn, Maliyah, can it wait?"

"Hell no! Wake yo' ass up and call Tia on three-way so I won't have to tell the story twice."

"I can't stand yo' ass! Hold on!" Kayla clicked over and called Tia. When she clicked back over, Tia was on the line.

"Kayla?"

"Make it quick."

"Tia?"

"Yeah, now what's so important, Maliyah?" Tia shot.

"I got fired yesterday."

"You like it cuz you got fired," Tia said. She was trying to be funny, imitating the scene from *Friday After Next:* "You like it cuz your son's a fag." That was our movie.

"Shut up. Listen, two niggas came to my job yesterday. I got in an argument with one of them that was testing my gangsta, and I got fired. But the nigga he was with, whose name is Don, was fine as hell! So I'm leaving, and guess who meets me outside, the nigga Don!"

"Fuck! Just get to the point! I'm sleepy," Kayla barked.

"Okay! Well, the nigga asked me out last night and I met him at the W Hotel for drinks."

"You a hoe!" Tia said.

"Call it what you wanna, but I didn't give up the pussy. He ate it and that's it. Now brace yourselves the best part. I woke up this morning to a note and three thousand dollars, and the note says there's more where that came from and to go buy myself something nice."

"Hell naw, I don't believe it," Tia said in disbelief.

"He got a friend?" Kayla asked with her thirsty ass.

"I don't know, but I'll find out. That's the question yo' ass should have been asking, Tia, so you can shake Floyd Mayweather."

"We ain't talking about me. So, let's get back to this nigga. Is he gay? Is his dick small? No, I know what it is, he's burning! That nigga got AIDS. Don't fuck 'em Maliyah," Tia exclaimed.

"Girl, shut the fuck up."

"So, what are you treating your best friends to with that three thousand dollars?"

"Good question," Tia added.

"Thirsty hoes. First, I'm paying my car note up for a couple of months. Then, I gotta go to the mall to get something to wear for tonight. Don wants me to meet him back at the hotel tonight."

"Okay, but what that got to do with us?" Kayla shot.

"Shut up, bitch!" They laughed. "I'll buy ya'll something. Get ready, I'll be there in a couple of hours."

"Okay," Kayla and Tia said with excitement before hanging up their phones.

CHAPTER 2
DON/MR. BO$$

Don and Tank rolled down Crenshaw Boulevard and debated whether to drop by Burger King or Taco Bell. Sticking to the script, they rolled around to the hood's fast food joints and tried to find the perfect naïve bitch to put on the payroll of trafficking drugs.

Tank looked to the left at Don in the driver's seat of his Cadillac Escalade. "You ready, Pretty Ricky?" Tank asked. Don couldn't help but laugh, letting his high get the best of him. "Which one? We got Tiffany at Burger King and Stacy at Taco Bell. Both supervisors are already paid in full."

Don placed his hand on Tank's stomach that looked like he was every bit of seven months pregnant. "I see whoppers," Don said, pretending Tank's stomach was a crystal ball. "I see onion rings, double cheeseburgers, and a king! I see a king!"

"Fuck you," Tank said. He pushed Don's hand off his stomach.

Don pulled into the shopping center on Cren-shaw and Slauson and scanned the parking lot for Tiffany's muffler-needing Nissan. "There it is," Don said. He noticed the bucket that seemed to have four different colors of red paint. Don sprayed himself with some Versace cologne and took one last look in the mirror at his gorgeous self before he exited the car.

Tank entered the busy Burger King and Don followed behind him on his phone. Tank spotted the pretty, chocolate, petite cutie taking orders, so he made his way to her line.

"Where's Sandra?" Don asked in a low tone.

"She told me that she works every day except for Thursdays."

"Her ass better be here." And as soon as Don said that, he spotted the supervisor, Sandra. When she noticed Tank, she winked her eye at him.

After every bit of fifteen minutes, Tiffany finally made it to the end of the line. "What can I get for you?" she said with a pleasant smile, unable to take her eyes off of Don.

"I ain't ready yet! Damn!" Tank barked.

"Okay, take your time," Tiffany said. She was admiring the sexy man who clealry had swag. But after about five minutes of Tank looking at the menu, she realized her line had become ridiculously long. "Sir, do you mind stepping to the side so I can take the next person's order, and when you're ready, I'll be glad to help you?"

"Bitch! Have you lost yo' damn mind? Do you really think I'm gonna step to the side and I waited about a week to get where I'm standing now with your slow ass!" Tiffany stood behind the cash register and tried hard not to let Tank have it.

"How much are the muthafuckin' onion rings?"

C'mon, bitch, break, say something, Don said to himself as he pretended he was talking on his cellphone.

"It's up there," Tiffany said. She pointed to the menu. "You should have memorized the entire menu by now."

C'mon, you're almost there ...

"Bitch, I didn't ask you that!" Tank barked.

"I'm not going to be too many more of your bitches."

We got her!

"Bitch! You gonna be what I want you to be, you low-budget-ass bitch!"

"Yo' fat ass don't know me to judge me, with yo' Biggie Smalls-looking ass!"

"Do we have a problem?" Sandra asked.

"As a matter of fact, we do," Tank replied.

"Tiffany, what has gotten into you? I've never heard you talk like this. Let me speak to you in my office. I'm sorry about this, sir. Your meal is on us," Sandra said. Her performance was like an audition for a Hollywood role.

"It's all good. That girl needs an attitude adjustment, because I was about to call that 1-800 customer complaint number," Tank said.

Afterwards, Don approached Tiffany in the parking lot. She was officially in the works. He asked her out on a date for the following day. The naïve girl accepted his invite just like he knew she would, forgetting all about losing the job that was putting her through college.

$ $ $

Getting the name Boss didn't come easy. Don had all the nickel-and-dime drug dealers under his wing. He was the re-up kingpin that got his weight at a seriously low price from his Jamaican connection. The problem rested in getting it from the islands back to the States. That's when Don came up with the idea of recruiting bitches, not just any bitch, but a "YBNB" a young-broke-naïve-bitch.

One thing about Jamaicans, they didn't deal with too many niggas. Don was persistent with getting a Jamaican plug, so when he was introduced to Rasta Mon—getting his kilos for $13,000, saving 8 grand—he handled business just how Jamaicans liked it, smooth and with no bullshit. Their operation was orchestrated perfectly. There were no mistakes in fucking with Jamaicans. A simple mistake could cost a man his life.

Jamaicans were some horny-ass niggas who loved American women. When Don brought his idea to Rasta Mon, he was totally with it. He had only one exception: that the bitches must be different every time, unless he said otherwise. Reading between the lines, Don understood it meant if she was a really bad bitch with some Grade-A pussy, she could come more than once. Don didn't mind. Shit, he was getting some good shit and saving money. Plus, he knew how Jamaicans worked. They liked to switch-up a lot, which mean never leaving a trail.

~~ROGER THAT~~

CHAPTER 3

I exited the fitting room of a boutique store. I had on a strapless mini dress. "Ya'll like it?" I asked. I turned around to check out my ass in the full body mirror, something most women did to make sure their asses looked good back there.

"It's alright," Kayla said with a look on her face like she smelled something. She was such an obvious hater.

"It looks like something you already have," Tia said.

"I was thinking the same thing. Come on ya'll! Help me, I need to find a sexy, freaky dress—something that says I'm that bitch."

"Well, maybe you're that bitch in the wrong store," Kayla said. "Come on, Maliyah, this nigga gave you three grand. Step yo' game up, baby girl, and go buy something legit. You think he wants a lame-ass broad who wears shit that you can buy in the alley downtown?"

"Mmm-hmm, she's right," Tia said. With her good co-signing ass, she made me sick. She always went with whatever Kayla said, cheerleading-ass hoe.

"Okay, I guess I can step out my element. Besides, he said there's more where that came from, right?"

"Exactly! So get used to that good shit."

"Roger that," I said. I turned to go back in the fitting room. Then I thought of something and turned back around. "Do ya'll believe in love at first sight?"

"What?" Tia said before laughing. "If you don't take yo' fairy tale, lame ass in that dressing room."

"You really like this nigga, huh? And he didn't even hit the pussy yet. That's deep, real deep," Kayla said and laughed.

"I don't know. I ain't never experienced that shit. I don't have a man."

"Well I got a man, and love at first sight is some bullshit. You need to get to know that nigga because the same nigga you think you're in love with ... can be yo' worst enemy. Trust me, I know."

$ $ $

The girls and I hit up almost every store in the mall until I ran past the perfect dress in bebe. It was a tight-fitting, off-the-shoulder mini dress, and I rocked it with some YSL heels from Neiman Marcus. I was definitely rocking the labels. I dropped Tia off at home after she got summoned by her man, Tommy, who stayed keeping tabs on her. So it was only Kayla left with me.

It was getting close to eight o'clock, so I called Don. He answered on the second ring. When I heard his voice on the other end of the phone, my pussy got moist instantly.

"Hi," I said with an innocent but sexy voice.

"What's up, Ma?"

"Nothing. I just wanted to make sure that we're still on for eight."

"Yeah, what time is it?"

"It's seven thirty now."

"Damn, time is flying. I guess time flies when you're working."

I giggled. I loved the fact that he was a business-man.

"Where you at right now?"

"At my best friend Kayla's house." Kayla shoved me. "Don't be telling nigga's my government name." I gave her a look like, *Bitch, please, you ain't nobody.*

"Why don't you bring her to the hotel with you? I got my homeboy with me."

"Okay," I said. I didn't even ask Kayla, knew her thirsty ass was gonna be wit-it.

"I'll see you later, baby. Make it eight thirty to give me time to finish up here."

"Okay," I said. I hung up with a smile from ear to ear. "He called me "baby"."

"Oh my god, kill yo' self."

"Oh, kill myself. That's pretty fucked up to say to a friend that just put you on."

"What the fuck you talking about?"

"Don told me to bring you with me to the hotel because his homeboy is with him."

"That's what's up! I need to find something to wear. Is his homeboy cute?"

"I don't know."

"Didn't you say he was with a friend when you met him?"

"Yeah, but I don't remember what he looks like," I lied. *Oh shit ... I hope it's not the fat greasy muthafucka,* I thought.

It was eight o'clock when I pulled up at the W. Kayla was in the passenger seat putting on MAC lip gloss. "How do I look?" she asked.

"You look aight. You ain't fuckin' wit me tho'," I said, then laughed. But the truth was Kayla really looked good. She went out of her way trying to compete with me. She was always competitive. I ignored it though. My mother always told me that people who have to prove things to others—floss, in other words—are not sure of themselves and are not used to having shit. So, I let Kayla have that one. Kayla was a little more out there than me. My dress was short, but Kayla's was ridiculously short. Plus, she didn't have on any panties, and wore some of those clear, stripper stilettos. She knew she couldn't outrank me in the looks department, so she just showed off all her goodies to get the attention that she demanded.

Kayla was a year older than me. So I would have thought that she would at least know the basics to making a nigga trick off some cash on her and come back. One of the basic rules was to make a nigga work for it, never show off too much, or give up too much. He had to have something to look forward to. Shit, Mama didn't raise no fool.

When we entered the lobby of the hotel, a handsome man walked toward Kayla and me. The way that he was dressed, I could tell he was someone important. I just knew he was gonna think me and Kayla were prostitutes by the way the bitch was dressed.

"Hello, I'm Edward Smith, the hotel manager here at the W Hotel."

"Hello," I said

"Hey," Kayla spoke.

"Mrs. Boss?"

"What?"

"Mr. Donnie Boss told me his wife, Mrs. Boss, should be arriving here at eight o'clock."

"Yes, I'm Maliyah Boss." I lied through my teeth. He then snapped his fingers and hotel employees came from every direction in the lobby with pink and red roses. It was every bit of ten employees, each carrying two dozen roses. I smiled, I couldn't believe it. Kayla stood in amazement, her mouth hanging open.

"Mr. Donnie Boss is a very loyal customer, and to show our appreciation, I'll be sending up a couple of bottles of our best champagne and strawberries."

When we entered the presidential suite, Kayla was in awe, just like I was the day before. This hotel was plush. It was a lot different than places we were used to, like the Snooty Fox and other hourly rate, hole-in-the-wall motels.

"Oh, so you fancy, huh?" Kayla said as she looked at me. I walked over to the bar and made myself a drink.

"Come fix yourself a drink."

"Any Remy over there?"

"No, bitch. That's some hood shit; you want a brown paper bag and a Styrofoam cup too?"

"Oh, you funny, real funny."

"Drink some of this Patron—it tastes good with limes—until they bring our champagne up here."

"Okay, Mrs. Boss." Kayla laughed.

"Maliyah Boss, how that sound? It's got a ring to it, huh?"

Kayla shook her head from side-to-side. "Get yo' life please," Kayla said in her best Tamar Braxton voice.

An hour later, the clock read nine forty-five. "Something's up. Maybe I should call him," I said to Kayla, who was good and fucked-up over by the stereo, dancing and carrying on, having a party by herself.

"Maybe you should, because these niggas got a real nigga fucked up!" Kayla yelled over the music with a drunken slur.

$ $ $

Hanging up from Don, I smiled. This nigga had me wide-open after only a day of knowing him.   "He said he'll be here in an hour."

"You tell that nigga to bring a lot of money with him!" she shouted over the loud-ass music that was play-ing.

"Kayla, get yo' self together and don't embarrass me."

"These fuckin' niggas already embarrassed you by being late." *Oh my God, it's gonna be a long night ...* I thought as I looked over at my drunk best friend.

~~TURNING ME ON~~

CHAPTER 4
MALIYAH

Kayla and I sang along to Ms. Keri's lyrics blasting from the stereo. We were having such a good time in the luxury suite that we didn't hear Don when he walked in.

"Damnnnnn!" he said. He stooed in awe and watched us pop our asses to the beat.

"That's how ya'll feel. Shit, shawty got some ass on her!" It was Fat-Ass standing beside Don and drooling like he'd never seen a bitch with ass before.

Fuck! He brought Fat-Ass. I tried to hide the annoyed look on my face.

"Which one is Don?" Kayla questioned with her hand on her hip. Whoever said liquor could make the ugliest muthafucka look good lied, because Kayla was wasted, but she knew an ugly muthafucka when she saw one.

"You look good," Don said and sized me up.

"Thank you. You don't look too bad yo' self," I said. I looked in Tank's direction. "Tank, this is my best friend, Kayla. Kayla, this is Tank."

"What's up?" Tank asked and nodded his head.

"Not a damn thing!" Kayla's ignorant ass said with an attitude. "Maliyah, let me talk to you! Now!" Once we made it in the room, she shut the door behind us and I burst in laughter. "Bitch, you knew his homeboy was fat and ugly!"

I was laughing so hard I couldn't say shit. "Okay, bitch, you wanna laugh and be stupid! Take me home right muthafuckin now, because you tried me!"

"Come on, Kayla, ugly niggas need love, too. Shit, you sleepin' on Fat Ass, but he might have some bread. Get this nigga's money and stop trippin'. But on the real, I didn't know Don was gonna bring him."

"Mmm-hmm" Kayla stood with her arms crossed, mad as hell. If looks could kill, I would have been a dead bitch.

"Are you gonna stay? *Please.* I really like this nigga. I'll buy you some more shoes," I begged and bribed the bitch. That's why it wasn't good to do that double-dating shit. It could easily fuck up what I had going on.

"What you gonna do, bitch?"

"I'ma stay, but the first time this pregnant man touches me, I'ma set it off in this muthafucka." Kayla meant just that. She was the complete opposite of me. I was a little more reserved, and more on the quiet side, compared to the rowdy, loud, neck-poppin' diva. She didn't bite her tongue for anyone and she said whatever was on her mind. Very blunt and didn't give a flying fuck. Shit, and if the price was right, she was giving up the pussy with no second thoughts.

"Bet," I said. I went in for a hug, but got stopped in my tracks.

"Don't touch me."

When we walked back to the living room of the suite, Don and Tank were sitting on the couch. Both niggas bobbed their heads and rapped along to Young Jezzy's CD, *The Recession.*

Tank was breaking down some sticky, green weed. He looked over at Kayla and me. "One of y'all got nails? Cut this Swisher Sweet and empty it." Kayla's chain-smoking ass didn't waste no time. She walked the short distance to the couch and got the grape Swisher from Tank. I wasn't a weed smoker, but that night I started. I'd hit a blunt before, but weed just wasn't my thing. I was more of a drinker. Kayla peer pressured me occasionally, and I'd hit the blunt once so she'd shut the fuck up.

After smoking two blunts, I was high as fuck. Don and I were vibin. I was sitting on his lap and giving him a lap dance. Usher was blasting out the stereo talking about making love in a club, I was ready to make love in this hotel, staring into the eyes of Don as he held my waist. I twirled my hips and practically fucked him with clothes on. He smelled so good. The Armani cologne he was wearing could have made any bitch weak, not to mention the fresh line-up he had. His White Sox's fitted hat was pulled up just enough for me to see that his it.

The mood was right. But there was one thing that was just fucking everything off: Kayla and Tank arguing like little-ass kids. I knew it was coming. To be honest, I was surprised they'd lasted so long

"Nigga, you will never be able to hit this!"

"You ain't my type anyway. The only thing you got going for yo' self is a little bit of ass, and to keep it on the real, you kinda look like a man. That's the reason I kept staring at yo' neck."

"Fuck you! Don't take it out on me because you haven't seen yo' dick in a minute. It's not my fault. Blame yo' stomach, you big-belly muthafucka!"

Kayla and Tank went back and forth for thirty more minutes, until Tank got fed up and knew he wasn't gonna get any pussy out of Kayla. He called it a night and left the hotel.

Now three was a crowd, but that didn't stop Don and me. We started fucking in the bedroom while Kayla listened to music in the living room. Don had me in a doggy-style position as he pounded every bit of his twelve-inch dick inside of me. "Oooooohhhhh! Don! Wait," I moaned. I nearly ran up the wall to get away. My little pussy wasn't used to a grown piece of meat, but I took it all in like a big girl. Gripping my ass cheeks, Don took it slow with long strokes. I kept hearing him say, "Shit! Damn!" He loved my tight pussy.

"Am I hurting you?" he asked, which made me like him even more.

"No."

"You sure?"

"Yes!"

"Okay." He went deeper and I got louder.

"Ahhhhh!!!!!"

"Ma, tell me if it hurts."

"Okay … it feels good, keep going." Don flipped me over and I shocked his ass when I grabbed his dick and put it in my mouth. I had to take charge. Fuck that, I wasn't gonna lie there and be a dead fuck. I was gonna put in some work. I deep-throated his long manhood and gagged on the mouthful. It was so embarrassing, but I knew sucking a big dick was a mental thing. I cupped his balls with his spare hand as he pulled my head closer. All I kept hearing was Tia's voice in my head: *"Shake them dice and roll 'em."* Something she used to say, trying to be funny about sucking a nigga's nut sack. I went farther down and put his nuts in my mouth. I started sucking on them. That shit drove him wild.

"Oooooh! Yeah!" he moaned. That made me roll my tongue across his nuts even faster. "Oh shit!" he shouted and pushed my head away, trying to warn me of what was coming next. He shot thick cum all over my neck and titties, giving me a pearl necklace.

I knew Kayla was on the other side of the door, rubbing her clit and getting off by listening to Don and me fuck. Next thing I knew, Kayla was standing in the room calling my name.

"Maliyah?" She was hoping to see something with her nasty ass. What could have been that important for her to interrupt the freakiness that was going down? *She wants a piece!* I thought.

"Oh, I'm sorry," Kayla said with a dumb look on her face.

"What you want?" I asked.

"I don't see no more weed. Ask Don if he got some more."

"Why don't you ask him since you already in here?" I was glad we were under the covers—so she couldn't see Don's dick

"Yeah, hold up. Here I come," Don said. "Ma, you wanna smoke too? We might as well smoke, then come back and finish where we left off."

"Naw, I'm gonna jump in the shower real quick."

$ $ $

Don sat on the couch staring at Kayla's ass while her back was turned toward the stereo.

"Oh, this my song," Kayla said. She threw her hands in the air and worked her hips. Kayla knew what she was doing. She had one of those stupid asses, so plump people would've thought it was fake. She turned around and noticed the lust in Don's eyes as he sized her up.

"You like what you see, huh?" Don nodded his head without saying a word. "Yeah, Maliyah's pretty, but she don't have one of these," Kayla said. She made her ass bounce one cheek at a time. Don's dick was rock hard as he fucked Kayla with his eyes.

"Look, this can be fast and easy. I'm not wearing no panties," she said and pulled up her dress revealing her pretty shaved pussy.

"Ooooh!" Don said, grabbing his dick. "I still hear the shower running. Bend over," he said, stood up, and dropped his jeans to his ankles. Kayla did as told.

"C'mon, I can take it, boo."

He walked the short distance, entering Kayla from behind, with no rubber. "Ooooh, you got some bomb-ass-pussy," he said in a low tone.

"I like it rough, Don. I'm not her—give it to me hard." The kinky Kayla turned him on. He shoved hard dick inside her pussy as deep as it would go. "Ooooh, that feels good .... Ahhhh!!!!!"

"Shhhh!" he shut her up, listening to see if the shower was still running. "Be quiet. I can't hear if you're loud," he said. He fucked her watching his dick thrusting in and out her pussy. As he looked at her *Nicki Minaj* ass from behind, he wanted to bust. When he didn't hear the shower running anymore, he went harder and harder, ramming his dick inside of her at a fast pace. "Oooh! I'm about to bust. Show me that you're down, sexy. Prove it to me and swallow my cum. Can you keep a secret?"

"Mmm-hmm," she answered. That's when he exited Kayla's pussy and entered her mouth. She swallowed every bit of Don's thick, creamy cum. "Yo' secret is safe with me," she said, wiped her mouth, then winked her eye.

$ $ $

The next morning, I sat up in bed scanning the room. For a minute, I forgot where I was. I had a terrible hangover. My head was pounding and I had the cotton mouth, thirsty as hell. When I entered the bathroom, a hotel robe hung on the hook right by the door. *This the type of shit I'm talking about ... that fancy Boss shit ...* I said to myself as I put on the expensive robe that felt good against my skin.

Entering the living room, I saw Kayla and Don sitting on the couch. "Hey, sleepyhead," Kayla said.

"Hey Ma, you was sleeping too good. I didn't want to bother you."

"I know, I forgot where I was for a minute. I was in a good sleep."

"Yo' mouth was wide open; you were snoring and drooling," Don joked.

"For real?" I was embarrassed because I knew I snored when I was drunk.

"Nah, I'm just fucking wit ya." He laughed and showed his gorgeous smile.

"I'm surprised, Kayla. You haven't been in there trying to wake me up."

"Don been doing good entertaining me," she smiled.

"I'm impressed because this one is very hard to please, let alone entertain."

"My mom always told me I'm a people person. I have this way about me that grows on people. For some strange reason, people like to have me in their presence."

"She's right, sounds like a very wise women," I said.

"You will meet her one day." I smiled.

"I got a terrible headache."

"You don't have any Tylenol?" Don asked.

"What? You don't carry Tylenol in your purse? What type of bitch are you?" Kayla went into her purse, pulled out a bottle of pills, and tried to show me up.

"A bitch that don't roll around with a medicine cabinet in my purse," I shot back. Fucking bitch.

"Ya'll ladies wanna have breakfast before we hit it?" Don asked. I loved how smoothly he changed the subject.

"Sure, why not?" I said. I looked over at Kayla, who was nodding her head in agreement.

After Don ordered room service, we ate everything in the breakfast column on the menu, smoked a blunt, and got so high we ate again. I sat next to Don. I waited on him by fixing his plate and giving him refills on his orange juice every time his glass got low. I did all the shit I used to see my mom do for my father.

$ $ $

Don couldn't help but to think that Maliyah would be a bad bitch if he could snatch her up and mold her into the bitch he wanted her to be. She was an eighteen-year old, innocent dummy with no street sense. He could tell her parents had sheltered her and were very strict.

Unlike Kayla. He could tell she'd been around the block a time or two. A nigga had already had his way with

Kayla. She was out there and the complete opposite of what Don was looking for.

$ $ $

     Don hopped in the shower, then put on his clothes. Kayla and I had already gotten dressed. He took his chain and diamond watch off the nightstand. I came up behind him, removed the chain from his hand, and put it on his neck. My little young ass was cold. I'd never been in a serious relationship, but I was determined to make Don wanna wife me.

     "Here." Don went in his pocket, pulled out a wad of cash and gave it to me.

     "What is this?"

     "Money."

     "I know that... I meant to say, what you want me to do with it?"

     "Give it back."

     Give it back! I handed the money back to him. He then gave it right back to me.

     "Sometimes it's best to say nothing and wait to be told."

     "Okay."

     "I can teach you some things, Ma," he said before he gave me a kiss. "Go spoil yourself a little." I stood mesmerized in this love spell that Don had put on me.

When Don left the room, he walked over to Kayla, who was still sitting on the couch. Going into his other pocket, he handed her five, one hundred-dollar bills. I stood watching from the bedroom door, stuck. Shit, I wasn't no hater; it just wasn't in my bloodline to hate. But I found it a little odd that Don was giving Kayla some money.

"Thanks, Don," Kayla said with a smile. "Mali-yah, Don is such a sweetheart."

"I know, isn't he?"

"This is for my sorry-ass homeboy. I should have known better than to bring that weirdo. Now ya'll go tear the mall down. Maliyah, check in with me at eight," he said, and then walked toward the door.

"Okay." I smiled, loving the fact that this nigga was trying to keep tabs on me.

Kayla looked at me with a smile on her face. "Bitch, you make me sick. Yo' ass done came up."

"I know, and this nigga is turning me on by the second," I said to Kayla, smiling from ear to ear.

$ $ $

"Maliyah, what are all these flowers doing in my living room like somebody died?" my annoying-ass daddy yelled, coming in from work to all the flow-ers that Don bought me. "Maliyah, come here right now!" I ran down the stairs wearing my McDonald's uniform that I hadn't yet returned in exchange for my last small-ass paycheck. I made my parents think I still worked. Shit, there was no need to tell them since I paid my car note up for a couple of months. Until I got up enough nerve to tell them, I was Tommy from *Martin,* frontin' like I had a job.

When I entered the living room, my big, beer-belly daddy was standing in the middle of the floor surrounded by pink and red roses. "Where did these come from?"

"How you know they mine and not Mommy's?"

"Because if Karen gets some roses like this up in here, I know they came from me, and I don't recall ordering no flowers."

*Shit! Why didn't I get rid of these ... Think, Maliyah ... * I stood dumbfounded. I really wasn't ever a good liar. That's why I always went to Kayla to help me come up with a good lie.

"I'm waiting, young lady," Daddy said. He, tapped his foot and waited for some answers.

"Tia's boyfriend beat her up again and he felt bad about it. He thought she was over here, so he sent them here." *Damn I'm getting good. I've definitely been around Kayla too long...*

"Mmm-hmm," he said, raising his eyebrow. "Well, get them out of my living room."

"Daddy, what am I supposed to do with them? It's too many to go in my room. They'll be in the way."

"I don't care what you do wit' em, but you better get' em out my living room, not now, but right now!"

"Yes, Daddy."

Now if that would have been my momma, she would have seen right through the bullshit. That lady, Karen, she didn't play. Thank God she was at work. I was my daddy's heart. He would turn the cheek on a lot of shit, and whenever my momma started trippin' on me, I ran straight to daddy because I was the only child and daddy's little girl.

~~CHOPPED AND SCREWED~~

CHAPTER 5
DON/MR. BO$$

Don sat behind his cherry wood desk, talked on the phone to his Jamaican connect, and puffed on a Cuban cigar.

Knock! "Boss!" The maid Maria entered his office. Don waved his hand with a frown on his face. She got the hint that he was busy.

"Sorry ... Sorry, Boss," Maria apologized as she exited the office in a hurry.

"Rasta Mon, check with the half-breed American girl from the West," Don talked code into the phone. That meant he could pick up the money that Don owed him from the Western Union. Jamaicans were very careful how they did things, and Don was just as paranoid. The Feds loved to catch a nigga slippin' on the phone, so for that reason, he had to watch what he said while on the phone.

Once Don hung up the phone with Rasta, he dialed Maliyah's number.

"Hello."

"What's good, Ma?"

"Nothing much. I'm at Kayla's house right now chillin."

"I wanna see you later on tonight."

"Okay, boo."

"Oh yeah, and bring some luggage, we're going on a trip."

"A trip?"

"Yeah, as in vacation."

"I don't know, Don. I gotta ask—" She paused, catching herself. She didn't want Don to know that she had to ask for her parents' permission to do certain things.

"What?"

"Never mind. Where we going?"

"I'll talk to you about that later on tonight. I'll call you around seven to give you the directions to my house."

"Alright, I'll talk to you then." When Maliyah hung up the phone, she was excited, but she couldn't help but wonder what her parents would think about her going on a vacation with a man who was twice her age.

"Shit, I'm grown!" Maliyah said. She sat on Kayla's bed and tried to pump herself up.

"Short-bus shawty, why you in here talking to yo' self?" Kayla said and she came back into the room.

"Fuck you." Maliyah shot Kayla the finger. "I just got off the phone with Don and he's taking me on a romantic vacation."

Kayla's facial expression changed instantly. Her nose all of sudden was turned up, being a hater in disguise.

"What?" Maliyah questioned. She easily felt the vibe.

"I didn't say nothing."

"Why you looking like you smell shit?"

"Because you're dumb, dawg. You know damn well Ms. Karen is not letting you go on a vacation with Don! And yo' daddy?" Kayla burst into laughter. "Girl, please," she continued.

"Wait, hold up. Wasn't you just telling me not too long ago to grow the fuck up. I feel you, Kayla, I'm a grown-ass woman, dawg! I am eighteen years-old, you feel me?"

Kayla laughed at a hyped Maliyah. "You grown now? Okay, if you say so," she said while laughing. The truth was Kayla was jealous of her best friend. She had been trying to stumble across a nigga like Don for a minute, and to see Maliyah with this man that was out of her element pissed her off. Kayla wanted Don for herself, and if it took coming between a friendship to get him, so be it. But, she wasn't stopping until Don was hers.

Maliyah pulled up to the gate of Don's San Fernando Valley estate in complete awe. "This is like a whole neighborhood," she said to herself.

"How may I help you?" A woman came on the intercom and scared the shit out of Maliyah.

"I'm here to see Don," she said to the pleasant-voiced woman. She looked up at the surveillance camera that was facing her car.

"And what is your name, Ma'am?"

Damn is this nigga a movie star or something? "Maliyah."

"Yes, Maliyah, he's expecting you."

Then you should have known it was me, asking all them goddamn questions like I'm trying to get in the White House to see Barack Obama, she said under her breath as the double gates opened.

"Follow the road, ma'am," the woman instruct-ed. Maliyah drove up the road, which led to a man-sion. Her mouth dropped. "He's rich!" she said to herself. From her Honda, to the Slauson Swap Meet outfit she was wear-ing, she felt out of place on a million-dollar property.

She pulled up to very large house that sat off in the cut. She exited the car to see Tank dressed in all black. "C'mon, Boss is waiting for you."

"Okay, you saw me coming? Damn!"

"Well, you ain't no senior citizen, are you?"

"Kiss my senior-citizen ass." As she walked through the double doors, she couldn't believe how beautiful Don's place was. A crystal chandelier hung from the ceiling like something she had seen in a movie. When they entered the office, Don was sitting behind his desk and looking through a cloud of smoke, looking like a true boss.

"What's good, baby girl?" He greeted Maliyah and noticed the discomfort in her face.

"Hey."

"Are you okay?"

"Yeah, I'm straight."

"Well have a seat with yo' fine ass." She blush-ed and walked the short distance to the chair that sat in the front of his desk. Don was so suave. Little did he know it was his presence that made her nervous. Where he lived was a surprise, but then again, any man that passed out money like Don had been doing since they met had to be sitting on a nice piece of change. She was more caught off guard than anything; it had finally sunk in that she was fucking with a man of money and power. Maliyah sat in the comfortable, very expensive Herman Miller leather chair.

"Look. Ma, lemme just get right to the point. I need your help."

"What's up, Don? Whatever it is, I got you."

That was all the sneaky, manipulating man needed to hear to take advantage of the young girl who wanted to prove herself to him. "Maliyah, baby girl, you're the only person that I trust enough to go meet a friend of mine to pick up something very important."

"Okay and where exactly am I going?"

"Overseas to Jamaica."

"Overseas! Jamaica!"

"Do you have to yell?"

"I'm sorry, but Don, I've never been out of California, let alone over somebody's seas."

"Baby girl, you don't have nothing to worry about. Do you trust me?"

Without hesitation, she nodded.

"As long as you fuckin' with me, I will protect you. I will never let anything happen to you, Ma." Maliyah sat soakin' up all the bullshit he was spittin' like a sponge. "My employee, Jasmine, will take you to get a passport tomorrow, and all you have to do is get this package for me and come right back."

"So, you're not going with me?"

He shook his head. "I got business to handle here."

"I'm going by myself? I thought you said earlier we were going on a vacation together?"

"I was gonna go at first, but something came up," he lied.   "You are a big girl, right?"

Smacking her lips, she said with an attitude, "I'm a grown-ass woman!"

"Okay, easy now. Let's keep it cute," he said, laughing. He knew he had pissed the young, neck- poppin' diva off. "My sexy, grown-ass woman gonna take that trip for daddy? It's easy, Ma. I'm looking for a woman that can make moves with me, you know wha' I mean? I need a ride-or-die chick on my team who's gonna meet me halfway. You know, complement my swag."

Maliyah sat contemplating. *I got to show this nigga that I'm all that he needs ... I'm that ride-or-die chick ... I can't let this nigga slip away.*

"So, what's up, Ma, you down?" he asked with a smile. And that alone did it, his sexy smile that made her melt every time he showed his pearly white's.

"I'll be your ride-or-die chick."

"So that's a yes?"

"It will always be yes. There's no other bitch that can do what I won't do. You wanna know why?"

"Why Ma?"

"Because there's nothing that I won't do." Mal-iyah came with some game for that ass, beating Don at his own game. He'd been laying game on women for a min- ute, and this was the first time someone ever hit him with something that made him think. *This youngin' is the truth ... he thought.*

"Mmmm, if that's the truth. I might be looking at my Mrs.," he said, licked his lips and rubbed his chin. "Jasmine!" he yelled into an intercom that sat near his desk.

A couple of seconds later, a tall, mahogany-colored woman entered the office. "What is it?" she asked with an attitude as if Don was working for her.

"This is Maliyah. Take care of her."

"That's it?"

He nodded his head as he puffed on his cigar. Jasmine then looked at Maliyah from head to toe, shaking her head.

What the fuck is her problem? ... Maliyah thought to herself.

"Follow me," Jasmine said. Jasmine was a Jamaican and very gorgeous. She could have been a model— she was just that bad. But her attitude was jacked up. She had a slight accent with a body of a goddess. Tiny waist and ass for days, with long curly hair that hung down her back.

After walking up a circular staircase in the beautiful mansion, Jasmine went into a room that had the stench of strong weed, burning incense, and Jamaican music blasting out of the speakers. Jasmine bobbed her head and snapped her fingers while getting her weed tray that sat on the top of the dresser. "Get comfortable while I smoke mi ganja."

Maliyah took a seat on the bed. She had a head-ache all of a sudden. She didn't know if it was from the loud music, or the smell of the burning incense.

"Do you smoke a little ganja?"

Maliyah lied and shook her head. She knew Ja-maicans smoked that high-power weed that would not only get her high, but have an American speaking their language. She was good on the ganja.

"So, you a friend of Donnie?" Jasmine questioned, firing up a fat-ass Bob Marley blunt.

"Yeah."

"Mmm, you like him, don't ya' now?" Jasmine continued, asking twenty-one questions.

Knock! Knock!

"Come in!"

"Jasmine, Boss told me to come ask you if you needed me anymore tonight because he's letting me off early."

"Yeah, get mi someting to drink and hurry up!"

"Puta," Maria mumbled.

"What ya say? I'll have ya in de unemployment line, keep it up, ya hear?"

"Pinche puta pendeja!" Maria shot.

"What you say? I can't understand that shit!"

Maria rolled her eyes and turned her attention to

Maliyah. "Hello, would you like something to drink as well?"

"No, thank you."

"I see some people have manners. Pretty girl, Bonita. Burger King, Taco Bell, McDonald's?"

"No thank you," Maliyah replied, not catching on. Maria stood looking at Maliyah like she was crazy.

"Get out of here! And go get mi goddamn ice tea!" Jasmine yelled.

Maria jumped, startled. "Puta!" she shot, walk-ing toward the door.

"No, you the puta, Bumbaclot. I know what that mean. About to fuck shit up, fuckin' Mexican!"

Maliyah laughed, still not catching on.

"I don't know why he hired that Mexican," Jas-mine said. She sized Maliyah up from head to toe. "You're about five-six and like a seven in shoes?"

"Damn, you good. That's my size. How did you know?"

Because I deal with dumb hoes like you all day, every day, Jasmine said to herself as she walked to the walk-in closet that looked like a Jamaican banner. Every-thing in the closet was green, black, yellow and red.

"When you get to Jamaica, you have to look like ya' on vacation or a Jamaican. I will pack yo' luggage with something from this closet. Everything on this side is your size". Now have fun at mi Jamaican boutique," Jasmine said in between hits from the packed blunt.

It didn't dawn on Maliyah that all the clothes were different sizes and with tags still on every garment. The huge closet was the size of Maliyah's bedroom. Maliyah was in materialistic heaven, trying on different outfits as Jasmine sat on the bed in deep thought—*This girl is beautiful, I know Don is fuckin' her...*

CHAPTER 6
MALIYAH

The next day I walked into the house from get-ting my passport with Jasmine. My head was pound-ing from the loud-ass Jamaican music that Jasmine was bumping from the time I got in her Range Rover Sport, to the time she pulled back up at my house and dropped me off. Damn, I was happy to be home. I went straight to the shower to wash my hair. I felt like I still smelled like Jas-mine's ganja, and the last thing I needed was for my par-ents to come home and smell weed. I wouldn't never hear the end of that shit.

After getting out the shower, I turned the TV to my favorite sit-com, *Gilfriends*—BET played reruns all the time. I'd probably seen almost every episode. I loved this fuckin' show, especially Lynn's crazy ass. She reminded me of Kayla. I grabbed my new iPhone, compliments of Don. The iPhone looked so much better than my beat-up Nokia. I hit up Kayla since the hoe had been blowing up my goddamn phone all day, like she was fucking me. I forwarded her calls to voicemail because I wasn't ready to tell her about the trip that was nothing like the romantic vacation I was throwing up in her face the day before. But I'd eventually tell her because that was my dawg, I didn't keep shit from my besties.

"Where the hell you been!" Kayla answered the phone, bumping her gums like I'd pushed dick in her the night before.

"Damn, what's up and how you doing, too?"

"Whateva. You talk to Tia?"

"No, why?"

"Tommy done beat her ass again. We been calling you all day, so you can go pick her up."

"Aww shit! I'll call you right back." I hung up in Kayla's face without waiting for a goodbye. When I dialed Tia's number, her phone rang once, then went straight to voicemail.

"This T, holla at yo' girl." *Beep!*

"Hey, Tia this yo' bestie. Holla at me when you get this." Once I left a message, I hit Kayla back up.

"What she say?" Kayla said, instead of a hello.

"She didn't answer. You know her and Tommy's ass too busy having some make-up sex. He done apologized by now. So what exactly happened this time?"

"Man, that nigga is straight off the looney van. She was over her mom's house and this nigga swore up and down she was with a nigga because when he called her, he heard the cable guy in the background. You know how Tina be having those fight night parties.

Mmm-hmm. She got some new high-definition boxes and the Comcast guy asked a question and that nigga Tommy lost it. When she got home he went upside her head."

"Kay, how long have we been telling Tia to leave that nigga Tommy?"

"I know, but she's still our girl."

"Yeah, but, c'mon, how many times you gonna let a nigga crack yo' cranium before you leave his ass?"

"We gonna talk to her."

"We'll be talking until we're blue in the face."

"However long it takes until she gets it," Kayla said, feeling Tia's pain, knowing how it felt to be in an abusive relationship.

I'd never been in an abusive relationship before, so I wouldn't know. Sometimes I thought it was because I grew up with a father in my home. My father always told me it was okay to be alone, and never settle for less. My girls came from a single parent home. They didn't have a father figure to warn them about men like my dad did with me.

Tia has been with Tommy for three years. She loved her some him. There was nothing Kayla and I could say to make her have a change of heart. Tommy got a hold of Tia when she was a senior in high school. Tia was just happy to be had, and be able to say she had an older man. Every young broad loved to brag about having a sugar daddy. But like my boy, Steve Harvey, said, "All sugar daddies ain't sweet."

I truly hoped the dangerously-in-love Tia got it one day. Because getting yo' ass whipped by a nigga was not a good look.

~~DOWN CHICK~~

CHAPTER 7
MALIYAH

Arriving at the LAX airport, I had bubble guts. I was so nervous, I had been shittin' all morning. I was hopping out of Jasmine's Range Rover with my luggage in tow. My flight was for one o'clock, but I arrived an hour early to give me enough time to get through security.

"Call mi when you get wit mi Uncle Rasta."

"Okay, I will," I said, and walked toward the entrance with my heart beating out of my chest.

Jasmine hooked my wardrobe up; she had me looking like I was from the islands. I walked through the airport looking like a Jamaican hoochie that just got through auditioning for a Sean Paul video. It seemed like everybody in the airport was looking at me.

Calm down, Maliyah, you're just paranoid. I tried to calm myself down. Standing in line at security, I could not be still, I was looking over my shoulders and fidgeting. *Why did I let Don talk me into this? I am so stupid! Fuck! I'm going to jail.*

"Take your shoes off, ma'am!" the airport flashlight cop yelled, and took me out of my deep thought. I wanted to let the hoe have it for yelling at me, but I was too nervous to talk shit. Instead, I did as told, and placed my wedge heels inside of the bucket as the bitch who took her job too seriously went up and down my body with a wand. The muthafucka started beeping and I almost pissed on myself. I just knew I was going down. "Ma'am, do you have change in your pockets?"

"Yes," I stuttered, scared straight.

"Didn't you read the sign? Step to the side and empty your pockets. Next!"

Once I emptied my pockets, the woman was occupied with someone else in the busy airport. She told her co-worker I was good and to let me through. I felt at ease that I passed the hardest part, getting through security. I felt my phone vibrating in my pocket. When I glanced at the screen, Kayla's picture flashed across it. "Sorry, Kay, I'll have to hit you back," I said, and put the phone inside my straw purse.

I made my way to Gate 12. When I boarded Caribbean Airlines, my face was dripping sweat. I sat in my seat and took a deep breath, then looked around at all the other passengers, trying to see if anyone looked like the Feds. I wouldn't have ever been as nervous as I was if I didn't have almost a hundred thousand dollars taped to my body. Something Don and Jasmine left out until the last minute. I had to do it for my boo; don't no nigga want no scary-ass bitch. He needed me, so I had to take this trip for daddy. Shit, if I didn't do it he would have found another bitch that would have been glad to. If I wanted to get Don to wife me, I had to be his down-ass chick. *Damn, where's Kayla with that peer pressure shit when you need her?* I thought. All I needed was a blunt, and boy would I be good. My nerves were bad. I was looking for the Feds, sweating, and even worked up a headache.

"Excuse me, ma'am."

I jumped. *Oh my God, I knew I was going down! I don't want to go to jail.* When I finally opened my eyes, I was looking in the face of flight attendant, who I just knew was a federal agent.

"Are you okay?" she asked with concern in her voice.

"Yes, I just get a little nervous when I fly," I said, cleaning that shit up good.

"It's gonna be a piece of cake; you don't have anything to worry about. But if you can be so kind. please put your carry-on luggage up here because this is someone's seat."

"Certainly, I am so sorry."

"It's okay. Would you like something to drink?"

"A water would be fine."

"Okay, a water coming up," she said before she walked off.

I was a fuckin' mess, jumping every time someone spoke to me. This shit wasn't for me. *God, please get me back home safe ... I want my mommy and daddy...* I closed my eyes and prayed, scared to death. It amazed me how I thought I was grown, but as soon as I felt like I got myself in some deep shit, the first thing I would say was, "I want my mommy and daddy." One thing I would always remember, something my mother told me on my eighteenth birthday: "As a young adult, there's gonna be some things that mommy and daddy aren't gonna be able to get you out of, so that's why you have to be a responsible young lady." I could imagine this was one of the things momma was talking about.

When I opened my eyes from the power nap I got in, I looked to the left of me to see a fine-ass man. *Damn, where you come from?* As I wiped the drool from the sides of my mouth, I wondered if my mouth had been open the whole time I was asleep.

"Hi," he greeted me with a smile.

"Hey," I said, sitting up in the seat, trying to get comfortable with all this damn money on me. This man was handsome. He was clean-cut and smelling good. The only thing—he was light-skinned. I did not like red meat.

"Did you sleep good?"

"Mmm-hmm," I dismissively said, trying to avoid conversation. I had to piss after drinking that bottle of water, and the fact that I was nervous and this man kept talking to me didn't help at all. I didn't want to take that chance of going to the bathroom and the money coming off, so I stayed parked in my seat, shaking my leg and rocking back and forth, trying to hold on as long as I could.

"The best sleep is on a flight. People don't think that, though."

"Yeah." *Damn, will he get the hint? Shut up already ...*

"I'm sorry, I'm just talking." *No shit!*

"I could at least introduce myself. I'm Terry," he continued. I thought he was gonna shut the fuck up, but since he didn't, it would have been rude not to introduce myself as well.

"I'm Maliyah."

"That's a beautiful name. I can tell you was born in the islands, but raised in the states."

I played along, not wanting to give my life story to the cute stranger. "Yeah, I come every now and then to visit family," I said, lying my ass off.

"My family and I vacation in Jamaica once a year. I'm always the slow one—they're already there. But they understand that school comes first with me."

"School?" I nodded my head, impressed. "What school do you attend?"

"University of Southern California."

"I always wanted to go to USC, but I'm starting at El Camino Community College for a semester or two."

"Yeah, I know where that is. In Torrance, right?"

"Yep."

"Prepare for landing," the flight attendant said. She walked past and made sure everyone was wearing their seat belts.

$ $ $

"It was nice talking to you, Maliyah. Time fa' mi to go, Mon," he said with a fake Jamaican accent.

I laughed. "Yeah, it was nice meeting you, Terry. Enjoy your vacation."

"Oh yeah, I'm about to act a fool on this island. And good luck to you at El Camino," he said, grabbing his carry-on luggage. He kept staring at me like he was unsure of something, or it could have been that I was gorgeous, too. He then reached in his pocket and pulled out a small piece of paper. "Can I leave this with you?" he asked so respectfully, and so not my type of brotha. He was the type of nigga my parents would have loved, lame. I grabbed the small piece of paper that had his number on it. "Call me sometime. We can talk about school. You know."

"School? That's the best you could come up with?"

"Well, I'm just saying," he said, smiling. He was a cutie, but I wasn't looking. I was content with Don. He would be cool for one of the girls. Well, Kayla because Tia was not leaving Ike Turner no time soon.   Once Terry left the airport, I sat on a bench and prayed as I waited impatiently for my ride to Uncle Rasta's.

$ $ $

Don and Kayla walked out the Mercedes Benz dealership, from checking on Maliyah's brand-new, custom Benz that Don would be surprising her with when she made it back from overseas.

"They supposed to be delivering the car at one o'clock tomorrow. The company is West Coast Customs," Don said into his iPhone, talking to Maria.

Maria was the maid that buzzed visitors in the gate onto the property during the day. She was not to let anyone through the gates without Don's permission first. So Don called his maid to let her know what to expect for the following day. Maria was good about things like that. If she didn't have an okay beforehand, the person on the other side of the gate was shit-out-of-luck, because she was one loyal senorita who took her job very seriously.

Ending the call, Don and Kayla jumped into his BMW and smashed off. "Thanks, Ma, for coming up here with me. If anyone should know what Maliyah likes, it should be you, her best friend."

"No problem. That pink and black is gonna be killing 'em. I know my girl, she's gonna love that."

Don felt the vibration of his cell phone and glanced at the screen. "It's Tank, just the nigga I've been waiting for," he said before answering.

"Ugh Tank" Kayla said under her breath.

"Call ATL," Don said, talking in code. "Two baked chickens," he continued into the phone before hanging up. Kayla sat in the passenger seat listening. Kayla wasn't as naïve and lame as Don thought she was. From past experience of fucking with drug dealers, she knew all the street codes, so when Don said, "Baked Chickens," she knew that meant two birds of dope.

I knew this nigga was pushing weight. Maliyah don't know no better, Kayla thought.

"That was yo' boy," Don teased, laughing.

"Don't make me throw up in my mouth."

"Tank ain't yo' type, shawty?" he asked, already knowing the answer, trying to be funny.

"Hell naw, look at me, and look at him. My type is you," she said, placing her hand on his lap and giving him a sexy wink. Kayla sat in the passenger seat with a hot pussy, staring over at Don with nothing but fucking on her mind.

"The other night wasn't enough for you, was it?"

"Not at all," she replied, taking off her knock-off Dior shades that were sitting on her nose, so Don could see the lust in her eyes. Putting them in her Dooney & Burke purse, she knew what time it was. She unfastened Don's jeans and put her face in his lap. Kayla took twelve inches of hard dick in her mouth and didn't gag once. Don took heed to that, knowing the nineteen year-old freak had to have a lot of practice not to gag on a piece of wood his size. She bobbed her head up and down as Don held back a nut that was trying to let loose in Kayla's mouth.

"Ahh ... you gonna ... Ahhh ... be my lil' secret freak?" he asked in between moans. People were blowing their horns as Kayla was blowing dick. Don swerved through traffic doing eighty-five in a sixty-five zone, trying to get his rocks off. Kayla had a technique for that ass, she made sure his dick was covered in her saliva, then she went up and down jacked him off, while she caressed his nut sack with her spare hand. She knew what she was doing, damn near causing Don to wreck his whip from the head she was giving him.

The quick dick-sucking session wasn't enough for the two. Don and Kayla made a detour to the Travel Lodge Hotel by the LAX airport. It went down in room 102. Kayla didn't have no shame in her game, as she put her back into it. She brought her "A" game, trying to show up Maliyah. On top of Don, she rode the shit out of him.

Don enjoyed the ride with his eyes closed. With a hand full of Kayla's ass, he gripped her cheeks and pulled himself deep inside the pussy.

"Ooooh Don ...," Kayla moaned. Don flipped her over, changing positions. He wasn't there to make love, he was there to get a nut off, so all the moaning and name-calling he tried to avoid. Ramming his dick inside with long, hard strokes, he bit down on his bottom lip as he beat the pussy up. He gave it to her just how she liked it, rough.

With a sore kitty and different walk, Kayla went into the hotel office to turn in the key. Don watched as she sashayed in the office. *Yeah, this pipe got her walking funny,* he said to himself, looking over to the left at the Denny's restaurant that was connected to the hotel and smelling the good food that had the whole parking lot lit up. He was ready to eat after busting that hell'va nut.

"Okay, you ready, baby?" Kayla said, walking up to Don.

"You hungry?"

"Shit, you know I am. All that riding I worked up an appetite." The moment Kayla and Don strolled in Denny's, the hostess, a dark, chocolate woman who was wearing some thick-ass glasses, eye-fucked Don, not acknowledging Kayla at all.

"Hi ... Welcome to Denny's," she said, grabbing one menu. "Follow me, sir," she continued.

"Um ... Excuse you! I know you see me standing here! You got all them eyes and still can't see," Kayla shot at the glasses-wearing hostess.

"I see you, but I just didn't think a man this fine would have a woman of your caliber on his arm," she shot back, grabbing another menu. "Y'all don't even look like y'all could live on the same block," she continued, and walked them to a table.

Damn I don't even need Tank ... Do we have us one? ... Don thought with his mind always on a million.

"Wait a minute, let me make sure you even talking to me because you looking everywhere with that eye that's cocked like a pistol. You fucked-up-eye-having bitch! Now excuse me, while me and my fine-ass man enjoy our meal. As a matter of fact, let me talk to your supervisor, yo' ass won't never put a little Shug Avery pee in my shit."

Her man? ... Don thought. That was the reason he didn't want to get fuckin' and making love mixed up, knowing young bitches tended to make something out of nothing.

"You're looking at the supervisor. How may I help you?" the woman said with a devilish grin.

Fuck! She's out, I thought we had one ... Don thought, always looking for a victim.

Kayla had a dumb look on her face, as the woman walked off. "Don, I'm not eating here. She's gonna do something to my food."

"You should've shut the hell up then, but I'm getting me something. If that would have been Mali-yah, she would have handled that shit back there like a lady, like you should have. Get it together, especially when you out with a boss like me."

This nigga done tried me ... Maliyah ain't shit! Kayla thought. *He's right, Maliyah probably wouldn't never made a scene. But I ain't her and she's not me.* "Well, Don, I'm sorry I'm not Ma—"

"I knew that voice sound familiar." Tia walked up to the booth where Kayla and Don were sitting. Kayla's mouth dropped, shocked to see her best friend standing in front of her. She had the caught-up, I'm-up-to-no-good look displayed on her face.

"I told Tommy that was you. Who the hell was you cursing out? I'm ready, where she at?" Tia said playfully as she took off her earrings. "You know I got yo' back."

"Yeah, way in the back. That four-eye hoe been gone."

"Who's yo' friend?"

"Oh him?"

"Yeah, him, crazy."

"Oh, I'm tripping. Tia, this is ... um ... Donald! Yeah Donald."

Don looked over at Kayla like she was crazy. "Hello," he greeted Tia. "What's up man?"

Then Tommy, playing along, greeted him with a head nod. "Hi, Kayla."

"Tommy," Kayla said, nonchalantly rolling her eyes. She wasn't really a fan of Tommy, because he stayed putting hands on her girl. But she kept it cordial by speaking when Tia brought him around. Tia loved to tell Kayla and Maliyah to stay out of her business but she stayed involving them. So, they did nothing but listen when she came around crying about him going upside her head, and hoped she would wake up and move on one day.

"Have you talked to Maliyah?" When Tia said Maliyah's name, Don choked on the water that he was drinking.

"You okay?" Kayla asked as she patted him on the back.

"I swallowed a piece of ice. I'm good."

"Yeah I talked to her earlier," Kayla lied, knowing she was overseas, still mad about it for having to find out from Don instead of her best friend.

"I gotta call her crazy ass. Alright, I'm about to get out of here, Kay. I'm full as fuck. I'll call you later."

"Okay, talk to you later, T."

"Oh, I'm sorry. It was nice meeting you, Donald."

"It was nice meeting y'all too." When Tia and Tommy exited Denny's, Don looked over at Kayla, who had her head down chanting "*Fuck! Fuck! Fuck!*" and repeatedly hitting herself in the head.

"Who was that? And how does she know Maliyah?"

"That's our best friend, Tia."

"Please tell me you're lying." Kayla shook her head.

"Well, good you was on point telling her my name was Donald," Don said, looking like he didn't have a care in the world.

Shit, if he's not worried about it... I'm not about to stress myself out.

$ $ $

Once Tia and Tommy made it to the car, Tommy looked over to Tia sitting in the passenger seat. "Did you see the look on Kayla's face when you asked her about that nigga she's with? And the fact that she had to think about the dude's name, that wasn't strange to you?"

"Not really baby, Kayla's strange. It's no telling with Kayla. Donald is probably somebody else's man. That's her get down. That's why her ass ain't got a man of her own, too busy borrowing someone else's," Tia said, not knowing this time the man Kayla was borrowing hit too close to home, being their best friend's man.

"And you call someone like that your best friend, have you ever heard, you are the company that you keep?"

"That's not true, especially when it comes to me and the girls' love lives," Tia said as she stared out the window.

Whap! It was the sound of Tommy's manly hand landing on Tia's left cheek. "What I say? You calling me a liar?" Tommy shouted. "Like I said, bitch! You're the company that you keep—if she's a hoe, you a hoe! Tia, I know you're fucking around on me!" he yelled, foaming at the mouth. *Whap!* "Fuckin' whore!" He slapped the shit out of her again.

Tia held her face with tears running down her cheeks. "No ... Tommy, I'm not calling you a liar. I love you, baby, you're the only one for me," she sobbed.

"Now look at what you made me do. If you wouldn't talk back, I wouldn't have to put hands on you. Damn, Tia!" he said, doing what he did best, turning the tables.

"I'm sorry, Tommy."

"Now you talking like you got some sense, because you are one sorry-ass bitch!" Tia sat in silence, scared to say anything and not wanting to piss off the abusive man with whom she was dangerously in love.

$ $ $

Jasmine knelt down on the ground. "Be still. Shit!" Jasmine said as she taped kilos of dope to Tiffany's body, starting from Tiffany's butt, working herself up to her stomach and breasts. Tiffany was petite, all bones, but after Jasmine got through with her, she looked like a full-figured woman. Once Jasmine was done duct-taping the drugs onto a pair of long johns she grabbed the Lady Footlocker bag, she pulled out the extra-large Nike jogging suit that she purchased earlier that day. "Put this on," Jasmine said, handing the jogging suit to Tiffany.

Tiffany did as told, putting on the pink and white Nike suit that was about three sizes bigger than her normal size.

"Do you feel comfortable?"

"Is that a trick question? What do you think?"

"No, what's gonna be the trick question is when you get in the airport and drugs fall off of ya', and a federal agent ask ya' if you know drugs is falling off ya' body, smart-ass. Now jump up and down." Tiffany did as told. "It's on tight."

Jasmine probably could have done this shit in her sleep. She was very good at what she did. That was the reason Don kept the rude Jamaican diva on the lingo. After watching her family overseas, she learned how to do it herself. Didn't nobody tape the weight like Jasmine. She'd probably done almost two hundred bitches for Don. She was what kept Don's business booming.

"Tank!" Jasmine yelled out the bathroom door of the motel. Don didn't feel safe bringing all the bitches he would get to traffic dope to his crib—just in case they got popped, they wouldn't know where to send the Feds when the Feds started putting deals on the table. A few seconds later, Tank entered the bathroom.

"You look like Big Momma." He burst into laughter. "Remember when Martin dressed up like that fat-ass woman in that movie *Big Momma's House*?" He continued laughing, as Jasmine joined in.

Tiffany stood, not finding a damn thing funny. *Why in the world would I let Terry talk me into this... He owes me big time ...,* Tiffany thought.

"Nah, all bullshit aside. You should land in ATL at about five o'clock. When you get to the Hilton, call Danny Boy and he's gonna meet you there. He's gonna do the same thing to you that Jasmine just did."

"I thought I was only taking one trip."

"Slow down Little Engine That Couldn't. Just listen: Danny-Boy is gonna tape money to yo' little stick frame. It should be fifty thousand dollars."

"Fifty thousand dollars!"

"Tell everybody—damn," Tank said.

"Fifty thousand dollars is not gonna fit on my body."

"You will be surprised. These nigga's know what they're doing."

"Okay, where's Don?" Tiffany asked.

"He should be on his way."

"I wanna see him before I leave," Tiffany said, doing a complete 360 in the mirror, making sure the drugs she wore weren't visible.

Jasmine sighed as she rolled her eyes, looking Tiffany up and down.

"Let me call this nigga," Tank said and left the bathroom. Dialing Don's number, Tank glanced at the time on his diamond Cartier as he waited on Don to answer the phone. After the phone rang forever, Don finally answered.

"Yo."

"Pretty Ricky, where you at? The bitch is getting scared. Come show yo' face."

"Nigga stop calling me that shit. I'm five minutes away."

"Aight," Tank said before slamming his phone shut.

Thirty minutes later Don was strolling into the motel. "There goes my babbbbbyyyy," Tiffany sang her favorite Usher song. The moment Tiffany laid eyes on Don, the swagged-out boss, all of her fright disappeared.

"Hey, Ma," Don said before he tongued Tiffany down.

"I wish you would've gotten here before all this shit was taped to me. I could have got a quickie before I left," she whispered into Don's ear. But just like most young women, there was no such thing as whispering, because Jasmine and Tank heard every-thing that was said.

"I had to make some moves, Ma, but damn you should have hit a nigga up. I would have made time to hit that good ol' pussy."

"It's cool, boo. I got something to look forward to when I get back."

Jasmine stood to her feet. "We don't have time for this shit! It's nine forty-five," she said, raising her voice. She grabbed her Fendi purse and threw it across her shoulder. "You fuckin' piece of shit Don! I'm tired of you, Bumbaclots!"

"What's wrong, Jas?" Tiffany asked, looking at the Jamaican diva in action.

"That's not mi name, it's Jasmine! Bring yo' ass before your baby be taking you to de airport!"

"You a psycho bitch," Tank said, shaking his head. Don stood looking across the room at Jasmine. He was about two seconds from whipping her ass for going against the grain and fuckin' with his bread.

"You a liar, Bumbaclot!"

"What's going on, Don baby?" Tiffany asked.

"Tell her!"

Don walked the short distance to where Jasmine was standing. He then grabbed her by the neck and slammed her up against the wall. "Hoe, don't try me. Go take Tiffany to the airport before I—" He moved in closer to whisper in her ear, "Beat yo' ass up in here. Now this is a warning and you know I don't do too many of those. Keep trying me, bitch, and I'll cancel yo' ass like Nino."

A tear fell down Jasmine's cheek as she brought her tone down a notch. "Come on, Tiffany, let's go before we miss your flight."

Tiffany looked at Jasmine, confused, then back at Don. She walked the short distance to where Don was standing and gave him a kiss. As she began to walk away, Don grabbed her by the hand, pulled her back into him, and gave her another kiss as he felt her up. With her eyes closed and on cloud nine, Don looked over at Jasmine and winked his eye while his tongue danced with Tiffany's in a passionate kiss. Jasmine wiped her tears from her eyes, stormed out of the motel and slammed the door behind her.

"Hurry Ma, before that crazy-ass Jamaican bitch leave you."

"Okay, but I'm only doing this for you because I'm a ride-or-die chick for my man."

"That's why you're the only person I trust enough to take this important trip for daddy," he said. The same rehearsed bullshit that he used on every other crash dummy.

"I love you, Don," Tiffany said before she walked out the door.

"I love—" Once the door closed he continued, "I love me too."

"Nigga, that's why I call you Pretty Ricky," Tank shot, laughing.

"Fuck you, nigga."

"You need to do something about Jasmine. That bitch is getting stupid."

"I know."

"Boss, all you got to do is say the word," Tank assured.

~~MY CHICK BAD~~

CHAPTER 8
MALIYAH

It was about a quarter after seven when I touched down at LAX. The flight on the way back wasn't nearly as bad as on the way there. The money that was taped to my body could have played a big part. When I approached baggage claim, I was instructed to go to the conveyor belt to pick up my luggage. I waited to see the luggage that Rasta gave me. The one he gave me looked identical to the one I brought, but I didn't ask no questions. Remembering what Don had told me: *It's better to say nothing and wait to be told.* So I did just that, and plus I was scared to death of the dread-wearing Jamaicans. But I did know it was something very important that belonged to Don.

Once I saw the luggage, I grabbed it and went on my way.

"Excuse me, ma'am!" I heard a voice behind me. I walked faster. "Mrs. Boss! Maliyah!" I had to turn around because whoever it was, they knew my future government name.

A man dressed all in black and looking like Will Smith when he played in the movie, *Men In Black,* stood before me holding a card that said, "MRS. BOSS," across it. How did I miss that? "Hello, I'm Andrew. I was sent by Donnie to be your chauffeur and take you wherever you want to go." he said and grabbed my luggage.

"How did you know I was Maliyah?"

"A light-skinned girl with long hair and a body of a goddess. Do you see any of that around us?" the man asked. "Oh yeah, I can't forget the red, yellow, and green I was told that you'd be wearing."

I looked down at my outfit and smiled. "I gotta take this shit off."

Once my new chauffeur and me made it out-side, a black limo was parked right in the front of the door. Andrew opened the door and when I got in the back, there was a Yorkie puppy sitting on the seat next to a colorful Louis Vuitton bag.

"Arf ... Arf ...,"she barked. She was gorgeous.

"Surprise, Mrs. Boss. Donnie told me to give you the puppy and tell you to read the card inside the purse."

"Thanks, Andrew."

He closed the door, and I didn't waste no time. I grabbed the purse searching for the card. Once I spotted the card, I began to read:

Baby girl,

*You looked out for daddy, so now it's my
turn to look out for you. Sit back and enjoy
the ride and your new puppy.*

Ask Andrew for your next surprise.

Don

"Andrew!" I tapped on the window that separated the driver from the passenger in the plush limo.

"You ready for your next surprise?" he asked, already knowing what I wanted.

"Yes," I said, and smiled like a child on Christmas morning.

"Right away, ma'am," he said with a grin. "Sit back and enjoy the ride."

I hated surprises. I was anxious. My palms started to sweat and I couldn't be still in the seat, wondering where in the hell this man was taking me. I glanced out the window, looking at all the people staring at the luxury limousine that I was rolling in, wondering who was the famous person sitting behind the tinted windows, and it was just plain ol' me.

Andrew merged onto the 405 Freeway. I felt high maintenance sitting next to my Yorkie.

"Are you okay?" Andrew asked.

"Mm-hmm."

"It's some Chardonnay and bottled water back there. Help yourself."

"Okay." I said, all into my new puppy.

"Did you think of a name yet?"

"What?" I said, annoyed.

"For the puppy. Did you think of a name yet?"

"No, not yet. She's so beautiful. I always wanted a puppy." I took the puppy into my arms, hugging her like an expensive designer bag that I always wanted. I was a handbag freak and never could afford the type of over-sized boss-bitch bags that I always wanted to tote around. Then out of nowhere it came to me. "Prada!" I said, "Her name is Prada."

"That's different. But why Prada?"

"Because I've always wanted a Prada bag."

"Okay," he said, looking at me through the rear-view mirror like my name was Kelly Bundy.

Forty minutes later, we pulled up to Saks Fifth Avenue in Beverly Hills. Andrew exited the limo carrying a black brief case. When he opened my door, he said, "Happy Birthday! From Donnie to you." I gave him a look like he was crazy, because it was the middle of October and my birthday was in July.

"But Andrew it's not my birthday."

"Donnie told me every day is his woman's birthday. Now open it."

I did as told, opened the brief case and my mouth dropped. "What in the world does he want me to do with all of this?" I shouted on busy Wilshire Boulevard as all the white folks that were walking by cut their eyes at me. I was appalled when my eyes saw stacks of crispy big faces.

"I'm glad you asked. Read this." Andrew went into his pocket and pulled out a piece of paper. He gave it to me and I began to read:

> *Baby Girl, go tear the mall down. Don't stop until it's all gone. When you leave Saks, ask Andrew for your next surprise.*
>
> *Don*

Tears had formed in my eyelids. I had to blink a couple of times to keep from crying. I began to think like Tia: *Something had to be wrong with this nigga 'cause he just too good to be true.*

"Where am I gonna put all this money? We can't just take it in there like this, somebody might rob us."

"Rob us, you playing right?" Andrew said before laughing. "You're gonna hand the brief case to me, and I wish a nigga would." Andrew got gangsta, pulling back his blazer jacket and revealing the pistol that sat on his waist.

I grabbed Prada and put her into my Louis Vuitton carrier. I looked like a ghetto-fabulous version of Paris Hilton. I got my fancy runway strut on, hitting the entrance and feeling like new money. I guess I looked like money too, because sales associates came from every direction. It was such a wonderful feeling to have them following me around for commission sales, instead of following me because they thought I was trying to steal something. *I can get used to this ...* is all I thought.

$ $ $

Kayla scrubbed her pink and white Reebok classics with a tooth brush, trying to get them as close to looking new as possible. That day she rocked Baby Phat. Everything about Kayla said low-budget, but to herself, she was project-chic. The denim skirt she wore complimented her ass and barely covered her pink G-string, which would give easy access to what little it covered. She sprayed underneath her skirt with some Bath and Body Works. Her braids were freshly dipped in hot water and baby oil, giving them a shine to match her shiny lips.

As she looked in the mirror, the picture of her and Maliyah at a Lil Wayne concert caught her attention. She reminisced for a second about the two wet-behind-the-ear little hoes that were so happy to be at their first concert, and a Lil Wayne one at that. Maliyah was lucky enough to get called on the stage by Lil Wayne when he and his Young Money crew performed the song, *Every Girl*. Kayla was mad as hell, just like almost every other girl in the crowd, because that girl on the stage wasn't her. Kayla would have given anything to be in Maliyah's shoes that night.

With Maliyah fresh on the brain, that reminded Kayla to make the call that she'd been putting off all day. She grabbed her Boost mobile phone as she sat on the bed and smacked on a piece of bubble gum. She scrolled through her contacts down to Maliyah's job number. Once the McDonald's employee answered with an up-beat voice, Kayla said into the phone, "May I speak to Misty?"

"She stepped out for a second. She should be back in about fifteen minutes. Would you like her voice mail?"

"Perfect!" Kayla said with a devilish grin.

You have reached Misty Fernandez, supervisor. Please leave a message with your name and number and I'll return your call at my earliest convenience.

"Ms. Fernandez, this is Maliyah. I want to come and pick up my check and return my uniform. When you get this message, can you please give me a call? If I'm not at home, it's okay to speak to my emergency contact, Karen, my mother."

Kayla hung up the phone and hoped it was true when people said she and Maliyah sounded just alike on the phone. When she heard a car horn, she peeked out the window and saw that the yellow cab she'd been wait-ing on forever had finally arrived. Kayla ran down the stairs and past her aunt, who was on the couch buck-naked with a man Kayla had never seen before. That let her know he was the chosen one to help out with the rent this mouth.

Kayla slammed the door purposely to wake the trick. "Check out time!" she yelled into the window before walking off toward the cab.

$ $ $

"It's Kayla! For the um-teenth time. Damn!"

"Ma'am I heard you before, but I don't think you heard me. Mr. Boss is not expecting you, so I can't let you through."

"Open this goddamn gate!" Kayla yelled at Maria through the intercom. After five minutes of wait-ing, the double gates finally opened for the yellow cab to enter. "About fuckin' time," Kayla said. She sat back in the seat and put on her shades.

"This sure is a nice piece of property," the cab driver said in awe.

"Yeah, yeah, yeah, how much I owe you?"

The cab driver looked at the meter, then at Kayla through the rear-view mirror. "Twenty-four dollars."

"Damn!" Kayla said, sucking her teeth and go-ing into her knock-off Fendi wallet.

"Well shit, ten of that came from just waiting to get through the gates. The meter doesn't stop run-ning. Gas is high as giraffe pussy," the cab driver explained.

"Whateva! I know you're trying to work me, but it's all good. This twenty-four dollars ain't shit. In a couple months, you can come back and work for me. You see him right there?" Kayla pointed at Don standing in front of his home.

"Yeah, and what?"

"That's my man and this is his estate. It's called the power of the pussy, now let that sink in." Kayla tossed him the twenty-four dollars and got out of the car.

Kayla sashayed up the walkway toward Don, right past the black Benz that had a big red bow on top of it. Being the hater that she was, she turned up her nose, pissed off at the fact that she just got out of a cab that had the smell of old bus seats, and there was a luxury car parked for Maliyah—who already had a whip—while she was stuck toe-nailing it. But she stuck to the script and let it ride, knowing her time to shine was right around the corner ... if she played her cards right.

Don stood with his arms crossed and watched as Kayla walked toward him. He took the time to give her something he liked to call a "Swagger Check," starting with the Reeboks. They were the first thing he noticed when she exited the cab. He hated a tennis shoe broad, being the old-school kat he was—a woman should always dress like a woman. Growing up, he could never recall seeing his mother in tennis shoes. It was always skirts, dresses and heels. There were exceptions for working out in the gym or if there was rain in the forecast, but with rain, a nice pair of boots was the appropriate diva attire. So, the Reeboks had to go.

"Hey, hon," Kayla said, going in for a kiss.

Don backed away, dodging the kiss. "What the fuck are you doing poppin' up at my shit?" Don barked, regretting the day he showed Kayla where he lived when they were car shopping for Maliyah. It wasn't until he pulled onto his property that he realized he had fucked up.

"I—," Kayla stood at a loss for words, shocked at how Don was coming at her.

"We ain't like that, Ma. I'm just fucking you! All this poppin' up at my shit is not what's up. Don't start this fatal attraction type of shit!"

"You got me twisted, nigga!" Kayla said, standing in her project-chick pose with one hand on her hip as she went in neck-poppin' mode.

"No, you got me twisted," Don said, and grabbed her by the neck and pushed her up against the Benz. "I don't know what type of niggas you fucked wit in the past, but I don't tolerate the bullshit. All that talking to me any kind of way, I ain't the one!" Still holding her by the neck with a tight grip, he looked her in the eyes, knowing Kayla was the type of wild bitch he had to tame by putting a little fear in her heart, or she was gonna get out of control and cause problems. "Do you understand?"

She nodded her head in agreement.

"Okay, now that we got that out the way, why did you pop up here?" he asked, releasing her neck.

She grabbed her neck now that it was free of Don's hands. "I—I wanted to be here to see the look on Maliyah's face when she sees her new whip that I helped you pick out."

"That's more like it."

Kayla walked the short distance to her cell phone, which had fallen out of her hand when Don ruffed her up, and bent over to pick it up. Eyeing the mocha-colored chick, Don licked his lips. Kayla's body was on point and she kept some shiny shit, like baby oil, on her chocolate-colored skin that gave it this smooth, creamy fudge look. She was bad, Don couldn't deny that. But her body definitely outweighed her looks. Only if he could put Kayla's ass on Maliyah's peanut butter, thick frame to match her good looks, he would have been alright.

Don was pissed off at her, but he couldn't resist the short denim skirt that was fitting so tight on her body that it looked like it was painted on. Lost in the trance her ass put him in every time he eyed that donk, sitting way up her back, his dick was soon poking through his True's. He thought about taking Kayla into the house to knock her down. Glancing at the time on his black diamond-faced watch, he saw he had ample time to push dick in Kayla before Andrew arrived with Maliyah. Then he thought about Jasmine, whom he had to put hands on for getting out of line with the Tiffany situation. Although she was asleep, he still didn't want to go that route. He looked over at the Benz. *Fuck it ...,* he said to himself.

"Get in." He opened the back door to Maliyah's Benz. Wasting no time, Kayla did as told and hopped into the luxurious whip that had the new car smell. Don sat back, as Kayla caught on quick and unbuckled his jeans. He put his head back on the leather headrest while Kayla did her thing. When Kayla looked up at Don with a mouth full she noticed he had his eyes closed, moaning in complete bliss. She slid off her hot-pink G-string and kicked it underneath the seat.

Maria stood on the balcony watching the freakiness go down like if she was watching a porno. The windshield was not heavily tinted, so she had a good view. The way Don had Kayla bent over in the backseat, while he hit it from behind. Maria found herself getting hot and bothered. "Oh, mio," she said fanning herself with her hand. After three years of working for Don, she finally knew how he got those beautiful women to risk their lives for him. It was the power of the pipe.

~~KNOCK YOU DOWN~~

Chapter 9

Keri Hilson's "Knock You Down" crooned out of the speakers as Tia sat on the couch puffing on a Black & Mild Wine. She was taking advantage of smoking while Tommy wasn't home. He would say smoking wasn't lady-like, but it was okay for her to smoke weed with him.

Tia bobbed her head as she sang along with Ms. Keri in between hits from the cigar. The words Keri sang in this song were the truth. Tia sat on the couch feeling like Keri was talking directly to her. She definitely was feeling her pain. Tommy had knocked her down in so many ways, but it wasn't that easy for her to get back up. Tia loved the man hard. She never thought she would love a man the way she loved Tommy.

A tear fell down her cheek as her mind reflected on the past, how she and Tommy used to be before his jail bid. After his trip upstate, he returned a totally differ-ent person. Tia blamed it on the new lifestyle he was forced to live. Tommy was used to living above his means, so when the time came to have to choose be-tween the dope game or his freedom, with the help of Tia talking some sense in him, he chose to do the right thing. Seeing the same niggas that used to look up to him now stunt on him in the dope game, it didn't sit well with the fallen kingpin.

Tommy was on his third strike. Something as little as stealing a piece of bubble gum out of the store could put him back in jail for the rest of his life.

Tia jumped when she heard the phone ring, almost dropping the lit cigar in her lap. She took off running toward the phone, scared to death, knowing if she didn't answer before the third ring, Tommy would put hands on her.

"Hello," she answered, out of breath on the fourth ring, waiting to hear Tommy start screaming on the other end of the phone and accusing her of cheating on him with another man.

"Is Tommy there?"

Thank you, God ..., Tia said to herself, glad that it wasn't Tommy checking up on her.

"No, may I ask who's calling?"

"This is Tank. Tell him to call me ASAP."

"Okay, does he have your number?"

"He should, but just in case, it's 555-5555."

"Okay, Tank, I'll tell him as soon as he comes in." Tia hung up the phone with a gut feeling that Tank was bad news.

By the time Tia was finished cooking tacos—Tommy's favorite—and cleaning the house, he was walking through the front door.

"Tacos again!" he said, throwing his jacket on the floor. He then kicked his shoes off and left them by the door.

"So much for cooking and cleaning," Tia mumbled.

Tia entered the living room to find Tommy sprawled out on the couch with the sofa pillows thrown all over the floor. Tommy already had her Febreeze-fresh living room smelling like stale corn chips from his stank-ass feet.

"Baby, somebody name Tank called you today."

"Aww, that's my boy I use to run wit."

I knew it ... Tia thought.

Tommy got up from the couch and went for the cordless phone. "He knows this guy that's opening a transportation company, and he needs a couple of drivers. He's gonna hook me up."

"Transporting what, Tommy?" Tia questioned, standing in front of him with her hand on her hip.

"Shit I don't know, and at this point I don't give a damn. I need some fuckin' money. I can't keep living like this."

"Living like what Tommy? We're good!"

"Tia, don't question me. I'm a grown-ass man. Step back before I reach out and touch you. Then you're gonna be walking around with a long mouth, crying and shit."

"Sorry for caring," Tia said and tossed the small piece of paper with Tank's number on it at Tommy before exiting the living room.

Trying to help a fallen kingpin that didn't know nothing but selling dope was useless. Tia stood in front of the stove and burned tortillas, too deep in thought to remember to turn them in the hot cooking oil: *He's right, he's a grown-ass man that knows the consequences and repercussions of getting back in the dope game ....*

Tia thought about all the weekends she ran back and forth to the prison for visits. Then there were the sunny summer days that she passed up going out with the girls, sat at home instead as if she were on lockdown, and waited on Tommy's collect call to come through. *Been there, done that for three years straight. I'm just gonna sit back and watch as he fucks himself with no lubrication.... Fuckin' dummy...*

"Girl, what the fuck you burning up in there?" Tommy yelled from the living room, bringing Tia back to reality.

"Oh shit!" she said, looking down in the skillet to a burnt tortilla.

Triple Crown Publications presents ... MR AND MRS BO$$

~~MY CHICK BAD PT 2~~

CHAPTER 10
MALIYAH

I was flooded in shopping bags. Sixty thousand dollars worth of designer shit. I finally got the Prada bag I'd always wanted, with some Prada shades to match. I even threw a couple of trendy treats in for my dawgs.

The last surprise was a spa treatment in Beverly Hills at a popular spot for the rich and famous. The spa parlor was connected to a hair salon. The deluxe treatment included a full body massage, a mani and pedi, and hair appointment. I wasn't too fond of just anybody doing my hair—I'd been going to the same salon since the ninth grade. My stylist, Rhonda, was the truth when it came to doing some hair, and she had some growing hands. I started off with sew-in weaves, but after a while, I started rocking my own shit. It was just as long as the eighteen-inch Hollywood hair I was getting sewed in my head. If Rhonda knew I was about to sit in somebody else's styling chair, that bitch would act a donkey.

After I got pampered—I had to come out of that Jamaican-hoochie ensemble—I figured the least I could do was get my sexy on for my man to show him my appreciation.

"Damn!" Andrew said as I walked out of the spa parlor wearing a dangerously tight, electric blue BCBG Max Azria mini-dress that I picked up from the store. My 36-24-36 body measurements complimented the dress, which stuck to my body. I set it off with a pair of Jimmy Choo boots. The lady that did my hair did her thing. I got some bangs cut in a baby-doll style with honey blonde highlights. I was definitely hot. The new and improved me was one bad bitch.

Andrew stood by the limo, lost in a trance from the moment he laid eyes on me. I was flattered at first, but after a while I started to feel a little uncomfortable. By Andrew's reaction to my new look, I knew Don was gonna love it.

I put an extra switch into my hips as I stomped the pavement in my expensive Jimmy Choo's. When I approached the limo, I heard a man calling Lauren London. So I started looking around because I loved the actress that played New New in the movie *ATL.* When I looked over at the man, he was holding a camera and looking at me yelling, "Over here Lauren, you're so beautiful!" Mistaking me for the gorgeous, deep-dimple actress? My dumb ass just waved, played along, and enjoyed the few seconds of fame. I mean, I had an audience—from the onlookers who thought I was someone famous to the drooling men. But my biggest fan by far had to be Andrew because this nigga was in a daze. From that day forward, my ego got as big as P. Diddy's. Don had created a monster with the fancy makeover and shopping spree.

"Are you gonna open the door?" I said, snap-ping Andrew out of it.

"Oh, my bad." He opened the door. The ride back to Don's was long. I kept looking at myself in the mirror and taking pictures of myself on my phone. I was happy with my makeover. I couldn't wait to show the girls.

The vibration of my cell phone scared the shit out of me. When I glanced at the screen, it was my mom. She had been blowing me up the whole time I was getting my hair done, but I didn't feel like hearing her mouth. I hadn't been home in three days. I could hear her bullshit now: *You think you're grown, but you ain't grown.* I wasn't for none of her shit. I was feeling good and looking good. It was time to go see my man that I missed so much.

Pulling to the gate of Don's estate, I hurriedly grabbed my purse and pulled out my Chanel lip gloss. I applied a little to get my lips dick-sucking-ready. Then I sprayed my body with some Heat perfume by Beyoncé.

After Andrew drove a mile or so, finally getting to the mansion that sat off in the cut, I noticed a black Mercedes-Benz with a huge red bow on top of it parked in front of the home. Fuck waiting for Andrew to open my door. I hopped out and ran over to the black Benz with black, color-coated rims and pink brake pads. I walked around the car with my hands over my mouth in awe. This was my vision. This was my dream car. I remember seeing this exact car in a magazine and telling the girls that I was gonna get me one of them one day, and them hoes gave me a look like, "Bitch, please" when I said it.

"You like it?" Don asked, walking out of the house. I was so into the car I didn't even see Kayla walk out behind him.

"Goddamn! Baby girl, you look good."

"Thank you! Thank you! Thank you!" I kissed him repeatedly, thanking him not for the compliment, but for my new car.

"Where's the ... the ..."

"Keys?" he said, pulling the car keys out of his pocket and hanging them in the air. I jumped, trying to get them.

"Gimme! ... Gimme!" I reached with a huge smile.

"You want these?" he teased.

"Stop playing, Don. Give 'em here."

He handed them over and I started screaming, "Ahhhh! I got a Benz!" Taking off to the car, I made it to the driver's door, stuck-on-stupid on how to use the unusual luxury key.

"Don, come here."

"It's the key, huh, Ma?" he said while walking the short distance over to the car and showing me how to use the key. I glanced over at the house and thought my eyes were playing tricks on me. Kayla stood on the porch with her arms crossed. The vibe she was giving instantly told me she was hatin' or it could have been that she was mad at me for not telling her about my solo trip overseas.

"Kayla! You told Don about the magazine and the puppy. You was behind it all, huh?"

"Yeah, thank Kayla, she picked out everything. I couldn't do it alone. And she's very good at keeping a secret. I just knew she was gonna tell you," Don said as he looked over at Kayla.

I ran over to Kayla and gave her a big hug and a bunch of small kisses on her cheek. "I love you, Kay! I don't know what I'd do without you."

"Mmm-hmm. Whatever," Kayla said nonchalantly.

Ignoring Kayla, I rolled my eyes and left her ass on the porch, going back over to my car. I wasn't about to kiss nobody's ass. Now I might suck some-body's dick, but it was gonna be the nigga that broke-bread for the shit. I wasn't paying attention to Kayla's bipolar ass. This was just a typical mood-swing that she did all the time. I told her ass to get some medication for that shit. She'd be alright in a minute.

Don was at the trunk of the limo with Andrew. He was all smiles, wheeling the luggage I got from Rasta into the house.

"Here comes her ass," I said out loud when I saw Kayla walking toward me. I sat in my whip and flipped through the Mercedes-Benz manual.

"Maliyah! Why did you keep it a secret about your trip overseas? I shouldn't have to find out shit about my friend from a nigga. I thought we were best friends. I tell you everything."

"Kayla, get off the gas. It's not that serious," I said and turned my attention back to the manual. When I looked back up, I caught her staring at my hair. She was diggin' my new do, but too mad to give me my props. "Oh yeah, tell me when Kayla returns because this bitch right here, I don't know her—with yo' bipolar ass," I said, pissing her off even more.

"Kayla told me to tell you this: yo' hair looks like a fuckin' wig and to kiss her monkey ass!"

I laughed it off, not letting Kayla get the best of me. She stormed into the house hotter than fish grease. I wasn't about to entertain the dumb shit. If I wanted to go back and forth with somebody, I would have answered the phone for my mom when she called.

$ $ $

"Mi eye is black! I can't see! Get away, Don!" Jasmine said to Don.

"Come here, baby, I didn't mean to black your eye. You have to control that attitude of yours. You could have fucked off my money, and that ain't cool, ma." Don shot that weak-ass game to Jasmine, who was sitting on the bed with her back to him.

She sighed before shouting, "Give me the damn suitcase!"

"See, that's exactly what I'm talking about," Don said, handing her the luggage from Rasta.

"How much longer, Don? How much longer do mi have to wait to get a wedding ring? Don'tcha love me?"

"C'mon, Jas, I don't feel like talking about this."

"Mi do, that's what's wrong wit ya. You don't care about no one but ya' self," she said with her voice starting to crack from holding back tears. "Why did'cha lie? You told mi that you don't sleep wit these women, business only, ya liar. You're sleeping wit Maliyah, too, tell the truth Donnie."

Don looked to the ground, unable to look Jasmine in the face. "I told you this is a business and I've made you my partner. What's the problem? You live good. You don't need for shit. What else do you want?"

"Tis don't mean shit. I come from money, mi uncles spoil mi rotten. All this means nothing, Don. Now answer mi question. Are you sleeping wit her? Why the Benz, boo, who does that?"

"You got a Range Rover."

"So now you're comparing mi to da trick."

"Oh my god, no! I'm not fucking her. You happy now?"

"Mi won't be happy until I get a ring that mi deserve," she said, going into the drawer and grabbing a screwdriver.

Kayla stood by the door and listened to the whole conversation. Jasmine took the screwdriver and went to work on the luggage-on-wheels. Unscrewing the screws in the handle, it came apart, revealing dope that was wrapped up in Saran Wrap.

"That's the shit!" Don said with a big grin, rubbing his hands together.

On the other side of the cracked door, Kayla couldn't believe what her eyes were seeing and her ears had heard. She'd seen a lot of shit by fucking with D-boys in the past, but never nothing like this. This was on some Frank Lucas type of shit. Kayla stood in disbelief. She would have never thought that much dope would fit in the handle part of a suitcase.

Drug dealers were some of the smartest, dumb muthafucka's, she thought as she watched Jasmine pull out the pure white cocaine that was stuffed into the rail. Don stood over her seeing nothing but dollar signs. He grabbed his iPhone and dialed a number. When he heard the voice of Shane, his stash-house worker, he said into the phone, "It's ready for you, man," before hanging up.

OMG

CHAPTER 11
MALIYAH

Don wanted to celebrate. When I asked him what was the occasion, he responded, "Our new relationship." He was in a good mood. That told me he was happy about getting whatever was so important in the luggage.

Kayla accompanied us. The bitch had returned and started acting like her regular old self. After I showed her ass the BCBG minis that I bought for her and Tia, she switched-up. She changed into the black, tight-fitted, back-out mini. The deep, low-cut design at the top of her ass made the dress look like it was designed specifically for the bootylicious diva; it was slammin'. Maria got us some bobby pins and I gave Kayla an updo and tried to jazz-up her micro braids (that I hated with a passion). I let her rock my Christian Louboutin stilettos and a clutch purse. The transformation from project-chic to red-carpet fab was a head turner.

We weren't the only ones looking good. Don entered the guest room and caught us off-guard, as we turned his maid out. "Hey! Pop it ... drop it ... make it clap!"

A tipsy me snapped my fingers, while Kayla and I showed Maria how to pop her ass.

"Am I doing it right, girls?" she asked. Getting no response, she looked up and noticed Don standing at the door. "I'm sorry, Boss," she said, startled.

"Hell, naw!" He laughed at the non-dancing Mexican mommie.

"Do y'all want some more drinks?" Maria asked, getting back to her job.

"Nah, we're leaving. Y'all ready?"

"Mmm-hmm," we said in unison.

"Maria." Don stopped Maria in her tracks.

"Yes, Boss."

"Stick to your day job," he said laughing.

"That's not funny, Boss," she said, going about her business.

Don was fly. He was wearing a brown and tan button-up, some crispy jeans, and tan Timbs. The brown and tan NY-fitted matched his fit, and he rocked it just how I like it on—lean.

We rolled to a Hollywood club in Don's black Phantom. Andrew drove us, while we sat in the backseat. Kayla and I WERE already tipsy, feeling ourselves. We were twirling our hips in the seat, ready to get on the dance floor and shut shit down. Don was respected everywhere he went. When Andrew pulled up to the club, we exited the car and the bouncer met Don at the car, giving him dap. "What's up, man?" the heavy set bouncer said, greeting Don.

"Nothing much, you know me, just trying to get it."

"I see ya, I wanna be like you when I grow up. Everybody else is inside," he said when he let us through. The hoes that stood in the long-ass line, cold as hell, trying to be cute in their skimpy outfits, rolled their eyes and talked shit because we cut the line on some VIP shit. I felt their pain, knowing how it felt to be standing in a long-ass line in the cold, waiting to get into the club. That was once the girls and me.

When we made it in the club, the DJ had the club jumping, playing all the club-bangers, getting everyone hype.

Trey Songz' "Say Aah" blasted throughout the club. That was the perfect intro song as the boss and I entered the packed club, looking like Hov and Bey.

We made it to VIP and Don was greeted by three niggas. Don nodded his head real cool-like. The niggas eyed Kayla and me like we were the only bitches in the club. "Who's yo' eye candy, Boss?" the yellow one asked, being thirsty.

"This one is off limits," Don said, grabbing me by the arm and pulling me closer to him. It felt good. "This my girl, Maliyah, but y'all niggas call her Mrs. Boss, and this her best friend, Kayla," Don introduced us. "And this light-skinned nigga is Craze, and that's Pablo and Mink."

"That nigga is a red-bone," Mink joked, busting Craze out.

"Fuck y'all. Light-skinned niggas getting hot again, ain't that right, ladies?"

Kayla and I just laughed, staying out of it. All three niggas looked like they were cake'd up. Craze and Pablo was going back and forth, fighting over who was gonna get Kayla, saying, "Nah, that's me." Mink kept staring at me. Every time Don turned his head, he winked his eye at me. I thought maybe I was trippin' though because the lights were dim and I was faded.

"Where's the Ace of Spades? What y'all nigga's waiting for?" Don shot, waving his hand and calling the lady over.

"What can I get for you, Don?" she asked, flirting sneakily with that googly eye shit. "Why did I ask? Two bottles of Armand de Brignac Brut Gold coming right up," the Spanish bitch said in a seductive tone.

"That shit is called Ace of Spades, all that fancy shit gotta go," Craze said.

"Nah, shut up nigga. I like the way she said it," Mink said, eyeing the chick.

"As long as you can afford it, it don't matter what you call it. What y'all drinking on?" Don asked Kayla and me.

"I'll have a Nuvo," I said.

"Me too."

"You got all that?" Don asked the Kat Stacks-video-groupie-looking ho.

"Mm—hmm. I'm not slow, just make sure you got my tip," she said before walking off.

"Money hungry ho," Mink shot.

"Nigga, you sound like Tank," Craze said.

"Speaking of Tank, where's that nigga? He knew we was supposed to meet up here."

"Lord!" Kayla rolled her eyes.

"Oh, I see you met Tank," Pablo said. He was Cuban or something, and fine as hell. Kayla better jump on that quick. I just wished Tia was with us so she could have hooked one of these niggas and kicked Tommy's ass to the curb.

"Baby, we're going to the ladies' room," I said to Don. When Kayla and I walked away, I couldn't get it out fast enough.

"Bitch, you better hook Pablo. He's fine as hell, and he's on your bumper tough. You know I don't do pink-meat, but damn!"

"He's too pretty. I don't want a nigga looking in the mirror more than me."

I looked at the bougie-acting Kayla. "What makes you say he's too pretty, because he's wearing stunner shades and you used to boys that wear white T's that fit like dresses?"

"No, it's his baby hair." We fell out laughing.

After applying lip gloss and looking at ourselves in the mirror, doing everything but use the bathroom, we made our way toward the door in the packed-ass bathroom. I stopped in my tracks when I looked to the left of me and saw this beautiful girl snorting lines of coke off a mirror. Kayla kept walking and talking for a couple of steps. When she didn't get a response, she realized she was talking to herself because I had stopped a long time ago to look at this chick that didn't have no shame in her game. She did it so openly, like smoking a cigarette.

"Why you stop? Got me looking like a weirdo, talking to myself and shit."

"Look at her."

"Yeah, I heard these hoes that be in these Hollywood clubs be all-the-way-live."

"What?" the girl said to Kayla and me. We were staring at her while all the other women passed her like it was the norm.

"Y'all want some?" she asked.

"This coke-head done tried us." I said, insulted.

"Naw, we're good," Kayla said.

"For now," she giggled. "Tell Donnie I said hello and I'm still in love with the white girl." She continued doing another line of coke.

"What the fuck is that supposed to mean?"

"Come on, she's a hater."

"You'll find out, and when you do, come find me. My name is Peaches. I come here all the time," she said and wiped the residue from her nostrils.

"I can't stand bitches!"

"I know you're not gonna let some junkie ho ruin your night." Kayla said, trying to talk some sense into me.

"Hell naw!"

"Well, I can't tell. Come on, fuck her."

When we made it back to VIP, Tank had arrived. "What's up?" He nodded his head at me. I waved. "Hey, Donkey Booty." He slapped Kayla on the ass.

"Nigga, don't play with me!" Kayla turned around hitting Tank on his arm.

"Oh, and she's feisty," Pablo said.

"Cuz, don't waste yo' time," Tank said to Pablo, who was jockin' Kayla something serious. She didn't pay him any mind.

After a couple of glasses of the expensive Ace of Spades, Kayla was wasted in her zone. I was doing the most, mixing liquor. I drunk some of the Ace of Spades, my whole bottle of Nuvo, and I was working on Kayla's.

Kayla got loose when the DJ played Luda's "Go Low." She did just that. And all eyes were on Kayla as she got low. My man was even looking as she got lower. I wasn't about to let her outdo me, so I joined her. We popped our asses to the beat, then we started freaking each other. Niggas loved that shit, seeing two sexy women grinding on each other.

"Dammmmmmnnnn!"

"Them some bad bitches!"

"Homie, look at her ass!" all the niggas said, watching us like they were at the popular Miami strip club, KOD

"Damn, Boss, you got some freaks on your hands," I heard Craze say.

"That nigga don't know what to do with that," Tank joked.

"Yeah, keep thinking that," Don said, not taking his eyes off the dance floor, watching as we got good ratings. I twirled my hips, giving Don a sexy wink. He smiled. Bitches hated and niggas watched, but Kayla and me wasn't stunnin' them hoes. Don and his crew started making it rain, more like a thunderstorm showing Kayla and me some love. I made my way to Don. I started poppin' my ass on his dick and felt it getting hard.

"You see what you did," he whispered in my ear. I bent over, getting lower. He leaned up against the wall holding me by the waist, and eyeing my apple bottom as I did my thing. Kayla glanced in our direction and grabbed Pablo by the hand, pulling him onto the dance floor. Kayla was freaking the shit out of him. He tried his best to handle the fat ass that came his way full-force but just couldn't keep up.

Mink and Tank was rolling. "Look at that nigga." Tank hit Don on his arm, getting his attention. Don looked through faded eyes to where Tank was pointing to see Kayla putting it on Pablo out on the dance floor. Don let go of my waist, letting me know he was tired of dancing. I got the hint and went to fix myself another drink. He called Pablo over the loud music. "Come here, nigga! Let's get this shit done!" he said with a firm voice.

Pablo came with sweat dripping from his face. "She put it on me dawg."

"We didn't come here for all of that," Don said.

"Why else would we come to a club?" Tank asked.

"Because I called a meeting. Who's the boss, me or you, nigga?"

"I'm just saying."

"Maybe that's the problem, don't say shit!"

I was dancing but listening at the same time. I was confused. Don had pulled one of Kayla's numbers. He was just cool, then all of a sudden, he flipped the script. I figured Gemini like Kayla.

Kayla came walking her loud-ass toward me. Now I wasn't gonna be able to hear what they were talking about.

"Ooooh, I'm tired. Why you leave, Pablo? Couldn't handle it?"

"We're talking right now!" Don said, giving Kayla attitude.

"Well *excuse* me, Don," Kayla said.

$ $ $

"Check into that ATL shit. Tank, have you tried calling her?"

"Yeah, from my number and yours, but still no answer."

"What about Danny Boy?"

"Yeah, that nigga said she was a no-show."

"What the fuck am I paying y'all for! Y'all should have been down there checking into this shit. I shouldn't have to call a meeting to tell y'all niggas some shit y'all should already know." Don looked all four niggas in the face.

"Go down there, look Danny Boy in his face, and if there's any sign of the bullshit ..." Don paused, and looked over at Kayla and Maliyah to see if they were eavesdropping their conversation.

"Yeah, Boss, we know what to do," Craze assured.

"Tank, you need to tighten up. Play wit it and one of these niggas gonna be my new lieutenant."

"Well, you're the boss."

"I'm glad you remember. This meeting is adjourned."

$ $ $

"Ms. Cooper, can you hear me?" the nurse said to Tia, who was lying in the hospital bed.

"Do you know what happened?" the nurse asked. "If yes, raise your left arm." Tia raised her arm the best that she could, still drugged up from the pain medication.

"Do you know where you are?"

Tia waved her pointing finger from side to side.

"You're at the hospital. You were rushed by the paramedics for second-degree burns from cooking oil."

Tia started panicking and tried to get up from the bed.

"No! Ms. Cooper, you have to stay in bed."

"Mirror ... a mirror," Tia said in between low cries.

"Ms. Cooper, you won't be able to see anything because your face is wrapped in medical bandages. Tomorrow you will be transported to a burn treatment center."

Tia's low cries turned into loud ones.

"Who did this to you?" the nurse asked.

Tia looked her in the eyes, wanting to tell her so bad that Tommy threw the hot cooking oil on her face. "I know who did it, but you have to say it. Help yourself, honey."

"Nurse, has my beauty queen woke up yet?" Tommy said, entering the room with flowers and a teddy bear. Tia burst in tears the moment that she laid eyes on Tommy.

"Can you please step out for a second?" the nurse said to Tommy.

"No, why?"

If it was up to her, she would have called security to put his ass out, but it was the patient's call. She then looked over at Tia and noticed the fear that was in her eyes. The nurse knew from past experience of being in an abusive relationship that Tia wasn't gonna tell him to leave. It was a waste of time to even ask because she was scared to death of this man.

"You're an asshole! You will reap what you sow. I hate men like you!"

"Lady, what the hell are you talking about?"

"You know, and she does too. And before she leaves here, I will get it out of her. Then I'm gonna call the police on your ass! Enjoy your last day as a free man!" the nurse warned Tommy. She then turned her attention back to Tia. "Ms. Cooper, if you need me, push that red button on the left side of you. I'll be right outside if this asshole tries anything." Tia nodded.

"Scum bag!" the nurse shot as she exited the room.

"Tia, what the hell you tell that woman?"

"Nothing, Tommy, I promise."

"You better not say shit! I told you I was sorry. I thought you were trying to burn down the house," Tommy said, making excuses for his actions, some-thing he did best. He was good at making it right when it was all said and done.

"Don't tell nobody, Tia. They'll put me away for the rest of my life. Don't even tell those nosy-ass friends of yours. Them miserable bitches are always trying to hate on our relationship because they're jealous of what you got. They want a man, but won't no nigga have them."

Tia lay in bed and listened to the same shit that Tommy recited every time he beat her ass. The shit started sounding like a broken record. It was really get-ting old. Tia knew that she was gonna be scarred from the second-degree burns. There was no hiding this from Kayla and Maliyah. They were gonna find out, just like everyone else that would see the noticeable scarring on the left side of her face. Tia didn't hide anything from her best friends, no matter how stupid she felt at the time. They had seen it all: broken arms, broken leg, broken nose, bruises, everything. It was just a matter of time be-fore they learned about the cooking oil incident, to add to the list of the many fucked-up things that Tommy had done to her.

~~BLAME IT ON THE ...~~

CHAPTER 12

After the party was the after-party. This was a night I will never forget, the night I was introduced to the party drug, ecstasy.

Soulja Boy blasted out of the speakers getting me and Kayla crunk.

I smacked Kayla on the ass as she threw it back on my pussy like I had a dick. Don sat in a leather chair with a Cuban cigar in one hand and a blunt in the other, loving the encore that Kayla and I were giving him of feelng each other up. We were all-the-way-live in the presidential suite at the W Hotel. When we left the club, we headed over to the hotel. Anybody else would've had to make a reservation for the presidential suite, but since Don was a faithful guest who brought the hotel a lot of money, when he strolled in at three o'clock in the morn-ing, he had that coming.

Now, at one point three was a crowd, but with some alcohol and weed, three became fun. I learned when ecstasy was in the equation, three is freaky, not-giving-a-fuck fun.

Don pulled a small Ziploc bag filled with colorful pills out of his pocket and tossed it on the table. I'd never seen an "X" pill nor took one. I'd heard of them before—living in Los Angeles, poppin' pills was the shit. If somebody said they were *rollin* or their *doors were wide open*, it meant they were high off the pill. A lot of my car-club members were pill-poppin' animals.

"Can I get some candy?" my naïve-ass asked.

"Me too, my mouth is dry. You got some gum? I need something in my mouth," Kayla said, high as a kite and didn't even know it.

"Baby girl, you ain't ready for this type of candy. This big-girl candy."

"Let's smoke. I'm thirsty," Kayla said with a twitch in her mouth.

"Drink this." Don gave her another bottle of orange juice.

"I think that's what's making me thirsty. After I drunk that first bottle, I got real thirsty. Fuck it, I'll drink it. Oooooh—this my song!" she said throwing her hands in the air.

"Ooooh—mine too, turn that shit up!" I said, hyped when Jamie Foxx's "Blame It" started playing. The mix CD Don brought up from the car was a banger.

"Now back to this big-girl candy," I said, taking a sip of Nuvo and Patron mixed together, and poppin' my ass at the same time.

Don said nothing, like he didn't hear me, as he lit another blunt.

"Right on time, pass that shit!" Kayla said, turning the bottle of orange juice up and taking it to the head. I looked up at the wasted Kayla, who was standing in front of me and Don twirling her hips.

I squinted through faded eyes. "What the hell is that in the bottom of that bot–"

"Ma, you looked so sexy tonight." Don cut me off and took my attention off the pill that wasn't fully dissolved in the bottom of the bottle.

"I love this new look you got going on. That's why I had to go floss you."

"You do?"

"Hell yeah, he do too," he said. He grabbed my hand and placed it on his lap to feel his hard dick that was trying to escape his jeans.

"You really want some candy?"

"Yep."

"Ma, it's XTC," he said having the upmost respect for me.

"I want one!" Kayla said from over by the stereo, smoking up all the blunt.

Don didn't waste no time; he grabbed the bag. "Which color you want?" he asked Kayla.

"Red!"

He handed the bright red pill to Kayla.

"What's that on it?" Kayla asked, putting the pill close to her eyes.

"A cherry."

"Ooooh a cherry. I like that," she said with the Bobby Brown-twitching, crack-head mouth.

"Ma, don't play with it, you ain't ready for this big-girl candy."

"Give it here."

"What color, Ma?"

"Um ... green!"

"Green apple, good choice. When I pop, that's the one I get."

"You gonna pop one with me?"

"If you want me to."

"Yeah, I do."

"Aight, go get us a orange juice out the refrigerator."

"Why orange juice?"

"Because it kicks in faster and keeps you rol-lin'."

"Mmm-okay." I'd never popped a pill before. I was gonna ask questions. I wasn't that fucked up. Kayla, on the other hand, said she hadn't either, but I bet she had. She kicked it in the trap with her nickel- and-dime-hustling, ex-boyfriend, Pee-Wee, and she didn't think twice when Don said he had them.

After about ten blunts, and a couple of bottles of Patron, we were rollin'. "X" made us chain-smoke. Don lit multiple blunts. I gritted my teeth so much I had to chew on some gum.

Me and Kayla grinded up against each other, both with hot kitty. Out of nowhere, Don said. "Y'all kiss." We did as told. I tongued my childhood best friend down like she was the opposite sex. I grabbed a chuck of her ass, and she grabbed mine.

"Hell yeah!" Don said, hyped.

Hearing Don, it pumped me up to take it up a notch. I allowed the pill to take over. I pulled Kayla's titties out and started sucking on each nipple. She moaned, letting me know she liked it.

"Dammmmnnn!" Don said. "Come over here," he instructed. We did as told, and walked the short distance over to the couch. That's when Kayla pushed me on the couch and slid my thong off. She then spread my legs apart and dived into my wet pussy.

"Oooooh!" I moaned. I looked over at Don, who was watching with his dick out, jacking himself off.

"Come here, I wanna suck it," I said seductively, as Kayla continued having a feast. Don came over to the couch and stuck his dick in my mouth. I sucked his dick so good that night off the pill, it turned me into a cold freak.

Don exited my mouth and entered Kayla from behind. Don grabbed Kayla by the waist as he rammed dick inside of her. I lay on the couch being a pillow-princess, looking my man in the eyes as he pushed dick into my best friend. The "X" made me cool with it.

$ $ $

The next morning, the sun shining through the curtains awakened me. When I sat up in bed, I grabbed my head that was spinning like crazy. Then I looked to the side of me to see my boo, and on the other side of him was Kayla.

"Oh my god, what have I done?" I thought, when I realized it wasn't a bad dream I was having— Kayla and I really did have a threesome with Don.

I grabbed the bottle of orange juice that sat next to me on the nightstand ... *and why did I do that?* It was just like poppin' another pill because all of a sudden I felt high. I craved a blunt. I climbed out of bed, and walked around to the other side of the bed to wake up Kayla, not wanting to reach over Don and wake him. I shoved the ho, who looked like she was in a peaceful sleep. "Bitch, get up!"

"No ... leave me alone."

"Bitch, get yo' monkey ass up!" I smacked her on the head. She looked up at me like I was crazy and looking ugly fresh out of a deep sleep.

"What?"

"I wanna smoke. Come roll me a blunt."

"You are officially a weed smoker; you need to learn how to roll," she said, talking shit as she climbed out of bed.

"Shut up and bring ya' ass," I said on my way out of the room. Kayla met me in the living room naked. "Damn don't nobody wanna see that shit. Why you didn't put on a robe?"

"Because I'm comfortable with my sexy. Don't be a hater all ya' life. You wasn't saying that last night," Kayla laughed. "Ooooh! Right there, Kay ... right there!" she teased, imitating me.

"Shut up, ho, I don't never, Evah! Evah! Evah! wanna hear 'bout this shit again. I only did it for Don, and you better not tell Tia."

"Why would I do that, so she could call both of us some dyke hoes?" Kayla rolled a blunt with the weed that was all over the table. Shit was everywhere. We turned the luxury suite upside down. Bottles of Champagne were all over the floor, me and Kayla's clothes, shoes and all.

"Hey," I said, greeting Don, as he strolled into the living room looking breathtakingly fine. He was wearing nothing but Dolce & Gabbana silk boxer shorts, showing off his six-pack that was washboard status.

"Damn, y'all couldn't wake a nigga up? I do smoke."

"I'm sorry baby, you were sleeping too good. I didn't want to bother you."

"Y'all put it on me last night. I feel violated. I've never got turned out before," he joked.

"Boy, shut up," I said playfully. He gave me a morning-breath kiss and that told me right there our relationship had grown from the episode last night.   We passed on breakfast since the pill left us without appetites. I had to go home and get right. The after-effect of Ecstasy was horrible. I felt like shit. I was sluggish, with cotton mouth, a headache, and I had the shits. That was a fucked-up combination.

Once Andrew drove us back to Don's, Kayla and I hopped into my Honda, leaving my Benz parked at Don's. I wasn't ready to have to explain the Benz to my parents. It was bad enough I had to hear their mouths about the M.I.A. stunt I pulled.

Don wasn't trying to hear none of that, saying, "My woman can't roll around in a muthafuckin' Honda. That makes me look bad. Get rid of it." He gave me a couple of days to tell my parents. Don had a reputation for being flossy, and he wanted his girl to be equal to his lavish lifestyle. Standing at the side window he went on. "Maliyah, I want a woman, not a little-ass girl that still has to get approval from Mommy and Daddy. Check it, Ma. Get grown or get gone."

"Don, my head is pounding. I'll call you later so we can talk."

That nigga had the audacity to give me an ultimatum. I had a lot on my mind leaving Don's estate.

"He told you. I sure wouldn't want to be in your shoes right now," Kayla said from the passenger seat.

"Shut up, ho!"

I dropped Kayla off at her house in Inglewood, then drove back to my parents' house across town. I begged Kayla's ass to come over to my house. Any other time she would have been all for it, fuckin' tramp. I had to clinch my butt cheeks together trying to keep from shitting on myself. I kept a tight ass the whole ride home.

When I pulled into the driveway, I snatched the keys out of the ignition and ran to the front door. I put my key in the door, and the son of a bitch didn't work. I stepped back, making sure I was at the right house. "Yeah, it's 53l9." I read the numbers on the side of the house, and tried my key again. "I know they didn't!" I knocked on the door. I had to shit so bad, my knocks turned into beating, trying to tear the bitch down to get in.

My mom finally came to the door. "Who are you?" she asked, peeking out the cracked door.

"Mama, stop playing, open the door. I have to use the bathroom."

"Maliyah, is that you? You got your hair all done up, in that skimpy little outfit. You grown now."

"Mama, open the door, please!"

"Maliyah, why you didn't tell me about losing your job? You lied to me, and then your father and I called up to the dealership and your little lying behind paid the note up for three months, so we wouldn't find out. What has gotten into you?"

Shit ... I wasn't prepared for this ... How the fuck did she find out? ... She must have went up there ... Damn! I stood in deep thought with the dumbest look on my face. I didn't know what to say.

"Maliyah!" She snapped me out of it.

"Mama, why are you talking to me from behind the door?"

"Because you can't come in here. You no longer live here. You're grown, remember?"

"Where's Daddy?"

"Oh, you don't wanna see him. He's so disappointed in you."

She shook her head staring at me. "Michael!" she called him. Then seconds later, my father came to the door.

"Daddy, tell Mommy to let me in the house," I said with my baby voice that always worked on my father.

"It's not my call, Puddin'. Your mother has already made up her mind. It's out of my hands."

"Maliyah, you already know your father is not gonna go against me."

"This is bullshit!" I sceamed.

"Wait, hold on. I don't care how grown you think you are, but you are not gonna disrespect me nor your father. You're never too grown to get your ass whipped."

"Whatever! I hate you!" When the words rolled off my tongue, I shocked myself. I couldn't believe I had the nerve to say that to my mother. I'd never came at my parents sideways. It had to be the "X." Looking at my mother, I saw the hurt in her eyes. Then I backed away, I wasn't no fool. Karen did not play. I didn't know what to expect.

"Move, Michael. You hate me? We raised you better than that!" my mother yelled as my father held her back.

"You think? I can't even talk to you, Mama! Y'all don't let me live my life. I'm not a baby any more!"

"Maliyah, as long as you live under our roof, you're gonna abide by our rules. Me and your mother made that very clear when you turned eighteen."

"And you better be glad we did that, because when I turned eighteen, I had to go. My mother wasn't playing that! But it's too late now. Anything that has to do with living in here, moving back in here, is a dead subject. You gotta go. You don't talk to me and your father the way you just did."

"But Mama."

"But Mama my ass!"

"Daddy." He put his head down. By the look on his face, I could tell my dad was totally against it, but my mother wore the pants in the relationship and what she said was final. "How can you guys do me like this? I hate you guys! I will never do my children the way y'all are doing me. Fuck you guys! Daddy, you need to man-up and wear the pants. You are the fuckin' man in the relationship! Stand up to Mama!"

"Maliyah, just leave," my father said.

A tear fell from my eye. I couldn't believe it. My parents were throwing me out to the wolves.

"I want you to come and get your things tomorrow! I'll have it all packed up for you, you little disrespectful wench! And when you come, come with some bus fare because I want the car too," my mom yelled.

I got in my car and broke down. I couldn't believe my parents had kicked me out of the house. Now where was I going?

~~I CAN FEEL IT IN THE AIR~~

CHAPTER 13
MALIYAH

I pushed it to the limit on the freeway headed back to San Fernando Valley. I was crying so hard I had the huff-and-puff's. I decided not to call Don. I wanted to tell him in person about what happened. He wouldn't have been able to make out a word that I was saying from me crying so hard anyway.

The ride to Don's was long and dreadful. When I pulled up to the gate, Maria came on the intercom.

"How may I help you?"

"Maria, it's Maliyah."

"One moment, Mommie," she said, opening the gates.

When I drove up to the house, Don was already standing outside talking to Tank. He walked up to my car noticing I had been crying from my swollen eyelids. "What's wrong, Ma?"

I broke down. "My par ...ents ... put me out."

"Why are you crying?"

"Because I don't have nowhere to go."

"Yes, you do, here."

"Here?" I didn't stutter.

"Maybe that's a good thing that they put you out."

"Huh?"

"Didn't you say these very same words when we first met, things happen for a reason? Well, maybe this is your reason. God don't make no mistakes. It's about time you grow up and live your life, Ma. Now go in the house and clean yourself up."

"Awww, baby, give me some," I said pointing to my cheek. He gave me a kiss. I loved him. He always knew what to say at the right time. I got out of the car and walked toward the house.

"Mal," he called me. I turned around.

"Hi to you, too," Tank said.

"Oh, my bad, Tank, what's up?" I said, then turned my attention to Don, knowing damn well he didn't call me just to speak to Tank.

"Yes, baby?"

"What are you gonna do about this piece of shit?" Don asked pointing to the Honda.

"My mom wants me to bring it to her tomorrow when I pick up my things."

"Okay, I'm going with you."

"I don't think that's a good idea."

"Well, I do, and I'm going with you."

"Okay, I am gonna need somebody to follow me while I drive the Honda."

"Remember what we talked about earlier? You're not driving that car any more. I'll arrange for someone to take it." I smiled, turned around and went about my business.

"Ay, Ma!" he called me again.

"Now what?"

"Do something with that barking-ass-dog. That damn thing been barking all day."

"Aww, Prada!" I said, taking off to the front door. I passed Maria outside watering the flowers.

"Hi, Mommie, you don't look too good. What's the matter?" she asked, noticing my flushed face and swollen eyelids. Sometimes I hated being light- skinned.

"Maria, I'd rather not talk about it."

"Maria!" Don yelled.

"Yes, Boss?"

"Show Mrs. Boss to the guest room."

"Will do."

I followed behind Maria, wondering how this was gonna work out, me staying with Don. I was happy and scared all at the same time.

"Maria, you're gonna be seeing a lot of me."

"That's wonderful, adds some personality to this house. It will be good having you around. But, Maliyah, between me and you," she said, coming a little closer to me, "make sure this is something that you really want to do. Just try it for a few days. And whatever you do, do not move out of your home just yet. Keep it. Let this be a trial period. Mommie, don't never jump head-first into something without knowing exactly what you getting yourself into. I have children your age, Maliyah, so I'm gonna tell you what I'll tell my own. Plus, I like you."

"I like you too."

"Well, this is it," she said, opening the door to the bedroom where I'd be staying. It was decorated in black and white, with a king-sized bed, a plasma-screen TV mounted on the wall, and a huge bathroom that sat close to a patio. Besides having to add a little color, it was perfect.

"Well, Mommie, get comfortable. If you ever need me, it's an intercom right here by the door. I'm only a push away. And if you need someone to talk to, and believe me you will, don't hesitate. My door is always open."

"Aww, thank you Maria." I gave her a hug.

"Now let me get back to work," she said, walking toward the door.

"Maria!" I stopped her in her tracks.

"Where's Prada?"

"Who?"

"My puppy."

"Oh, baby, she's in my TV room. Let me go get her," she said, exiting the room.

I took a hot shower to try to ease my mind. As much as I tried, I couldn't stop thinking about what went down. The shit was eating me up inside. I was very close to my parents. It was just a shame we had to fall out over something so petty.

When I got out of the shower, Tia crossed my mind, so I decided to give her call. I went for my phone and dialed her number. It rang once before going straight to her voicemail, which was strange. "That's why I don't call her ass," I said, and waited to hear the beep so I could leave a message. "Tia, it's Maliyah, yo' best friend, remember me? Call me when you get this message, bitch. That's why I don't call yo' black-ass because you don't never answer. Tell that fuck-nigga Tommy that you do have friends. Call me ASAP. It's a code 10," I said, then disconnected the call. We had codes that we went by. Code 10 meant it was kinda-sorta an emergency, really just needing someone to talk too. Tia always answered my code 10s, unlike Kayla.

Don sent Maria back up to the room to organize my closet with all the new shit from the shopping spree. Maria put my closet in alphabetical order by designer name. I loved the idea. I was just mad that my Valentino blouses had to be at the end of the huge walk-in closet.

I threw on a pink and white, Juicy Couture tight-fitting jogging suit that had "Juicy" written on my ass. I unzipped the jacket just enough to see my matching Victoria Secret bra, which added some sexiness to the comfortable look. Keeping it comfortable-chic, I slid on a pair of sequin flip-flops that showed off my French-tips and the toe ring that looked so cute on my toe. "I'll be right back, Maria. I'm going to talk to Don."

"Okay, Mommie."

When I walked out the room, I ran into Jasmine in the hallway.

"Hey, Jasmine."

"What are you doin' here?" she questioned me like she was the owner of this house. I looked at her mangled eye and wanted to ask her so bad who in the hell she pissed off. But I decided not to ask the Jamaican bitch shit, who was staring at me with her nose turned up. "Hello, is anybody home! What are you doin' here, and walking around without someone watching you?"

Oh no she didn't, I thought, wanting to go ham on this ho, but I chose to go the other route and play this bitch with kindness. She would never find a piece of my hair around this house and do voodoo on me. I knew how them Jamaicans got down. "As a matter of fact, someone is home, because this is my new home. And for the record, I don't need nobody walking around watching me. I don't steal, if that's what you were getting at."

"Your new home? Donnie!" she yelled, running to the room and grabbing a walkie-talkie. The eight-bedroom, ten-bath mansion was so huge they needed to use walkie-talkies to find one another throughout the home.

"Donnie, I need to talk to you not now, but right now!" she yelled in the walkie-talkie.

"Tell him me too," I chuckled, walking off. *That bitch Jasmine is gonna be a problem, I can feel it,* I thought. I just didn't get her position. And why did she have to live here? I definitely needed to talk to Don about her because something wasn't adding up.

"Now, where is this nigga so I can get a pill," I said, talking to myself, lost trying to remember how to get to the front door.

When I finally found Don, he was standing outside talking to Tank and Craze. The driveway was bumper-to-bumper with limousines like someone had died. Craze was standing next to a Lincoln Town Car with some type of advertisement to a business on the side of it. I tried to get a glimpse of it, but Craze was standing in the way. When I walked up to Don, the look on his face said that he was pissed off about something.

"Baby–" Before I could finish my sentence he grabbed me by the arm and damn near dragged me off to the side to talk to me private.

"What the fuck are you wearing?"

"Juicy Couture, what's wrong with it?"

He looked down at my feet in the pair of flip-flops and that did it. "Did you just leave the fuckin' nail shop or somethin'?"

"What's wrong with it?"

"Everything. I'm having a business meeting here, so that means we're gonna have a lot of company. Take yo' ass in the goddamn house and make yo' self presentable! And when I say presentable I mean some heels, a dress, something of that nature. And get rid of this project-chick, low-class bullshit that you're wearing!" he hissed as he released my arm from his tight grip.

"Okay, I'm sorry, baby. I didn't know you were having company," I said and rubbed my sore arm. It was definitely gonna leave a bruise being that I was one to bruise very easily.

"Where is Maria?"

"She's in the room organizing my closet."

"Well, she should have told you. That's the reason I sent her ass up there with your clothes. She will be dealt wit. I'm sorry, Ma, we're gonna charge that one to the game because you didn't know," he apologized and gave me a kiss on the cheek before walking off. I brushed his anger off instead of paying attention to something that should have been a sign to run—and run fast.

As I headed back in the house, the advertisement on the side of the Lincoln caught my attention. It read: BOSS LIMOUSINE AND TRANS-PORTATION SERV-ICE.

"Well that explains the limousines," I mumbled to myself, finally finding out what type of business Don was in.

$ $ $

The next day came too fast. I kept turning to look out the back window at Craze following behind us in the Honda. My heart was beating out of my chest as I sat next to Don in the back seat of his Phantom while Andrew drove us to my parents' house. When we pulled up to the front of the house, I took a deep breath and looked over at Don. "Here goes nothing. Stay right here—I'll be right back."

Bringing Don didn't do nothing but add fuel to the fire. I think it would have turned out a lot different without bringing Don, but he insisted on coming. Andrew opened the door and I exited the car.

"Andrew, follow her and get her things," Don ordered.

Andrew did as told, on my heels like dead skin. Walking up the walkway I had an audience. I can't stand nosy-ass neighbors. They sat on their porch and looked over at my parents' house, hoping to see some action.

"Hey Maliyah, I see you stumbled up on some money. Good girl!" Tameka said, walking past and pushing one of her ten kids in a stroller. I called her Dashiki from the Wayans Brothers comedy, *Don't Be A Menace,* because she had a bunch of kids like the ghetto baby momma in the movie. I rolled my eyes at Tameka's food stamp, WIC-getting ass, and kept it moving. As I approached the door, I lifted my hand up to knock and noticed it was trembling. I don't know why I was so scared. It was just instilled in me to be terrified of my parents. I was still geeked from the pill I popped two nights before, so shit was moving fast. I knocked once and my mom swung open the door. I quickly moved out the way before I got hit by one of the flying Hefty trash bags.

"Where's my suitcases? Why did you put my things in trash bags?" I questioned.

"Who bought those suitcases?"

"Man, I'm not even gonna go there with you."

"Mmm-hmm, that's what I thought."

When my mom stopped to catch a breather from tossing six full trash bags out the door nonstop, she noticed Craze sitting in the Honda. "Who the hell is that?"

"Oh, I'm Andrew." Andrew extended his hand.

"No, not you. Him, sitting in my goddamn car!"

When it all registered, she looked back at Andrew, then back at me. "Who the hell is Andrew? Who are these people, Maliyah?"

"They're—" Don cut me off.

"Maliyah, come on. You don't owe her an explanation. She's throwing her daughter's shit out of her house in trash bags! What type of mother does her own child like that? I know mine wouldn't!" Don shot.

"Yeah, he's right! I ain't gotta tell you a damn thing!"

She then called my father. "Michael!"

"Mama, just give me the rest of my things."

"Where's my goddamn car keys? Give them up right now!!"

"Craze, give this lady the car keys to this piece of shit. Lady, I can buy you a car lot of these," Don shot.

My father came to the door. "What now Karen?"

"Your daughter has brought these thugs to our place of residence."

"Puddin', who are these men?"

"Oh, I'm Puddin' now?" I chuckled. "That's my boyfriend, Don, and these are his employees. Are you happy now? Can you please tell Mama to give me the rest of my stuff?"

"Your boyfriend?" my dad asked, rubbing his head in confusion.

"Her man," Don added, standing next to his Phantom.

"That explains why she's been acting the way that she has. Staying out for days, not working, probably out with this thug!" my mom said, throwing bag after bag outside, as Andrew put them in the trunk.

"Don't worry, Pops, I'll take good care of her," Don said with a devilish grin, then winking at my dad.

"You son of a bitch!!" my dad yelled, running toward Don.

"Michael!" my mom screamed.

Craze and Andrew pulled their pistols from their waistlines like trained goons. "Uh-uhh, Pops, you don't wanna go that route."

"Stop! Are you guys crazy?" I screamed at Craze and Andrew, who had my father at gunpoint.

"Maliyah, get these men off my property right now before I call the police," my mom yelled. My dad stood staring at Don with his fists balled, breathing hard as hell.

"Alright, big man, we can handle this like men. Do I have your blessing to ask your daughter for her hand in marriage?"

Oh my god is he serious, is all I thought, as I looked at Don then back at my father.

"You are filth! You fucking pervert! This is my baby you're talking about!!"

"Daddy, that's just it. I'm not your baby anymore."

"Don't talk back to your father, with your fast ass!" Karen said, before slapping the shit out of me. I held my face; then my reflex made me swing at my mom but my father jumped in the middle and took the strike that had my mom's name on it.

Craze held my mom at gunpoint. He was one of them coke-head, crazy-ass-niggas. That's how he got the name Craze.

"Boss, you want me to do her?"

"Stop!" I screamed, knowing Craze was just insane enough to kill my mother. My dad tried getting away from Andrew, who had him in a choke hold.

"Put the gun down and let's fight like real men, you little bastards! Just let my wife go! Maliyah, tell them something!" My dad shouted.

"Man, kill the noise. Yo' wife got more heart then you," Andrew said to my father.

"Boss, do you want me to waste the bitch?" Craze said, trigger-happy.

Don looked at me and said, "It's yo' call, Ma."

"No! ... No! Look at what you're asking me. Do I want them to kill my parents? Just come on and let's leave before one of these nosy-ass neighbors call the police."

"Alright," Don said, walking over to my father. "I tried, old man. Your baby is now my woman. Later,

Pops," Don said, patting my father on his shoulder, then walking the short distance back to the car.

"Maliyah, you listen to me, and listen good. Don't you ever step foot on this property again! I will be going downtown to get a restraining order against you! When things don't work out between you and that asshole, don't call us. The only thing I want you to do is remember this day!" my father shouted.

Don grabbed me by the hand and helped me into the car. Craze followed, putting his burner back on his waist.

"Damn, I thought we were gonna set it off!" Craze said, disappointed. "Today is y'all lucky day. Thanks, Mrs. Boss, because if it was up to me, she would be collecting some life insurance real soon."

"Craze, shut up, and please get in the car," I yelled from inside the car.

Craze did as told and climbed in the back seat as Andrew drove off. I looked at my parents through the tinted window with tears in my eyes. My mother stood speechless as my father carried on, foaming at the mouth.

"Don't worry about them, Ma. You got me and as long as you got me, you won't need a muthafuckin' soul." A tear fell down my cheek as I continued staring out the back window until I couldn't see my parents any more.

THEY SMILE IN YOUR FACE

CHAPTER 14

Tommy couldn't believe his eyes as he followed Tank into the beautiful Hollywood Hills mansion they called a stash house.

"Y'all use this big, nice muthafucka as a stash house?" Tommy asked and looked around in awe.

"It throws them alphabet boys off."

"Okay, I get it. If they see limousines rolling on a piece of property like this, they're gonna automatically think it's a famous person inside, and not a bunch of dope."

"Exactly," Tank said.

"I like the concept, y'all did that," Tommy said, nodding his head.

When they entered the living room full of weed smoke, Shane was sitting on the couch, puffing on a blunt and watching the Lakers game highlights on ESPN. Surrounded by surveillance monitors, Shane didn't have to turn around to know Tank was standing right behind him.

"Don't come up in here with that Laker-hater bull-shit," Shane shot.

"No need, you see it. Them Lakers got their ass whooped last night." Tank laughed, knowing Shane was a die-hard Lakers fan.

"Man, you gonna have to get off the Lakers," Tommy chimed in.

"Aww, nigga you too? Fuck that, you fired," Tank said, clowning.

"I like you already, my man," Shane said, giving Tommy some dap.

"When they play Miami next week, they gonna tear Kobe a new asshole."

"Nigga, fuck Miami, they ain't hittin' on shit!" Shane said, hyped.

"Fuck you and fuck the Lakers," Tank said, walking over to the bar and grabbing a bottle of Grey Goose. "Tommy, you want something to drink?"

"Nah, I'm straight."

"Shane, this our new driver, Tommy. He's gonna be doing the transporting to this spot."

"Aight, cool, because Boss had me coming to pick up the other night. I only did it because we were short of folks."

"No, you only did it because you wanted to keep yo' job," Tank said.

"Nah, fo' real fo' real, that was a dangerous situation, driving back by myself. I was the perfect lick for the perfect sucka."

"You sound scared," Tank said.

"Fuck you, nigga."

They all laughed. Tommy sat on the couch in deep thought. *This is supposed to be me. I had the game in a choke hold.*

"Nigga, what you over there thinking about?" Tank snapped Tommy out of his deep thought.

"Shit, nothing. I was watching TV," he lied.

"Nigga, you was staring at them football players like they were some fine-ass bitches."

Shane fell out laughing.

"How long did you do in the pen again? Don't tell me those niggas took yo' cornbread," Tank clowned.

"Oh, this nigga got jokes," Tommy said, laugh-ing. "This is all the time with his fat ass."

After Tank gave Tommy the run-down of his new job description, they gave him a tour of the huge mansion. Every room in the seven-bedroom house stored drugs, money and guns. Shane was in charge of the stash house. His job was to cook up hard white and monitor the house. Instead of doing his job himself, he had his baby momma, Heather, and her twin sister, Halley, cooking dope for him.

Tommy was caught off guard when they entered the kitchen and his eyes laid on two bad, naked, white bitches cooking up dope.

"Tommy, that's my baby momma, Heather, and that's her sister, Halley." Shane introduced his fully nude baby momma. Both girls waved and went right back to work.

"Nigga, you already know Boss don't like them around none of the shit after what happened with Peaches. Just don't let Mink or Craze see it."

"As long as it gets done, it shouldn't matter. That junkie bitch, Peaches, was one of his hoes," Shane shot.

"Heather, have you been over to the cave to see Tif?" Tank questioned.

"Yeah, she's cool."

Shane shoved Tank, then cut his eye at Tommy. "Oh, he's straight. That nigga too busy drooling over them pink toes—he ain't heard shit. Ain't that right, Tommy?"

"Huh?" Tommy said, playing dumb.

"My point exactly," Tank said with a smile.

"Still, tighten up and make sure when this shit is all over wit you and that fuck-nigga Pablo run me my ten stacks along with Heather and one of those expensive-ass bags that she likes."

"That's why I love you, Daddy" Heather said, blowing a kiss in Shane's direction.

Tommy stood listening to everything that was said. He knew some shiesty shit was in the making, but he just couldn't pinpoint it. Playing dumb was gonna get him the scoop. So he did just that.

~~THEY SMILE IN YOUR FACE~~

~~PT 2~~

CHAPTER 15
MALIYAH

Sometimes I thought Kayla and I kicked it entirely too much. We had been tight since Audubon Middle School. We took our tight friendship to Cren-shaw High School and from Crenshaw we never went a day without seeing each other.

I lay on the bed next to Prada wishing that she could talk. I needed someone to talk to. Tia wasn't answering her phone and Kayla said she'd call me back over an hour ago. She was up to no good at one of her D-boy's trap houses, trying to milk a nigga for some bread. My phone started ringing and Prada started barking. "Hush, girl," I said to Prada. When I glanced at the screen, Kayla's picture flashed across it. "It's about time!" I answered the phone instead of a hello.

"You gonna get my hair done?" Kayla asked.

"Hell no."

"Shut up then. I'm over at Pee Wee's house trying to get some money out of his ass. So what's up with this code 10?"

"Oh, it took you so long to call back, I almost forgot. Karen and Michael kicked me out of the house."

"You lying, Maliyah."

"Nope, true story."

"For what?"

"I guess she called up to my job and found out about me getting fired. Then—you know Karen with her investigating ass—she just had to get down to the bottom of things. She found out about me paying the car note up for three months."

"Damn, that's all bad. Look, dawg, you can come stay with me and Aunt Shell."

"Thanks, but no thanks. I live with Don now."

"What! When did that happen?"

"After I dropped you off, I went home and Karen wouldn't let me in. They changed the locks and all, can you believe that shit? Anyways, I went back to Don's and he said I can stay with him. Gurl, we took the Honda back to my mom today, and she gave me my stuff, well some of it. Because it got ugly between them and Don."

Nothing but dead air from Kayla.

"Kayla?"

"Yeah! I'm here."

"Well, I'm gonna need for you to say something, baby."

"Bitch, finish telling me!"

"Okay, this is where the code 10 come into play. Don asked for my dad's blessing to marry me!" I heard a loud noise on the other end of the phone.   "Hello, Kayla?"

"Yeah, I dropped the phone."

"I think I'm getting married, dawg! 'If He Liked It, Then He Shoulda Put A Ring On It!'" I sang some Beyonce.

"Married, girl please! You are so dumb, you don't even know this nigga."

"I thought you'd be happy for me. You are my best friend, right?"

"My best friend wouldn't have put a man before her parents. And now you're staying with him and that Jamaican bitch, his so-called employee. I bet you he's fuckin' her too. Listen, and you better not say nothing," Kayla said, the intro to gossiping.

"What? Tell me!"

"The day you came back from overseas, I caught a cab over to Don's so I could be there when you saw the Benz. When the cab drove in, I caught that Jamaican ho and Don getting out the back seat of your Benz. She was fixing her clothes as she got out of the car, fuckin' tramp.

I just forgot to tell you. But you know what goes down in back seats, stay in back seats."

"Mmm, I ain't stunnin' that ho, but I'll keep a close eye on them."

"And you still gonna marry that nigga?"

"Shit, I don't know. He didn't even ask me yet. Maybe he was just trying to piss my dad off. And if I do, I'm gonna be wifey. Then I really won't be worrying about the next bitch."

"You are the dumbest bitch I know. Let me get off the phone with you before some of that shit rub off."

"Then you probably will get a ring from Pee Wee," I shot.

"I don't need a goddamn ring for a nigga to show me that he loves me, know that!"

"Damn, why you getting serious on me?"

"Because sometimes you say some of the dumbest shit. Now, let me go work on getting me a ring. Bye!" Kayla yelled in the phone before hanging up.

That girl has not been herself lately. She had to have gotten a blood transfusion, because she had some hater blood pumping through her veins. This was not the girl I made my best friend. I sat my phone beside me on the nightstand and my mind drifted off in deep thought. *Why is she just now telling me about Jasmine and Don getting out the back seat of my car? She forgot ...?*

That's a bunch of bullshit ... Why do I even kick it with her?

$ $ $

He's gonna marry her! Kayla said to herself in the bathroom. *This was not supposed to go down like this. Fuck! Fuck! Fuck!*

Kayla was pissed when her plan backfired on her. Kayla had thought Karen would have put Maliyah on punishment for awhile when she found out about Maliyah losing her job. That would have given Kayla some alone time with Don so she could try to win him over. Never was he supposed to move her in, or even marry her. *I gotta do something quick,* Kayla thought, getting herself together before leaving the bathroom.

Kayla re-entered the living room to Pee Wee and his boys doing what they did best: trapin'. "Trapin' ain't dead, niggas just scared," Pee Wee said in the kitchen as he taught Tiny Mac how to cook up hard white. *Damn he looks familiar ...* Kayla thought, staring at the youngsta as he got his Betty Crocker on.

Surrounded by pots and Arm & Hammer baking soda, Pee Wee went on-and-on with Tiny Mac's undivided attention like he was a professor at Harvard teaching Trapin' 101.

"Y'all wanna make some money?" Kayla knew just what to say to get all five niggas' attention.

"Hell yeah. Is that a trick question?" Pee Wee shot.

"How much you talking about?" Slim asked. Slim was Pee Wee's partner-in-crime.

"It's negotiable."

"So, what's up, shawty, what we gotta do?" Pee Wee questioned.

"Get rid of somebody."

"Oh, that's gonna cost ya," Slim added.

"I ain't trippin' on the money."

"Oh, you ain't trippin' on the money. If you got it like that, why you up over here asking me to get yo' hair done?" Pee Wee demanded.

"That nigga gots a point," Tiny Mac chimed in.

"Listen, when I say get rid of somebody, I don't mean kill them. I'm talking about kidnapping them for ransom. Then if you wanna kill her after we get the money, that's cool too."

"Where they do that at?" Pee Wee laughed.

"Shut up, Pee Wee," Kayla said. "Look, you can sleep on it if you want, but the nigga got bread and he's gonna pay."

"Who are we supposed to be kidnapping?"

"This girl named Maliyah."

"Why does that name ring a bell?"

"Because that's my best friend—well, she was my best friend."

"And who's the paymaster?"

"Her fiancé, Don, he got bread."

"You trying to get us all killed? That nigga front me my dope! You lost yo' goddamn mind!" Pee Wee said.

"You on yo' own Jojo," Slim shot, grabbing the X-Box joystick and restarting his game. Slim wanted no part of what Kayla was talking about once he heard the name "Don."

"Pee Wee, you know I got to take this back to Boss. I was working for him before I was working for you, but I think we can work something out," Popeye with the lazy eye said rubbing his chin.

Pee Wee looked at Kayla, giving her a look like, *You know you done fucked up.*

Pee Wee knew exactly what Popeye was getting at. Popeye was a nigga that didn't get no pussy, and every time Kayla came around, he went into the bathroom for long periods of time to masturbate. He wanted Kayla bad.

Popeye got up from the couch, walked up to Kayla and grabbed a hand full of her ass. "Pee Wee, I'm first," Popeye said, ready to push his hard dick inside of her.

"I'm after him," Slim called his spot in line.

"Then me, I know Don, too," Tiny Mac said from the kitchen.

"Come here, Kayla." Pee Wee started walking toward the bedroom. Kayla followed behind him with her heart beating out of her chest. Pee Wee slammed the door behind them, looked at Kayla and shook his head. "You called this one on yourself. Why the fuck you didn't tell me by myself, instead of throwing yo' self out there like that!"

"I don't know! Pee Wee, help me! What are they trying to do to me?"

"It's either help you and die in the process, or help myself. Because it's obvious that you don't know Donnie Boss. Look, how can I put this? Basically, these niggas wanna fuck you, or they're gonna take this back to Don, and he will get one of his goons to murk you."

"What should I do?"

"Shit, snort this," he said as he pulled a small Ziploc bag out of his pocket. "And drink this, that should get you right." He handed her the rest of the Hennessey that he was drinking on. "Do what you gotta do."

"Man, I ain't never did that," Kayla shot. She tried to hand the Ziploc bag back to him.

"It's just a little dust."

"You got *X*?"

"Nope. If you can do 'X,' you can fuck with the powder."

Man what have I got myself into? What should I do? Think, bitch! Think! Kayla stood, stared at the pure white coke in the Ziploc bag and contemplated what she should do.

"Kayla, what are you gonna do?" Pee Wee questioned, snapping her out of her deep thought. "Gimme some more of that shit. Fuck it! I gotta do what I gotta do."

$ $ $

After snorting two lines of coke, and downin' the Hen, Kayla took all four lubes, and wanted more.

Pee Wee was used to running trains on hood rats with his boys, but watching them have their way with Kayla didn't sit well with him. Although Kayla was his ex-girl, he would still double-back and knock her down every now and then. Pee Wee liked having Kayla on the lingo, getting her to come by the spot, and his boys drooling over how good she looked. Just like every nigga, Pee Wee loved the props he got from his boys for having a bad bitch like Kayla on his all-star line-up. But after witnessing all his boys run up in her, he was good on Kayla's road-kill pussy. Kayla lay sprawled out on the couch, asshole naked, playing in her pussy.

The coke and Hen turned her into a real freak. "Ooooooh!" she moaned, twirling her hips as all the niggas stood hyped with hard dicks. "Who wants seconds of the good stuff?" Kayla asked with a seductive tone.

"Me!"

"Me!"

"Me!" They all shot one after another.

"You, Tiny Mac," she pointed at the lil nigga.

"Back! Back, I'm getting some more before all of y'all niggas. I'm the one that got shit crackin,'" Popeye said, coming out of his jeans.

"Now, calm down boys. It's enough for all of ya," Kayla said mischievously.

"Aiight, dog, it ain't that serious, it's just pussy," Tiny Mac shot.

"Don't trip, cuz, this nigga don't get pussy on the regular. Let him enjoy because it's no telling when he might get some again," Slim clowned.

Popeye walked up to Kayla and manhandled her. He pinned her up on the back of the couch, spread her cheeks apart and entered her virgin asshole. "Take it," Popeye said into her ear.

"Ahhhh! Wait ... Go in the pussy!" Kayla said from the pain.

"Shut up, you can take it, girl."

"Okay, go slow," Kayla said tolerating the pain from the numbness of the coke and Hen.

"This nigga fuckin' the dooky-shooter. Get the pussy and come on, Popeye, damn! My dick is getting limp watching this shit," said one of the trap star's finest.

"Y'all niggas ain't shit." Pee Wee exited the living room sick to his stomach.

$ $ $

The worst sleep was in the trap. Nigga's had to sleep light to stay on point for the jackers. After they all had their turns with Kayla, they passed out, leaving Tiny Mac on duty to make all sales.

He didn't mind, though. Tiny Mac loved the life as a trap star already. The bitches with good pussy, the money and the reputation of a D-boy.... He was living the same shit he would hear rappers talk about on some of his favorite songs. This was the life and he was living it.

"Pee Wee!" Tiny Mac called Pee Wee, who was sleeping on the floor next to his pistol.

"What, cuz?" Pee Wee jumped up.

"Listen for the door. I gotta go to the bathroom."

"You woke me up for that shit? Just hurry up nigga. I'm tired. I've been up all night."

When Tiny Mac got into the bathroom, he pulled his Nextel out of his pocket and dialed his cousin Craze's number.

"C'mon nigga, answer," an impatient Tiny Mac said, waiting to hear his cousin come on the line.

"What's hood?" his cousin answered.

"Ay Cuzzo, let me ask you something. The other day you said something about going with Boss over some bitch house, what was that ho's name?"

"Watch yo' mouth nigga, just because you got hair on your nuts and making money now, you still young as hell."

"Fuck you."

"You talking about Maliyah, that's Boss's lady."

"Craze, you're not gonna believe this shit, man. I'm at Pee Wee's trap. Tank sent me over here so Pee Wee could show me how to play with the pots, because you know I'ma be running the lab."

"Nigga, you know I know. I'm the one that put you on."

"Man, this hood rat bitch came over here trying to hire niggas for a ransom hit."

"For who?"

"Boss' girl! Nigga where's yo' antenna," Tiny Mac said, busting him out.

"Fuck you, nigga, when did this happen?"

"Like two hours ago."

"What's her name?"

"Man, nigga you know I smoke too much weed to be remembering shit like that. Oh, but she did say it was her best friend."

"It's that bitch from the club!"

"What club?"

"Nothin'. I'll hit you back. Keep ya' ear to the street."

"All the time. Aight, one." Tiny Mac discon-nected the call.

$ $ $

"Pablo, man, you wouldn't never guess who that was," Craze said, smiling from ear to ear.

"Who?"

"Tiny Mac. Somebody is trying to get 'em before us."

"What are you talking about? And pass the blunt! Over there babysitting."

"Oh, my bad." Craze took two hits from the blunt before passing it.

"That bitch with the fat ass from the club, Mrs. Boss' home girl."

"Yeah, what about her?"

"She just was at Pee Wee's trap trying to hire nig-gas for a hit to knock Mrs. Boss out the way. I told you Boss was fucking her. I peep'd game when you was dancing with the bitch, that nigga got one-time hot."

"I wasn't even stunnin' that broad. I wanted Mrs. Boss—now that bitch is bad!" Pablo shot.

"Hell yeah!" Craze gave Pablo some dap.

"This is gonna be a lot easier than we thought. That's what his ass get for hatin' on me when I was danc-ing with the bitch."

"Boss always let his dick get him in some shit," Craze said, laughing.

"Because he tells these hoes that he loves them, that's something you don't do."

"One man's slip-up is another man's come-up. We got his ass," Craze said and nodded his head with a devilish grin.

"Chuuch!" Pablo shot before hitting the blunt.

~~LOVE IS BLIND~~

CHAPTER 16
MALIYAH

"Why, Tia? Why?" I cried looking at my best friend, who now resembled the character Two-Face Harvey from the all-time classic, *Batman*.

Kayla paced the floor, unable to look Tia in the face. "This is bullshit! Where is he? Where's the mutha-fucka?"

"Y'all calm down. This is the reason I didn't want to call y'all. Maliyah, you promised me that you'd behave. Kayla, please do the same. All I need is for these people to tell Tommy y'all was in here cursing and carrying on," Tia said from her hospital bed.

"What the fuck? I'm out. I can't stay in here any longer. Something is really wrong with you!" Kayla said, then stormed out of the hospital room.

"Don't worry about her Tia, look at me. Look at me!" I shouted, grabbed my purse and dumped every-thing out on the bed. "Where's my goddamn mirror!" I cried. I searched through the many things that were in my purse, trying to locate my MAC compact. "Look at yourself! Look!" You can't keep doing this to yourself!" I cried, holding the mirror up to Tia's face so she could see the scars up close.

Tia cried and pushed the mirror away. "No!"

"You're gonna see this! Look!" I shouted, putting the mirror back to her face. "Press charges, Tia. If you don't stop it here, next time he's gonna kill you."

"Stop, Maliyah! Please! He didn't mean it— he's just going through something right now. It's nothing you can say or anyone else to make me put someone in jail for life. That's not our call. We don't have that type of power. If God wants that for Tommy, He will put him there!"

I stood speechless and looked at Tia. There was nothing else I could say or do to convince her that Tommy was a dangerous man who needed to be put back behind bars. The power an abusive man had over a woman was unbelievable.

"Now with that said, will you guys please let me handle this on my own. I know you guys are concerned, and I love you and Kayla for that, but if y'all really love me, y'all will leave me alone and let me deal with this. I'm a big girl!"

"Ms. Cooper, can you and your visitors please keep it down? Other patients are trying to get some rest, and to be honest, you should be getting some rest yourself."

"Yes, Nurse Cathy, my visitor was just about to leave so I could do that."

"Okay, Ms. Cooper, if you need anything I'll be right outside the door at my desk," the pleasant nurse said as she exited the room.

I collected my things off the bed and tossed everything in my purse. I slung it on my shoulder and grabbed Tia's hand. "I still love you. I just pray that you do the same and love yourself as much as I do." I kissed her on the hand and exited the room.

When I made it to the entrance, Kayla was puffing on a cigarette as she walked toward a bench that sat next to an ashtray. *Ugk! Cigarette smoke. When did she start smoking cancer sticks?* I thought. I hated the smell of cigarettes. It was crazy. I could tolerate the smell of weed and a Black & Mild, but the smell of cigarettes gave me a headache. I snuck up behind Kayla as she held on to the side of the bench, sitting down carefully like she was in some type of pain.

"What's wrong with you?"

"Shit!" She jumped startled. "That's how muthafuckas get killed—creeping up on ya'," she said.

"Kill me with what, cigarette smoke? Second hand smoke does kill. When did you start smoking cancer sticks, dawg?"

Kayla exhaled, being the bitch that she was, and blew a big stinky poof of smoke toward me.

"Ugh! You know that shit stay on your clothes. Why cigarettes, Kay? Ugh!"

"That bitch Tia got my nerves bad. Her with that Tommy bullshit will push you to start smoking crack." Tia threw the cigarette butt on the ground and stomped it with her House of Dereon peek-a-toe pump. "I had to get a cigarette from somebody. I left my Blacks in the car," Kayla said.

I noticed she was walking a little different than usual. "Why the hell you walking like that? And you was sitting down like an old-ass woman back there."

"I got cramps."

"We start our periods at the end of the month. It's the first."

"I know you're gonna let my period come when it feels like it!"

"Whateva, just come on." I pressed the unlock button on the car and slid in. I put in Beyoncé's CD and threw on my YSL shades as I sang along to Bey.

$ $ $

"Fuckin' Mexican!" Jasmine said. She looked through her clothes hamper for her Roberto Cavalli jeans. Throwing clothes all over the floor, she searched for her favorite jeans that snugged her ass just right. When she got to the bottom of the hamper, she sighed and took off to the walk-in, where she scanned the jeans section of the packed closet. "This bitch!" She stomped her foot, and put her hand on her hip. Storming out her closet, she hit the button on the intercom and yelled at the top of her lungs. "Maria! Get your fuckin' ass up here now!"

A couple of minutes later, Maria entered the room and found Jasmine standing in the middle of the floor with her arms crossed. Maria looked around at all the clothes on the floor. "What happen?"

"Where's my Cavalli jeans?"

"In the washer."

"I knew it! How many times do I have to tell you, do not wash my clothes? You fuckin' dummy! Dry cleaners only. You only wash my panties, bras, sleepwear, shit like that," Jasmine lectured the remedial maid. "Just get the fuck out!"

"I'm sorry, Jasmine."

"Get out! And I'm gonna tell Don to deduct it out of your pay so I can take a trip down to the Just Cavalli store!" Jasmine took off to the door behind Maria.

"What you say?" Jasmine screamed.

"Nothing!"

"I thought I heard you mumble something. Say it in English! Keep it up and you won't have a pay for Don to deduct!" Maria passed Maliyah, coming up the stairs.

"Hey, Maria."

"Hello, ma'am."

"I told you to stop that *ma'am* stuff," Maliyah said with a smile.

"Oh my god, dumb and fuckin' dumber!" Jas-mine shot, going back Into her room and slamming the shit out of the door.

"That girl has a serious problem," Maliyah said, shaking her head.

"Yes she does," Maria said in agreement and they both laughed.

"Mommie, would you like me to get you any-thing?"

"No thanks, I'm tired. I'ma try to get a nap in. It's been a long day."

$ $ $

Jasmine sat in her Jacuzzi-style tub taking a soothing bubble bath. *Don tink he's slick*, Jasmine said to herself as she thought about the quickie Don just put on her. Jasmine was purposely loud, hoping to wake Mali-yah, who was sleeping in the room down the hall. Don knew what the devious diva was up to, so he cut it short.

Jasmine was pissed off about Maliyah staying in the house. But she refused to let Don go that easy, espe-cially to a young-ass lame like Maliyah, so she was gonna stick it out and stay. Jasmine had invested too much time into Don just to up and leave.

Don gave her some weak-ass lie about using Maliyah to traffic dope, but Jasmine knew what was up. Her womanly intuition was telling her different. Maliyah was beautiful and weak-minded, just how Don liked 'em. And out of the many girls he had used in the past to traffic dope, he had never brought any of them to his home. Maliyah was different.

Jasmine got out of the tub and dried herself off. She glanced down at the Victoria Secret panties that she had just taken off and noticed brown discharge in the seat of them. "WHAT TE BUMBACLOT!!!" She grabbed the panties, putting them up to her nose. "Eww!" she said, smelling the horrible, unusual stench. "Oh no!" she shot, running out of the bathroom and grabbing her cell phone.

"Dr. Hall's office."

"Hello, this is Jasmine Coley. It's an emergency. Can I please come in to see Dr. Hall today?"

"You sure can, Ms. Coley, as long as you can be here by two o'clock."

Jasmine took the phone from her ear looking at the time displayed on the screen. It read one o'clock. "I sure can."

"Okay, see you in a bit," the pleasant receptionist said before hanging up. Jasmine ended the call and tossed the phone on the bed.

$ $ $

"From what I can see and what you're telling me, I think it's gonorrhea, Ms. Coley, but don't quote me. I have been doing this for a while, but we still must follow the proper procedures and wait until your gram stain results come in," Dr. Hall said.

"But Doc, just from what you're seeing in tis underwear, it looks like gonorrhea," Jasmine pleaded, sitting on the hospital bed and holding the pair of panties that she brought along.

"Ms. Coley, I'll give you a prescription for an antibiotic, because we both know something is not right. Now get dressed and I'll leave your prescription at the front desk."

"Thank you, Doc."

When Dr. Hall left the room, Jasmine burst into tears. She couldn't believe this was happening to her. "A fuckin' STD!" she said, stripping off the patient gown and putting on her clothes. Jasmine had always made this promise to herself: if she ever caught an STD, the nigga and ho that gave it to her would pay.

It was bumper-to-bumper traffic on the 110 Free-way. Jasmine drove in silence all the way back home. All she could think about was Don and Maliyah infecting her with an STD.

"Pussy hole! Bumbaclot!" she mumbled to herself with her strong Jamaican accent. After an hour drive Jasmine finally pulled through the gate. The tires on her Range Rover came to a screeching halt. She hopped out of the truck, leaving her keys in the ignition.

"Jasmine, are you okay?" Maria asked, as Jasmine pushed past her and headed straight up the stairs to Maliyah's room. Out of breath from running up the stairs three at a time, Jasmine burst through Maliyah's bedroom door and woke her out of a deep sleep.

"What the fuck are you doing?" Maliyah asked. She sat up in bed and stared into the face of a deranged Jasmine. Everything around Maliyah was moving fast as she came out of a deep sleep in slow motion. The hood in Maliyah told her to grab some-thing to clobber Jasmine upside the head but it was too late. Jasmine was on her ass like flies on shit.

"You nasty ho!" Jasmine barked as she pulled Maliyah out of the bed by her hair.

"Let me go! Let me go, you crazy bitch!" Maliyah yelled, trying to fight back. Jasmine was in full-blown beast mode, whooping Maliyah's ass.

Maria peeked into the room and saw Jasmine on top of Maliyah. "Get off of her!" Maria said, running into the room and trying to break up the fight.

"Bitch, if you touch me, I'll beat the beans out of your ass!" Jasmine snarled at Maria as she kept striking Maliyah in the face.

Maria didn't want to test the crazy bitch so she took off yelling into her walkie-talkie, "Boss! Boss!"

Maliyah was able to get ahold of Jasmine's face. She dug her nails into Jasmine's flesh. Jasmine screamed from the pain. "Ahh! Let me go!"

"No! You let me go!" Maliyah yelled and dug her nails in deeper and deeper.

Jasmine lost it when she saw blood and started beating Maliyah in the head. Don finally ran into the room and dragged Jasmine off of Maliyah.

"Get the fuck off of her!" Don said.

"You dirty dick bumbaclot!" Jasmine shot as she slapped Don. She startled herself, thinking about what she just did for a moment. Don gave her a look that she had never seen before. That's when she heard the voice of Dr. Hall: *We both know something is not right.* That right there put her back in not-giving-a-fuck-mode. "Don, you and this nasty ho gave me gonorrhea!"

"Bitch, I ain't gave you shit!"

"I thought you weren't fucking her, Donnie!"

Don stood speechless with the dumbest look on his face, knowing the cat was now out the bag.

"What are you talking about? This is my man!" Maliyah shot. "What is she talking about Don?" Maliyah looked over at Don and raised one eyebrow, then put her hand on her hip and waited for an answer.

"Yeah, what am I talking about, Don? Bitch! Did you miss the memo? He's fucking your nasty pussy ass, and me. It's obvious that he fucked you bareback because he gave me a fuckin' STD!" Jasmine said as she wiped the dripping blood from her face.

Jasmine reached over Don and slapped Maliyah in the face.

"Didn't I tell you to stop?" Don grabbed Jasmine by the neck. "Now, I'm gonna have to let her hit yo' ass back, because that was a sucka-punch," Don said, still holding her by the neck. "Maliyah, come over here and get a good one in."

Maliyah didn't waste no time. With a balled fist she punched Jasmine right in between the eyes, hoping to black both eyes.

"You bitch!"

"Now y'all even," Don said, releasing her neck. "You better stay put, because you don't want me to hit yo' ass." Maria stood by the door watching as the love triangle drama unfolded.

"Don, how can you do this to me. I thought you loved me," Jasmine sobbed.

"Shut the fuck up, Jasmine!" he shot through clenched teeth.

Kayla was right ... Maliyah thought. "Is that true Don? Do you love both her and me? Because you told me the same thing."

"I don't remember telling you that."

"Ha! Bitch, he don't love you!" Jasmine shot.

"I don't love you," Don looked over at Jasmine, and her smile turned into a frown. "The truth is—I'm in love with Maliyah."

Jasmine stood with the dumbest look on her face. "Oh, is that right! What happen to all that shit you was talking: 'I'm only using her to traffic dope.' Huh, Don? Bitch, you are a crash-test dummy. He got you fired from your job so you can go get his dope! It was all a set up!"

Don slapped her to the ground, lifting his size-ten Gucci sneaker and stomping her.

A tear fell from Maliyah's eye as she stood in disbelief. "Is that true, Don? So, you're the reason all this went down between me and my parents! How can you do this to me?"

Don stopped trouncing Jasmine out like he was starring in the movie *Stomp The Yard*, and looked over at Maliyah. "I helped you out. I changed you into an overnight celebrity," he said.

"That's how you feel?"

"Yeah, I upgraded you from a Honda to a Benz, and from a ghetto wardrobe to Sak's," he continued. Maliyah stood frozen, unable to utter a word.

"Now, you can bounce, leaving all of my shit behind, or you can stay and enjoy the good life, here, with a man that loves you."

"What about Jasmine, and the gonorrhea thing? Don, I'm only sleeping with you and I think you know that."

"Don't worry about her. She's canceled already, a dead subject. And, to be honest, I think she's lying. But to be on the safe side, we'll make appointments at the doctor to get checked out," he said, then kicked Jasmine one last time in the stomach. "Maria!" he called.

Maria came right in from listening outside the door. "Yes," she said.

"I know your nosy ass was out there listening."

"No, Boss."

"You lying. I saw you. Go call Tank and tell him to get over here now."

"Right away, Boss," Maria said and exited the room.

~~THE GOOD LIFE~~

CHAPTER 17
MALIYAH

Yeah, I chose the good life here with a man that loves me. I stood in front of my vanity mirror looking at all the bruises and scratches all over my body from the fight with Jasmine. I heard a voice in my head that said, "Just leave." But it was the voice of Maria as she stood over me with a first-aid kit.

"It's not that easy, where am I gonna go?"

"Back to your parents' house."

"You don't know Karen. She's not gonna let me come back and, besides, my dad made that very clear before I left with Don."

"I don't know, Maliyah. It sounds like a bunch of excuses to me. Because as a parent, I know if your child comes back home, we might talk a lot of shit, but we're gonna let ya' back in. Trust me."

"Nah, Maria it's about time I grow up. I'm a woman now."

"Okay I can respect that, just don't tell Don about this conversation we just had."

"You straight."

"What?"

"That means, you're cool."

"If you young kids say so." Maria smiled.

Don had kicked Jasmine out of the house, so I had my man all to myself. Come to find out, Jasmine was telling the truth about the STD. Don and I were infected with gonorrhea, a sexually transmitted dis-ease. We both were taking an antibiotic. In the doc-tor's words, "It's nothing that a little antibiotic could not clear up."

Don put two-and-two together. He said Jasmine gave it to us. She just tried to use me as a cover up for her whorey-ass-ways.

Anyhow, I forgave Don. He explained the whole story to me. I now know what it is that Don does for a living and I'm cool with it. We laid by the fireplace last night and he let it all out, all the secrets that he held inside. I listened to every word that Don said. He told me about his father that was sentenced to life in federal prison where he later died, which left Don having to feed in the streets.

Don and I stayed up to the wee hours of the morning, geeked up off a pill, telling each other our life stories. Ecstasy made you tell all of your business. We ended up making love and Don finally told me that he loved me. Imagine that! It was on some R Kelly type of shit, because it was the best sex I ever had.

The next morning I woke up to Kayla screaming in the phone. She went on about me never having time for her since I shacked up with Don. So to shut her ass up, I planned a girls' day out.

It was hell getting Tia out of the house. Now that Tommy had a job and was gone all the time, Tia had a lot of time to herself. She had made a drastic change. Tia went from P Diddy feelin' herself to hiding in her one-bedroom apartment, ashamed of the scars on the left side of her face. She called herself ugly and tried her best not to be seen in public, saying people were always staring at her. The old Tia longed for attention from others; now she was running and hiding from it. But after begging her for hours on the phone, Tia finally agreed to come along.

I made a pit stop at the carwash on Crenshaw before going to get the girls. I had to shine the Benz, getting her right. As I exited my car, I heard a bunch of kids sitting by their parents saying, "Ooooh, that's my car!" and pointing over at me. I laughed, remem-bering when I used to do that as a kid.

"I see your new car, Mommie," Jose said as he walked toward my car with his spray bottles and rags in tow.

"Hmmmm," I smiled and sashayed to the waiting area. All eyes were on me. I read the onlookers' minds—

some haters, some just wondering what it was I did for a living to have a car decked out like that.

I paid for a deluxe wash, a Dasani water, and a *Sister 2 Sister* magazine to catch up on the latest gossip as I waited on Jose's slow-ass to finish with my car. If he would stop looking over at me smiling and showing off that fucked up grill of his, maybe he could hurry the hell up. He stayed flirting with me every time I came to get my car washed. He made sure that he was the one washing it. He would blow kisses and wink his eye at me the whole time he was washing my car; that's why I tried hard not to look his way. Mexican men were the biggest perverts. He disgusted me. That's why he never got more than a dollar tip.

Jamie Foster Brown had my undivided attention as I read an interview that she was having with Tiny and Toya. "Ooooh, them shoes are hot! Ooooh, and I love that red in Tiny's hair." It was impossible for me not to talk to myself while looking through magazines. It was a habit that I needed to break because people in the waiting area were looking at me like I was crazy.

"Maliyah!" I heard someone calling my name. I looked up to see the college boy I met on the plane. "Maliyah right?" He was now standing in front of me.

"Yeah, hi um ... um."

"Terry."

"Yeah, Terry. I'm sorry my memory is shot."

"That's okay. So you up here getting your car washed?" he asked, trying to make small talk.

Nah, I'm up here selling bootleg CD's ...Why else would I be at a carwash? I thought. "Yeah, it needed it."

"So, how have you been?"

"I've been okay."

"What about school? You over there at El Camino right?"

"It's ... um..." I started to lie, but then thought, *Why lie, who in the hell is he?* "To tell you the truth, I haven't got around to it yet."

"You gotta put that on your to-do list, Shawty."

"I know. I'll get to it."

"I know something else you need to put on your to-do list," he smiled. That boy had a sexy smile and now that I wasn't scared shitless, I was able to get a good look at the brotha and he was definitely easy on the eyes. He looked a lot better than he did on the plane.

"And what is that Terry?" I asked, catching a glimpse of his shoes on the slide, and yes they were fresh out the Nike box, ready.

Grill ... CHECK ... Shoes ... CHECK ... *Wait what am I doing? I got a man*, I said to myself, interrupting my swag radar that sometimes did its job auto-matically.

"Calling me, that's what you need to put on your to-do list, under 'Priority,'" he said, trying to mack me up for the second time.

"I lost your number," I lied, knowing I threw that shit in the trash somewhere overseas.

"Where's your phone? So I can store it in."

He's persistent, I thought, pulling my iPhone out of my purse and handing it to him. "What about now, do you have time to go get a quick bite to eat? We'll call it a lunch date."

Okay, persistent is turning into bug-a-boo. When I heard my car horn blow, I was saved by the bell. Jose was signaling for me to come by waving a towel while smiling and showing off his rotten 32's. "I'm sorry Terry, I already got plans with my girls. But I'll call you."

"Make sure you do that."

I sashayed to my car, adding a little switch to it, knowing that Terry was eyeing me from behind. I glanced over my shoulder and checked to see if he was watching. He was watching me like a hawk, just like I knew he would. I smiled, then turned back around and walked toward my car. I dreaded this part of my carwash, handing Jose his dollar tip and smelling that stank-ass breath.

"All clean," he said.

"Did you spray some cherry air freshener?"

"Yes, si."

"Okay, thank you Jose." I handed him one crispy dollar bill.

I checked my mirrors, then looked for the perfect theme song to dump as I pull off. I loved doing that. Rihanna and Jezzy's *Hard* was perfect.

I tossed the *Sister 2 Sister* magazine on the back seat. *What in the hell?* I thought when I saw a hot pink G-string on the seat, and it damn sure wasn't mine. I reached in the back, grabbed them and noticed they had brown discharge in them. "Ugh!" I threw them bitches back where I got them from. "That disrespectful muthafucka!" I said knowing exactly where they came from, Jasmine. Kayla was telling me the truth all along.

I can't wait til I get home. Don got a real bitch fucked up! Fuckin' dirty pussy bitches in my ride!

$ $ $

"What's wrong with you? Why you so quiet?" Kayla asked me from the passenger seat.

"Nothin'. Just thinking."

"About?"

"Damn, business. Get some," I shot.

"Well, kill yo' self then," Kayla shot back, and I couldn't help but laugh. But after the he-he's and ha-ha's, I went right back into deep thought about the G-string I put in my trunk. I decided to keep the G-string and gonorrhea ordeal from Tia and Kayla. I couldn't handle the jokes and comments just yet, and the famous "I told you so."

One thing I'd learned from Tia and her relationship drama is never tell friends and family everything that goes on in the relationship, especially when the man has done something wrong. Because if you're planning on staying with him, all you've done is cause controversy between your boo and your loved ones, and they will eventually end up hatin' his guts, how me and Kayla hate Tommy's ass.

Pulling up to Tia's, she waved from the window. "See, that's what I'm talking about, promptness. Yo' ass be taking forever."

"Tia ain't as fly as me."

"Look, you know she's been feelin' some type of way about her scars. Don't say shit like that right now, you don't wanna hurt her feelings."

"Shit, she lets Tommy hurt 'em."

"You a disrespectful bitch. Shh! Here she comes."

"Hey y'all. Maliyah, gurl, this is fly! I love it," Tia said, giving me my props as she got in the back seat.

"Thanks girl!"

"You got that Beemer, Benz and Bentley pussy," Tia joked.

"Girl, shut up."

"Please, Pinto Pussy," Kayla shot.

"Fuck you." Tia playfully hit Kayla in the back of her head.

We all laughed. Everything was back to normal. We were busting each other out, laughing, just acting a fool. But every time I looked in my rear view mirror at Tia in the back seat, it hurt me to see my best friend looking like that. Tia wore a bone straight wrap that was combed to her face, trying to cover up the scars the best that she could.

Tia was puttin' on for me and Kayla. She tried too hard, acting like everything was normal and nothing ever happened. What she failed to realize is that I was her best friend before anything, and I could see the hurt in her eyes, and hear her soul crying out for help.

I once heard a wise man say, "You can't help someone that don't want to help themselves." Then I thought about all the chaos that had been going on in my life. Here I was infected with an STD and hiding bruises on my face with concealer. Luke 6:41 in the Bible says "Why do you look at the speck of saw dust in your brother's eye and pay no attention to the plank in your own eye?" That was so true. Who was I to judge Tia?

We arrived at the Beverly Center ready to do some damage. Shit, I knew I was with the Platinum American Express card that Don gave me. He added me to his account as an authorized user when I explained to him that a brief case full of money wasn't gonna work for me every time I wanted to go out and shop.

I never knew the joy of saying, "Charge it." Damn, it was it a wonderful feeling. Me and the girls were in the Gucci store surrounded by sale associates, shoes, and handbags. We picked out a pair of shoes and a purse to match. I simply said, "Charge it!" and pulled out the American Express. I felt like the rapper Fabolous: "Just throw it in the bag." Now I know what he was talking about. The lady handed me a receipt to sign that said twelve thousand and some change.

Twelve thousand! I screamed to myself, but signed the receipt like it was nothing.

When we exited the store carrying big bags that said "Gucci" in big white letters, Tia looked over at me puzzled. "Bitch, who is this nigga you fuckin', Barack Obama?" I laughed and looked at her through my Prada eyewear. Before I could reply I was rudely interrupted by this nigga.

"Mmmm, what's yo' name?"

"Damn, that was rude. Don't you see me holla'n at my girl?"

"Aww, my fault. Excuse me Ms. Lady." He apologized, but I wasn't trying to hear it. "Now, is that better? What's yo' name, lil ma'ma? You fine as hell."

"First name: Annoyed; last name: By you. Now kick rocks and keep it moving, playa'."

"Damn, I always pick the bitter one out of the bunch. Where's the sweet? Uhh?" He looked at Tia and quickly turned his attention to Kayla.

"Okay, I see a little sweetness," he said with that lame-ass game, sizing Kayla up. "What's yo' name sweet thang?"

"First name: Sick; last name: Of you. I'm related to her," Kayla shot. We all laughed and walked off, leaving the skinny jean, Van-wearing lame standing there looking dumb.

"Okay, now tell me all about Barack," Tia said, trying to be funny.

"His name is Don, and, T, I think I'm in love."

"Awwww! Really?"

"Yes, he's so sweet. The way he touches me, the way he treats me. I just love everything about him."

"Don't forget the way he wines and dines you. The Benz, the new look. Girl, he sounds like he's an all-the-above brotha."

"Kayla already met him. I can't wait until you meet him. He's so good to me and my friends. Oh, that reminds me. His birthday is in a couple of weeks and I want to throw him a surprise party and I need y'all to help me." Kayla looked over at me, trying to act like she didn't hear me. Whoever she was texting on her phone, she was writing them a fuckin' book.

"You talking to me?" She glanced up from the screen.

"Nah, I'm talking to you. The bitch that had a fit because I don't find time for her, and now she don't have time for me, ain't that a bitch! Over there writing a damn book."

"Gurl, shut up. Let me just finish this message, hold up," Kayla said, typing away.

"Who you texting?" I asked, looking over her shoulder and trying to get a quick look.

"Move wit yo' nosy ass." She covered the screen.

"You don't have to hide it. I already know you're a pimp."

To Donald Daddy—I miss u too. Make sure your on time. Don't leave me waiting like the last time. i'ma ride that dick all night. I should be mad at yo' ass. Why I didn't get an American Express??? Your pussy on the side should get treated equally to yo live-in pussy. We need to really have a serious talk about some things. But anyway, thanks for the Gucci purse and shoes. I love it :) She spent twelve thousand. She spent only four on me. See u later daddy.

SEND. Kayla tossed the phone in her purse. "Now, what was yo' ass talking about?"

"Who the hell you texting? Because I know it ain't Pee Wee. He can't get away from the scale, Ziploc bags, and dope fiends long enough."

"You worried about the wrong thing."

"It's probably that lil chocolate cutie that I seen her with at Denny's a couple of weeks ago."

"Who? You mean to tell me you got a new piece that I don't know about? You foul for that," I shot.

"Gurl, they were lovie dovie at Denny's. I didn't know you had it in ya Kay, to bump a nigga that fine. I'm so happy for y'all. Liyah, you got a man that treats you like a queen, and Kay you found a good looking brotha that looks like he's the opposite of the trap star wanna-a-be thugs that you usually fuck wit. You can tell he has some thangs, and he actually takes you somewhere beside the trap spot. What was his name? D, Derrick, Deway–"

"Donald," Kayla said cutting Tia's forgetful ass off.

"Yeah, Donald. I knew it was something that started with a D."

"He ain't nobody," Kayla said with a slight smile.

"Yeah, whateva. You can make Maliyah believe that bullshit because she wasn't there, I was. You had a glow to ya that I've never seen before," Tia continued rubbing it in.

"Hmmm, you foul Kayla." I rolled my eyes.

"I'm glad to know we're keeping secrets now," I said walking ahead of them toward the Hot Dog On A Stick to get me a cherry Lemonade.

"Gurl, kill yo'self, ain't nobody keeping no secrets," Kayla said, walking behind me.

Walking from the food court, niggas approached me and Kayla left and right. After about the tenth nigga we turned down, Tia excused herself, going to the restroom. After about five minutes, she exited the bathroom, looking like she had been crying. Tia was a red bone like myself, so it was noticeable when we had been crying because our face turned a reddish pink. I felt bad for Tia, and started to feel uncomfortable for her every time a nigga approached me and Kayla, so I decided to bounce from the mall.

We passed Macy's on the way out, and I had an idea. I hated to see one of my friends feeling down about something. I thought. *Damn this Mac concealer is doing a hellva job because they haven't noticed the bruise and scratches that was on my face from the fight yet. I bet they got something to hide them scars on Tia's face. But how was I gonna tell her I wanted to buy her some make-up to cover up those terrible scars without hurting her feelings. I got it!*

"I need to run in MAC real quick. I'm almost out of lip gloss."

"Oooh, and I need some foundation," Kayla said. After we looked around and I paid for my lip gloss, I suggested that we get our faces made up.

"Okay," Kayla said. I knew that ho was gonna be all for it.

"Let me think, did the doctor say I can wear makeup? Yep, I remember he said once my face heals."

"It's healed right?"

"Yeah, I guess."

"Okay, let's get our faces done, then we'll go get mani and pedi's."

"You are so booughetto," Kayla shot.

I gave that ho the finger, still mad about this new nigga Donald that she hadn't told me about. Kayla was first to finish and she looked good. I was done not too long after Kayla. When I looked in the mirror I was out done by the beautiful art.

"Damn Debra, you did that!" I said. I've never been one to just make up my face with all that eye shadow and shit. I was naturally pretty, give me a little lip gloss and I'm good to go.

"For real, you like it? I thought you were gonna be one of those picky customers," Debra said in between smacking on some gum.

"It's bangin'!"

"See pink looks hot on you, with your complexion I can work with a lot of different colors. You have almond-shaped eyes. I love doing a nice eye," Debra said, talking make-up talk. I couldn't stop looking in the mirror. My make-up was flawless, not too much, it was just right. The girl had skills.

"Walah!" the MAC make-up artist said that was doing Tia's make-up once she finished.

"How it look? Does it look good?" Tia asked me and Kayla, who was staring at her with our mouths wide open. Tia looked amazing, you could barely see the burn scars. That girl did some fuckin' surgery on Tia because she looked like she never had second degree burns. "Say something!" Tia said, hesitant to look in the mirror. "Shit, let me see the mirror." She got out of the chair and took a look at herself up close and personal. "I look pretty a ... again," she said, getting teary-eyed.

"What are you talking about Tia, you've always been pretty," I said getting teary-eyed myself.

"Bitch, I'm jealous! Yours look better than mine," Kayla shot.

"C'mon y'all keep it one hundred, y'all won't hurt my feelings. Since the accident I look like a totally different person, huh? I do not look the same."

"Yes you do."

"T, yes you do. Now stop before we all fuck up our make-up from crying," Kayla said.

Tia turned looking at the girl's name tag that did her make-up. "Thank you, you got talent Amber. I love it!"

"Girl, like I tell everybody, you make the make-up, the make-up don't make you. Because under-neath all of this you're beautiful."

"Aww thank you girl."

"Amber, I wanna buy everything that you used on Tia's face."

"Liyah, that's gonna be too much. This stuff is expensive."

"Uh uhh, charge it! Just throw it in the bag," I said pulling out the Platinum card.

"Oh lord, you're gonna spend all Barack's money," Tia shot.

$ $ $

Tommy sat in front of Tank as he nervously anticipated meeting the head nigga in charge, Donnie Boss. "Damn, this nigga! He should be coming any minute now," Tank said, tapping his Air Jordans anxiously, and looking at his diamond-face time piece every couple of minutes like he had some where to be.

"I ain't trippin' homie," Tommy said admiring all the pictures on the wall of Scarface, Al Capone, Al Pacino, and he even had one of Frank Lucas up there on the king-pin wall of fame, in the room they called "The Chop-it-up Room."

"Tank, why the Chop-it-up Room?"

"Because, this is where we chop it up at. We discuss the moves we make in this room, at that long-ass table where you're sitting. Unless, Boss calls a meeting at a club or sumthin.'"

"Oh." Tommy shook his head. He was ready to meet the man that everyone called Boss and spoke so highly about. *I wonder if I know this dude,* Tommy thought. He had been out the game for a while, but he was still well known in the streets of LA for the moves he made back in the day before losing it all to the system.

Don entered the room puffing on a cigarillo. "Sorry for the wait," he said looking over at Tommy sitting at the table. "Do I know you?" Don asked, trying to figure out where he knew Tommy from.

"Nah, I don't think so. But you probably do, it's no telling. I used to be in these streets wild'n," Tommy smiled, reminiscing for a second about his old life.

"I just feel like I've seen you somewhere before. You probably knew my Pops."

"Who dat?"

"Goldie."

"Goldie, yo' pops man!" Tommy said hyped.

"Hmmmm," Don nodded his head, as he puffed on his cigarillo.

"I can see it, just by the way you handle yo' business. Yo' pops was about his bread. As a lil nigga in the game I looked up to your pops. I used to make moves for him. Them pussy-ass Feds threw the book at ya' pops like that, that was fucked up. May he rest in peace."

"Tank tells me you were in the can."

"I was in State, thank God. If the Feds would have got a hold to my case, I'd still be jammed up. The price was hefty though."

Don looked through a cloud of smoke. "So, this our new guy. He seems cool and he knew Pops, so that's a plus."

"Yep, this Tommy, Boss. He's the driver for Shane's stash house, and I guess we can use him as a OT driver too."

Don looked Tommy in the eyes. "Can you be trusted?"

"Hell yeah! I'm a real nigga."

"Aiight, you a limo driver, dress like one. A black suit at all times, and give Tank yo' Social Security number so I can get you a paycheck stub made, make it look legit. I like to be on point at all times."

"Just like Goldie."

When Tank seen Craze's number flashing on the caller ID, he looked over at Don. "Excuse me Boss, let me get this," Tank said before answering the phone, knowing Don hated for nigga's to take calls during a meeting. Don nodded his head giving him the okay.

"Yo," Tank answered. "What! Y'all nigga's is dumb! I told y'all to stop doing jobs high because of shit like this.

Y'all niggas are already retarded, being high just makes y'all numb and dumb! I'm on my way over, fuckin' numb and dumber!" Tank disconnected the call. "DAMN!"

Don looked over at Tank. "Everything aiight?"

"Man, these stupid ass niggas did the job in the car. The 48 Hours is up on Florence as we speak."

"What! It's registered to this address."

"I know, don't trip Boss. I'm gonna fix it."

"How the fuck you gonna fix that?" Don yelled. Tommy sat listening trying to put two-and-two together. He knew the hood term for "48 HOURS" was homicide detectives.

"Well, don't just stand here. Go check it out. Tommy can take the limo home."

Tank did as told exiting the room in a hurry. Don walked over to the intercom pressing the button. "Maria!"

"Yes Boss," Maria replied.

Don looked back at Tommy. "You want some-thing to drink man?" he asked.

"Yeah, water is cool."

"Bring my cigars, and something to drink in the chop room."

"Right away Boss."

Don walked the short distance back to the leather chair at the head of the conference table.

"I never forget a face. You the dude from Den-ny's."

"Donald."

"We both know my name is not Donald, but that's gonna stay between us, right?"

"I ain't built like that. I told you Boss, I'm a real nigga. Real nigga's do real things, ho-nigga's do ho-nigga shit. That's none of my business."

"Good answer, my man." Don extended his hand. Tommy stood up from his seat to go shake his hand.

"Long distance man." Don stopped him in his tracks with his hand still out. Tommy sat back down in the chair and extended his hand giving Don a long distance hand shake. They both laughed at the thought.

"You're now employed by Boss Limousine and Transportation Service. Tommy, you're gonna fit in just fine," Don said with a smile.

What the fuck was all that about. What is this nigga hiding? I'm lost, Tommy thought on some ho-nigga shit.

~~BUTLER NO BS~~

CHAPTER 18
MALIYAH

Speeding in the fast lane with the pedal to the floor, I gripped the steering wheel tightly, being my own hype person and saying shit to pump myself up. *How he just gonna disrespect me like I'm some average chick? Who in the hell this nigga think he is?*
As hard as it was to, I blocked the G-string out of my head while with the girls. But the moment I dropped them off at home, all I could think about was getting home to check Don for fuckin' some tramp in my ride.

I pressed the remote clamped on my sun visor and the gates slowly became ajar. I drove through the gates and tears came to my eyes. *Stop it Maliyah with the bull-shit!* I cursed myself, as I put the emotional shit in the back seat.

I popped the trunk, grabbed the nasty G-string, and stormed in the house. I went straight to his office. Without knocking, I barged in. "Donnie!" I stopped when there was no sign of the bastard. Still on the prowl to find him, I ran into Maria. She seen the rage in my eyes and the underwear in my hands. Going with her better judgement not to pry in my business like she usually did, she simply pointed in the direction of the conference room and said in a low tone, "He's in there."

I ignored the sign on the door that read, "DO NOT DISTURB. BEWARE OF BOSS."

"Fuck Boss," I mumbled barging in. "Don come here!" I shot with a little neck, hiding the G-string behind my back. When I caught a quick glimpse of the nigga that was sitting at the table with him, I thought my eyes were playing tricks on me because it was fuckin' Tommy.

Don turned his attention back to Tommy and paid me no mind. "I know you hear me Donnie!" I shot, standing in my baby momma pose.

"What's up Maliyah?" Tommy greeted me with a smile.

I turned, giving him the dirtiest look. "I don't like you, and you know that, so please don't say shit to me," I shot, rolling my eyes on a war path. Don continued to ignore me and I lost it. I walked the short distance over to where he was sitting and tossed the hot pink G-string on the table in front of him. "Read my lips, you're the nastiest, most disrespectful muthafucka I have ever met!" I said, then stormed out the room and slammed the door behind me.

Upstairs, I sat on the balcony sipping on a Hennessy and Coke and tried to unwind. I thought about the half-smoked blunt in my purse that me and the girls were blazing earlier. I went for my purse as Prada followed behind me. It was obvious that my puppy missed me while I was gone. I grabbed the blunt and lighter, taking them to the balcony.

I noticed Tommy leaving the house. I stared him down, thinking to myself, *Only if I had a sniper.* He felt my eyes burning a hole through him as he walked toward one of the parked limousines. Tommy waved and smiled being the asshole that he was, trying to annoy me. He did a good job at it. I shot his ass the bird and continued smoking on my blunt. And waited on Don because I know he was on his way up here now that Tommy was gone.

"*In Ten ... Nine ... Eight ... Seven*" I counted down in my head and by the time I got to one, Don was dragging me off the balcony by my hair.

"Bitch, don't you ever disrespect me like that in front of one of my guest!" he said on top of me, stuffing the G-string in my mouth. "Bitch! You'll have these nigga's thinking it's cool to try me!" he continued.

I gagged from the nasty G-string that was getting stuffed down my throat.

"Now get yo' ass up!!" he said, grabbing me by the neck and standing me up like I was a dummy doll.

"You muthafucka!" I said, ungagging myself, then throwing the G-string at his face. He dodged it, which pissed me off even more.

WHAP! I slapped the shit out of him. He came back so fast slapping me back on some Three-Stooges type of shit. "When yo' **ass** hit me expect to get hit the fuck back!" he shot.

I held my warm face that probably was fire engine red with the imprint of Don's hand. "So nigga when you fuck a bitch in my car, expect for me to fuck a nigga in yo' shit! Since we playing by those rules!"

"Play wit yo' life if you wanna."

"How could you fuck that nasty bitch in my car?"

"Who? What are you talking about?"

"Who else, unless it's someone else!"

"Man Maliyah, miss me with this shit," he shot, walking toward the door.

"Nah, nigga we gonna talk about this!" I ran standing in front of the door.

"Talk about what?"

"You fuckin' Jasmine in my car, nigga?"

"Jasmine?" he chuckled.

"What's so fuckin' funny?"

"Yo insecure ass, you stunnin a bitch that no longer exist. Get it together, Ma."

"So how the fuckin' panties get in my back seat then Don!"

"Shit I don't know, they probably yours."

I walked the short distance grabbing the G-string off the ground. "Nigga, do it look like I'll wear some cheap shit like this?"

"Yeah, before you got wit me."

"Oh, you trying to be funny nigga? Donnie keep it funkie wit me? Did you fuck the bitch in my car?"

"No! Now stop asking me the same question over and over again sounding like a fuckin' broken record!" He pushed me out the way, then stormed out the room.

"Donnie, I'm not finished wit yo' ass! We gonna get down to the bottom of this shit!" I followed behind him. He went into his office and sat behind his desk. I burst through the door out of breath from trying to keep up, with the G-string in my hand.

"Now, you out of bounds! Maliyah get the fuck out!"

"I ain't going no muthafuckin' where!" I screamed with my hand on my hip, meaning what I said.

He sighed, standing up from the leather chair that sat behind his desk, walked over to where I was standing and said with a calm serious tone, "I'm not asking you. I'm telling you. Now get the fuck out."

"And I'm telling you, I–ain't–going–no–mutha-fuckin'–where!" I said it in syllables for his ass.

WHAP! I never seen it coming, the back hand that landed on the left side of my face.

"Ahhh!" I screamed and blood slung from my busted lip.

"Hard headed bitch!" he barked.

I panicked once I seen blood and took off to my room.

$ $ $

Don grabbed the G-string off the floor once Maliyah took off, placing it up to his nose. The strong scent of Bath and Body Works Sweet Pea was still in the G-string right along with discharge stains, which told Don two things: that they belonged to Kayla and that she also was infected with the STD. *This bitch burn't me,* he thought.

$ $ $

Jasmine Sullivan crooned out the speakers as I sat on the couch crying and holding a cold towel to my fat lip.

Don leaving me home alone and staying out all night was starting to become a ritual. Any other night he'd just leave and wouldn't return until the following morning around check-out time. But this night in particular he told me not to wait up for him. Walking out the door smelling and looking good I knew off the rip there was another woman. But who? Why would he kick Jasmine out of the house to fuck with her on the low? Shit everything was out in the open here. He should've just let her stay if he was gonna creep around with her anyway.

I chased him out the door trying to make everything right before he left, but he wasn't trying to hear anything I had to say. He turned the tables, making me believe it was all my fault that we got into the huge fight in the first place. Surrounded by Kleenex, I sipped Ciroc straight from the bottle, going hard in depressed mode.

"Mrs. Boss! Mrs. Boss!" Maria came running in the living room like a crazy woman. "The people are here to see you," she said taking off back toward the front door.

"What people?" I asked, getting up from the couch and following behind her to get no answer. Once I made it to the front door there were two men dressed in suits.

"Here she is," Maria said to the short chubby one when I walked up.

"Hi Ma'am. I'm Detective Daniels and this is my partner Detective Murphy." Both men flashed their badges. "Is it alright if we come in?"

"No, you're fine right where you are."

"Okay then. I'm here to ask you some questions about Jasmine Coley."

"What about her?"

I caught the slim detective that'd been standing in silence staring at my busted lip. "What happened to your lip?" he asked.

"What about Jasmine?" I ignored his question turning my attention back to Detective Daniels.

"Ms. Coley was found murdered in her car this afternoon."

"What! I just seen her!" I spoke too fast.

"Okay, that was my next question," Daniels said pulling out a writing tablet and pen from his pocket.

"I can't remember. Uhh, a couple of days ago."

"Now you don't remember. What is your relationship to Donnie?"

"How we get on me and Donnie when this is about Jasmine?"

"Ma'am, just answer the question," he said with a firm tone.

"Donnie is my man," I said with a little bass. He wrote something down in his tablet.

"So, you and Donnie aren't married? Because the maid called you Mrs."

"No we're not married."

"Okay, and what was Ms. Coley's relationship to Donnie?"

"I ... don't know." I choked up for a minute.

"Are you sure?"

"Yeah, I'm sure."

"Now, I guess my question would be, what type of relationship did you think Donnie and Ms. Coley had?"

"Like I said, I don't know!"

"I was told by Ms. Coley's close to kin that Donnie was her fiancé. So, that takes me back to the question that Murphy asked. What happened to your lip?"

"I'm not answering no more questions."

"I think you're hiding something."

"You get paid to think, detective?"

"No smart-ass, I get paid to break little-ass girls like you down. Now you can cooperate or next time I see you it will be with a warrant for your arrest. Because it's mighty funny that Ms. Coley had scratches and bruises on her face and I come over here and you look like you've been in some type of physical altercation. Now, did you and Ms. Coley get in an argument or anything physical? Because that's what I think, and what I think does matter to the prosecutor." He chuckled before continuing. "You and Ms. Coley got into an altercation because Donnie was seeing the both of you."

"Look, I don't know what you're talking about!" I shot, getting agitated and scared all at the same time.

"When should you be expecting Donnie?"

"I don't know."

"Well give him this, and tell him to contact me at any one of these numbers as soon as possible." He handed me one of his cards. I grabbed it with my trembling hand, scared to death. He turned around and began to walk off. "Oh yeah, for the record, I get paid to get down to the bottom of things, and know when someone is lying to me. I have a strong feeling that I'll be seeing you again. Have a good night," he said with a devilish grin before walking off.

I slammed the door. "Maria, get Donnie on the phone now!" I yelled.

"Mommie, that's what I've been trying to do, but he's not answering."

"Shit!" I said, going for my phone to get the same result, Don's voicemail. "He's mad at me; he's not gonna answer a call from my number! I'll send him a text."

"Aye yai yai," Maria said, placing her hand on her forehead.

"Okay I sent it. Hopefully he'll call back."

"Mommie, did he say where he was going?"

"No, after we got into that fight he just up and left. I thought he was with Jasmine, but if she's dead, where could he be? With someone else?"

Damn she boss'd up ... Don thought, walking behind Kayla as they got on the hotel elevator headed up to their suite. Don adjusted his hard dick that was standing at attention in his jeans.

"You sure are wearing that dress, Ma," he complimented Kayla's thick frame in the tight-fitting Herve Leger by Max Azria mini that snugged her curves in all the right places.

"Really, you like it daddy?" Kayla asked, easing up against him, rubbing her ass across his dick. "Does he like it?" she said mischievously.

"Why don't you ask him."

She looked up and nodded her head toward the surveillance camera that was in the elevator.

"So," he shrugged. "Now if you scared I understand," he continued, using reverse psychology and hoping that it worked.

"Did you forget who you're talking to?" she said, tugging at his jeans, pulling out the anaconda and placing it in her mouth. Don pushed the 18th floor to give him enough time to get his jolly's off. He put his head back and enjoyed the ride as Kayla went to work on every bit of 12 inches like a pro. "Ooooh!" he moaned, looking down at Kayla on her knees with a mouth full of dick. He smiled, thinking to himself. *Bitch you burn't my dick so I'ma burn yo' mouth.* After doing a little research, he learned there is such a thing as gonorrhea of the throat.

Don was almost certain that Kayla gave him the STD, because she never confronted him about giving it to her. But almost certain wasn't good enough to beat Kayla's ass. He had to know for sure. Don didn't really know where he got the STD from because he ran-up in every last bitch he was fuckin' on bare-back.

Oooh, I won't kiss you in the mouth, but you damn sure can get it, Don thought, feeling himself about to cum in Kayla's mouth.

Sex with Kayla was mind blowing because she was down for whatever, whenever. She was like a pink-toe in a black girl's body. White girls are known to have the most fun. Kayla was every bit of nigga. She was just a natural born freak that partied like a rock star.

Don was beginning to fall for the freak, especially now that she stepped her game up, 86'n her project-chick micro braids and Reebok classics. She still wasn't wifey material, but she was the perfect jump off. When playing house with Maliyah got boring, Don would creep with Kayla for excitement. In the suite, where they finished what they started in the elevator, Don laid out of commission.

"Don, get up we need to talk."

"Look, I'm tired. Just because you're high off that powder on energizer bunny status don't mean I feel like being bothered," he shot.

Kayla stood over him not taking no for an answer. "C'mon Don, get up and talk to me."

"You got enough coke, weed and drink. Let me rest up for a minute until I'm ready to knock you down again." Kayla sighed, sucking her teeth, and plopped down on the couch, pouting like a child that can't have their way.

"I'm tired of this shit! You come kick it wit me to fuck like rabbits and go right to sleep. You could do that at home with yo' bitch!" she said, hoping to get a reaction out of Don.

"Laying over there looking like a broke dick dog!" she continued.

RING! RING! Don grabbed his phone off the night-stand and glanced at the caller ID.

"Oh, but you can talk to that ho! Not on my mutha-fuckin' time you won't," Kayla barked, snatch-ing his phone out of his hand. "If you can't talk to me, you won't talk to her!" She powered the phone off. Kayla was one of those wild bitches that liked to get choked up and slapped around by a man. It turned her on, especially when she was high off the dust. She would try hard to push Don's buttons, hoping to get a reaction out of him, so he could choke, spank and pull her hair while fucking the dog-shit out of her. The cocaine made her like it rough.

Don laid on the bed, staring at Kayla and shaking his head. "See, that same attitude right there is what makes me think you purposely put those drawers in the car."

"First of all, niggas wear drawers, bitches wear panties. And I already told you that I must have acciden-tally left them in there. I'm so used to not wearing none at all. It must've slipped my mind. Shit, Maliyah so stupid you can tell her they're hers and she'll believe it." Kayla stuck with her lie.

But Don was not buying it. "Yeah, sounds good," he shot with sarcasm. Don liked to believe God had blessed him with the power to see through the bullshit.

"What's that sarcastic shit suppose to mean? I know you believe me right?"

"I believe you on that bullshit, that's what I believe. But I'm a let you have this one. Now if something like this happen again, I'm cutting you off for good because I'm not wit all that drama. And one thing you're gonna do is respect my girl."

"Respect yo' girl?" Kayla fell out laughing. "You don't even respect yo' girl. You call me sucking yo' dick on the elevator, and meeting me at a hotel every week-end respecting yo' girl? Nigga, you got life and everything else all fucked up."

"No dumb-ass, you need to lay off the dust. You know what the hell I mean, stop throwing fuckin' salt in my game. You and Maliyah play two different positions. She can't play yours, and you damn sure can't play hers."

"It's no need, Boo. I have you just as much as she do."

"Well, if you wanna keep having me as much as she do, play yo' position as my other bitch. That means no BS."

$ $ $

I managed to calm myself down while Don was out all night up to no good. When he strolled in the house, I didn't even bother to ask him where the hell he'd been. My only concern was making sure that I wasn't a suspect for Jasmine's murder. Going to jail was my biggest fear. The thought of me rockin' some County blue's made me nauseated.

I watched as Don paced the floor with the detective's card in his hand. "You are never supposed to talk! Always request for your lawyer to be present," Don said, trying to cover up the fact that he was upset with me for talking to the pigs. But how was I supposed to know? I'd never been in any type of trouble a day in my life. I put my head down, closed my eyes, and took a deep breath. I was tired of watching Don pace back and forth. He was beginning to make me nervous. Everything was too much to grasp at once. Murder, the detectives, and now I have to talk to Don's big-shot attorney.

"Maliyah, are you listening to me?"

I raised my head. "Yes Donnie. Never talk. Always request for your lawyer to be present," I said, letting him know I got everything he said. I put my head back down, thinking to myself that the information that he was giving me was useless because the damage was already done.

"Ma, I'm sorry. I should've been here with you."

You think? I thought with sarcasm.

"Them muthafucka's wouldn't never got shit out of me."

"Mr. Boss, Ms. Goldstein is here." Maria came through the walkie-talkie that was sitting on the table.

"My pit bull is here," he said with relief, walking the short distance and grabbing the walkie-talkie. "Okay set us up in the chop-it-up room," he spoke into the walkie-talkie.

"I will do that."

Don walked over to the couch where I was sitting. "Baby you don't have nothing to worry about." He kissed me on my lips, and at that moment I felt safe.

I sat beside Don at the conference table, shaking my leg anxiously underneath the table as I waited on the high-power attorney's grand entrance. When she entered the room, the first thing that came to mind was money. She wore a Dolce & Gabbana pants suit, draped in pearls, with a nice, classy cut bob.

"Mr. Boss," she greeted Don, as she slammed her brief case on the table. "I'm in trial so we're gonna have to make this quick," she said, taking a seat across from me. "Hello, I'm Dana Goldstein, and you are?"

"Maliyah." I reached across the table, shaking her hand with my sweaty palm and went right back to fidgeting.

"Mr. Boss, Daniels really has it out for you," Dana said, looking over at Don with her permanent mean-mug that she wore on her face.

"Yeah, but with you on my team he doesn't stand a chance."

"You got that right," she said, turning her attention back to me. "Okay Maliyah, what is your last name?"

"Brent, I'm sorry. I'm just a little nervous."

"There's no need to be nervous. I'm on your side; I work for you. Now, let's get down to business. I want you to tell me everything that you told the detectives without leaving anything out," Dana said assertively with an intimidating mean-mug that made it hard for me to look her in the face.

As I recapped everything that was said between me and the detectives, Dana sat listening and jotting down notes on a legal note pad. When she wasn't writing, she was tapping her pen on the table, making this aggravating noise that was driving me insane.

"Okay, let me make sure I'm understanding what you're saying. You never told Daniels nor Murphy about what happened to your lip?" Dana probed.

"No," I replied, getting agitated. *I know I'm speaking English ain't that what I just said,* I thought to myself. Attorney's would ask you the same questions over and over again like you're retarded. This snooty non-facial-expression-having bitch was starting to get on my damn nerves.

"And you and Ms. Coley did in fact get into a physical altercation?"

"Yes."

"When did that take place?"

"A couple of days ago."

"Something is not adding up. If you and Ms. Coley got into a physical altercation a couple of days ago, why is your lip still swollen? The swelling would have gone down by now, don't you think?"

I looked over at Don, then back at Dana. I was confused on what to say. I didn't know whether to lie or tell the truth. This lady was still a cracker, and wasn't the friendliest person that you would ever want to meet. I didn't know who to trust at this point.

"Ms. Brent, I've been a criminal defense attor-ney for a while now. I already know what happened to your lip. I'm just trying to build some type of trust here. Like I told you before, I'm not working against you, I'm for you. Ms. Brent, I'm your best friend and you don't even know it. I'm often in the position of knowing that my clients are guilty," Dana said, glancing over at Don. "No offense Mr. Boss, but he's one of them. Sorry for throwing you out there, but it's the truth."

"Don't worry about it," Don said cool, calm, and collected.

"Like I was saying, I still fought for them be-cause they were innocent in my eyes."

"Me and Donnie got into a fight, but it was all my fault!" I blurted out, feeling some type of relief.

"Now, was that hard, Ms. Brent? That's what I've been waiting for you to say. I'm going to ask you one more question and I want you to be honest. If you don't remember, just say you don't remember. Did you tell the detectives what you just told me about the fight you and Mr. Boss had?"

"No!"

"Are you sure?"

"Yes!"

"The reason to all the questioning is to prepare a defense. If the prosecutor files a charge against you, I'm already on top of things. In order to prepare a good de-fense, it's imperative that I know everything that was said with no surprises. Ms. Brent, leaving me in the dark about anything is expecting me to operate a vehicle blindfolded. With that said, from this moment on, if you're ever ques-tioned by law enforcement, don't say anything. Just hand them one of my cards and I'll handle it, it's that easy. I always like to tell my clients, I do all the talking and you do all the check signing."

"Dana, are you done with her?" Don asked, read-ing my mind.

Dana briefly looked over her notes and said. "Yes, I think we covered everything."

"Baby, can you step out for a minute while I talk to Dana in private?"

"I sure can." I quickly got up, damn near running toward the door, but then I thought to myself, *What the hell is so important that he has to talk to her in private?...*

Exiting the room, curiosity got the best of me. Don's track record wasn't good. I couldn't trust him as far as I could throw him. I put my ear to the door listening to everything that was said.

"Mr. Boss, it's obvious that Detective Daniels is making it personal between you two. Since we beat that attempted murder charge with Peaches Armstrong, he's been working diligently to get you behind bars. If Ms. Brent did not say anything like she claims, I can assure you that you have nothing to worry about."

On the other side of the door, I stood more confused now than when I was in there. *Peaches ... Peaches ... Why does that name ring a bell?'* I said to myself. *Who's Peaches?*

I know who will be able to tell me, I said, continuing to talk to myself. I glanced at my Fendi watch that sat pretty on my small wrist. It read ten o'clock. "I know exactly where she is," I mumbled to myself. When I entered the laundry room Maria sat at the folding table with her eyes glued to the TV. Like clockwork, Maria had the TV tuned in to the Maury Povich show.

"Be a man! Stand up and take care of your children!" she shouted at the TV like she was in the studio audience. "You ARE the father!" Maria said.

"You are NOT the father," Maury said right behind Maria.

"Aye yai yai, and now she runs off the stage. Girl I was rooting for you," Maria wailed.

"Maria!" I got her attention, startling her to death.

"Oh my, Mommie you scared me," she said with her hand on her chest.

"My bad." I laughed. "Maria, I need to ask you something, you got a minute?"

"Always for you, besides I need a break from these stupid women on this TV. Now if it was *The Wendy Williams Show,* you would've had to wait until a commercial."

"How you doin'," I said mimicking Wendy. "Maria what you know about it?"

"Como estas," Maria said with her lips spread and all. She had Wendy down pat. We both laughed.

"So, what's going on, Mommie?"

"Maria, I need some information."

"That's if I have the information that you're looking for."

"I'm pretty sure you do. Who's Peaches Armstrong?"

When the name rolled off my tongue, Maria put her head down, putting too much into folding a towel, which let me know she had the 411.

"I knew you would know."

"That girl is nothing but trouble," Maria said, shaking her head. "Well, when Boss first got a hold of her she was actually a very nice girl. Look Mommie, whatever I tell you has to stay between us. I like my job and love my pay."

"I pinkie promise," I said, extending my pinkie finger.

Maria locked her pinkie with mine, and started singing. "Boss was dating Peaches for a while. He later took her under his wing when she got put out of her parents' house. Sounds like someone?"

"Hmmm—me."

"Boss put his trust in Peaches and gave her a job at one of his stash houses. He put that lil young girl through it with his lies, cheating, and of course the Jasmine in-house drama. Peaches started using cocaine every other day. Then with the help of all the stress that Boss was putting her through, every other day turned into everyday all day. That girl turned into a junkie ..."

"Peaches! The coke-head junkie in the bathroom at the club!" I cut Maria off when it finally came to me.

"Huh?" Maria said, confused.

"Nothing, just finish telling me."

"Okay," Maria said, continuing from where she left off. "Peaches got so strung-out that she started stealing Boss's dope. He found out and got his shooters to cancel her, as he would say. It didn't quite pan out like that though, because Peaches survived. The same short, chubby detective that came questioning you was assigned to that case. The poor girl was so terrified of Boss and his men that she didn't talk. Peaches told detectives some men tried to rob her, but they knew she was lying. Which left Daniels and the prosecutor with no evidence to convict Boss. Daniels was pissed."

I stood listening in disbelief. Maria had given me the 411 and some. I was outdone. "Maria, do you think Don killed Jasmine?"

"Do I think he killed her? No. Now, do I think that he got one of his men to do it? I wouldn't put it past him."

ALL EYES ON ME

CHAPTER 19

They say money bring bitches and bitches bring lies, one nigga gettin' jealous and muthafucka's die ...

2 PAC – *All eyes on me*

Heather pulled up to a run-down house on Main and 50th Street in the heart of the slums. The Audi that she drove stood out like a sore thumb on the east side of LA. Niggas broke their necks looking when they spotted the silver Audi pulling up. Not to see if the person in it was the Feds or a come-up, but to see the white girl that had the swag of a hood chick. When they saw Heather, the first thing that came to mind was the model CoCo. A pink-toe with a black girl's ass.

Heather grabbed the Denny's To-Go bag off the passenger seat before exiting the car. She walked toward the front door with an audience of fans. They would stare all day long and give her hand claps as she passed, but wouldn't dare try her, knowing that she was off limits by Shane, a crazy-ass nigga that was well-known in the turf.

With her hood-chic style, she rocked big round-the-way-girl earrings, cornrows, a short denim skirt and knee-length boots. Looking through a pair of Versace shades, Heather nodded her head, greeting a couple of hood niggas that was posted up at the house next door.

"What up y'all?"

"Heyyyy Ms. Parker," they all said in unison. *When you gonna let me fuck you, Ms. Parker?* all three niggas said to themselves. They respected Heather's gangsta in a real way. She wasn't one of those pink-toes that tried too hard to be down; her swag came naturally. That's what made niggas infatuated with her.

Approaching the door, "Shit!" Heather stomped her Gucci boot to the pavement. When she glanced down at her key ring and noticed that she didn't have the key to get in the house, she dug into her over-sized Gucci bag and tried to locate her iPhone to call inside the house. "Oh my God!" she shot, mad at no one but herself for having a whole lot of unnecessary bullshit in her purse that was making it hard for her to locate her cell phone.

"Fuck it!" she shot, kicking the door. BAM! BAM! BAM! Heather saw her friend, Tif, peeking through the blinds like a tweaker.

When Tif saw that it was Heather kicking the door like she was crazy, she tried rushing her Public Defender off the phone before letting Heather in. The talkative Public Pretender went on-and-on until Tif just hung up the phone in her face. Tif finally opened the door for Heather.

"Damn! I thought I needed a password to get in!" Heather shot, as she walked in.

"You do. The password is use yo' fuckin' key," Tif shot back.

"I should've just left yo' cave-woman ass in here starving."

"You don't have it in your heart to do your friend like that."

"Hmm, keep thinking that," Heather said, perk-ing her lips, then rolling her eyes.

"Shane done turned yo' ass out. I remember when I first met you at Burger King. My first day at the job, you was such a pleasant cracker, now you just a salted cracker with an attitude," Tif joked.

Heather couldn't help but laugh before giving Tif the finger. "Ho! How many times I gotta tell you I'm not a cracker? I'm a fuckin' albino."

"Yeah, whateva', cracker."

"Fuck you, you wanna blaze one before I hit-it?"

"I'm good, I don't feel like smoking right now." Heather walked the short distance over to the couch where Tif was sitting, placing her hand up to her fore-head. "You feel okay?"

Tif pushed her hand away. "Ha ...ha ...ha! Damn, a bitch can't turn down smoking."

"Not you, Snoop. Alright, I'm gone on your boring ass."

Heather got up and walked toward the door. "Come lock this. I'll call you later."

Tif locked the door behind Heather, then went for her phone. Glancing at the screen, she had four missed calls from her attorney.

"Good my phone was on vibrate. This bitch is so smart that she's stupid," Tif said, talking to herself while dialing her attorney's number.

"Gloria Cater's office," the receptionist answered with an upbeat voice.

"Ms. Cater please."

"May I ask who's speaking?"

"Tiffany Barker."

"Let me see if she's available." A couple of seconds later the receptionist came back to the line. "Ms. Barker, I'm gonna transfer you to Ms. Cater, one moment please."

"Tiffany, what happened?" Ms. Cater came to the line.

"I had to hang up. Someone was at the door."

"Oh okay. Ms. Barker like I was telling you before the call was disconnected, I know the govern-ment is asking for a lot, but if you want to walk away with no jail time you have to cooperate in order to get the 5K1."

"Ms. Cater, I think I've done more than enough. The agents took pictures of the drugs that was taped to my body. I've been hiding out over in this piece of shit, excuse my French."

"I understand Ms. Barker, but you're looking at some serious time. They're coming down pretty hard on these white collar crimes, and with the amount of losses in your bank fraud charge, I'm afraid you might get the book thrown at you. On top of that, you have priors, which places you in the career criminal category, and you have an open state case for identity theft. I'm gonna be completely honest with you Ms. Barker, it doesn't look good. You're definitely gonna need this 5K1," the public defender said, doing a great job marketing the 5K1, better known as the snitch deal with the Feds.

"Okay Ms. Cater, but I need to see something in black and white that says I'm not getting no jail time, and that I'll be placed in the witness protection program, because these are some dangerous men that I'm dealing with. I'm playing both sides here. I have my friend's boyfriend thinking that I'm working with him by stealing the main man's drugs, and I'm working as an inside job with the Feds to take the main man, Donnie Boss out. In the end of all of this, I need to make sure that I'm gonna be good, because there's gonna be a lot of people getting taken down by the Feds when it's all said and done."

"Ms. Barker, don't worry. Just do what you have to do, and everything is gonna work out for the good. Make sure you comply with your pretrial officer, don't do any drugs, and check in with the agent every day."

What have I got myself into. This is too much, fuck what she's saying, I need a blunt, Tif thought as she ended the call.

~~RIGHT THRU ME~~
CHAPTER 20
MALIYAH

After Maria exposed Don's hand, I walked around the house on egg shells. I tried hard not to be spooked by the man that I loved dearly. The informa-tion that I'd learned about the real, dangerous Don should have been enough to make me have a change of heart, but instead it made me love him even more. Crazy huh?

Once I came to the realization that there was an-other woman I became very clingy. I reminded myself of the woman from the movie *Coming to America:* "Whatever you like." I tried my best to make Don happy at home, so he wouldn't want to creep with his side line ho and stay out all night.

I even suggested that we share the same room. I got tired of having to choose between my bed or his every time we wanted to make love. Don didn't like that idea though. He enjoyed having his privacy. He even said, "Only married couples should sleep in the same bed every night."

I disagreed, but my opinion no longer mattered, not like it ever did anyway. My reply to everything was, 'It's up to you, I don't care, it doesn't matter' and one that I used quite often, 'whatever you like.' Big ol' mouth me became very passive.

The next couple of weeks, Don treated me like a queen. I guess he felt bad about busting my lip and leaving me home alone while the pigs interrogated me. He copped us his and her Ferrari's. I was so overwhelmed when I saw the pink and black Ferrari F430 with the license plate that said, "Boss's Girl" that I immediately called up the girls for a night out on the town for strictly flossin'.

However, I wasn't the only one that got a new whip. When I called Kayla for a code 10 she broke the news to me that Pee Wee's cheap-ass got her a Lexus. It was very hard to believe. We're talking about a nigga that barely wanna come out the pockets to get a bitch hair done—a Lex—*O, hell naw* is what I thought. But when me and Kayla met up at Rosco's Chicken and Waffles, sho' nuff' she was sitting in a brand spankin' new pearl white Lexus with paper tags. The power of pussy, is all I could say.

One thing about me, when my girls got something new I never hated on them like I'd catch Kayla doing all the time. I've always been the bitch to give props when props was due. I praised my girl, as we caravaned to Sunset Boulevard to floss.

$ $ $

Don's birthday had finally come. I gave Maria the day off and served him breakfast in bed since breakfast was the only meal that I knew how to cook. Don loved it. He licked his plate clean, then he licked my pussy dry. The birthday sex was so good that I thought July had rolled around and it was my birthday.

Shit, after the birthday sex, I'd say the day had started off good. Until Don killed it by calling a meeting at the house. I was mad as hell because I had the whole day planned out for us to celebrate his birthday. I used the quick intermission for Don's stupid little meeting to relax. God knows I needed it after all the running around for Don's surprise party. I was worn out. I laid poolside, looking at the water with no intentions on getting in to get my fresh hairdo wet. I sipped on Red Berry Ciroc, regretting that I let Maria off because she made the best Bahama Mama's that would have been perfect for this setting. I grabbed my phone to call Tia.

"What up, ho?" I asked into the phone.

"Bitch, you're gonna live a long life, I was just thinking about you. Gurl, I don't know what has gotten into Tommy, but he said I can come to the party!" Tia said with excitement.

I held the phone thinking to myself. *After he done
fucked up your face now he wanna let you go out to the
club with his insecure bitch-ass.*

"You hear me, ho? He said I can go!"

"How am I not gonna hear you, when you're
screaming in my damn ear."

"My bad, I'm just excited bitch!"

"He's probably coming, so he can watch yo' ass
like a hawk. Remember I told you, I seen his bitch-ass
over here a couple of weeks ago? Shit, I wouldn't be surprised at all to see that fuck-nigga strolling in the party.
Gurl, the guest list is bananas. I don't know half of the
muthafucka's on it. Don's ace helped me out with the in-
vites and he must have invited all of LA, and a couple of
more hoods while he was at it."

"Nah, I don't think Tommy is coming. He men-
tioned something about having to work, and plus he ain't
really a club scene type of nigga."

"That's because he's weird as hell. Well, he'll be
doing me a favor if he don't come, because I can't stand
the sight of h–." I stopped when I heard static in the
phone. "T, what the hell was that?"

"This cheap-ass phone. It's been trippin' all day. I
gotta make a trip up to Walmart."

"Can you hear me now? Can you hear me now?"

"Yeah, bitch!"

"Good! Remember that Verizon wireless commercial?" We both laughed. "Like I was saying. If Tommy's bitch-ass don't come, I'ma hook you up with one of Don's boys."

"Oh no! I'm straight. I'm happy with my boo. Tommy has been good these days and blowing my back out on the regular."

"Ugh! TMI, bitch."

"He's not that bad Liyah, fo' real. I hate that I always tell y'all the bad things he do and never the good"

"Name one good thing? Please do. I really wanna hear this."

"Um ..."

"Exactly, the bad outweighs the good. Don't rack yo' brain. If it doesn't come right to ya that means you're thinking too damn hard."

"So, what time are you coming to pick me up tonight?" Tia changed the subject knowing I was about to dig in that ass. But I let her have that one.

"I'ma be too busy trying to hide the surprise from Don, so I'll send our chauffeur Andrew to come and get y'all. I don't know if Kayla's pushing her whip or not. If she does you wanna just catch a ride with her?"

"That bitch drink like a muthafucka! She won't never kill me, shit I love me. Now back to this chauffeur, I didn't know black folks have those. I can't wait to see this shit. Barack's money is long," Tia joked. "I can't wait to meet Barack Obama."

"It's gonna be a whole lot of Barack Obama's there. If you just kick Tommy's no-good ass to the curb."

"Here you go. Bye bitch," Tia shot before hanging up the phone.

"Don't like the heat, stay yo' ass out the kitchen then," I said to myself, tossing the phone on my lap and continuing to sip on my Ciroc, that was kicking in full throttle because I started to talk shit like I'll always did when I got a little tipsy.

$ $ $

Hatin' ass bitch! You hate the sight of me. I'm not gonna be the only one that you hate after Tia tells you Don is fuckin' yo girl. You nothin' ass bitch! Tommy thought as he hung up the cordless phone from listening to Tia's conversation with Maliyah. Tommy had it planned to use Tia as his mouthpiece to put shit on blast. That was the only reason he was letting Tia go to Don's party.

$ $ $

Silence filled the room as Don stared into the faces of six trigger-happy goons that looked at Don as their god. "Y'all keep yo' eyes and ears to the streets. If you see that bitch, Tiffany, flat-line that grimy bitch on the spot!" Don gave direct orders to his shooters. "Whoever gets her head first will get a nice reward. I want the job done mob-style too, bring me back a finger, a toe or sumthin', get creative. I wanna know this bitch suffered as much as I suffered my loss. This meeting is adjourned." Don dismissed his goons, still puffing on his favorite Cuban cigar, certain that one of his loyal shooters would be returning with a finger or a toe of Tiffany's.

$ $ $

I staggered into the house wearing my Gucci bikini, Gucci heels adorning my pretty French tip toes. I ran into Pablo and Tank huddled up by the front door engaged in a conversation. With suspicious looks on their faces, they stopped talking when they noticed me. Pablo eye-fucked me, grabbing the bulge that appeared in his jeans. I gave him a look like, "You wish you could hit this," and kept it moving right past them. As I walked up the stairs I read Pablo's lips: "Damn she's bad."

Then I overheard Tank snapping Pablo out of his trance. "Fuck her, nigga. We got more important shit to worry about." Tank kept his eyes glued to the door of the chop-it-up room where Don was with the rest of his men. Tank continued as he moved in a little closer to Pablo, looking like he was up to something. "We're gonna have to keep Tif low-key a little while longer. Boss done put a price over her head and niggas is hungry out in these streets."

"Nigga, don't tell me you getting paranoid. You knew Boss was gonna have niggas looking for the bitch. This is what we're gonna do, we gonna let it die down a little, then were gonna take her ass to Atlanta so she can show us where she stashed the dope, and after that it's lights out for that bitch." Pablo said.

"Shh, here he come," Tank said, when he noticed Don exiting the room.

Me, being me, I stood my nosy-ass at the top of the stairs, listening to what Tank and Pablo was talking about. *Who's Tif?* I thought for a second, then went on about my business not thinking nothing of it.

THANK ME LATER

CHAPTER 21
MALIYAH
BOSS'S BIRTHDAY BASH

Me and Don got out of the rented Aston Martin Vantage looking like Hov and Bey. Don was decked out in an all-black tailor-made Hugo Boss suit with Gucci loafers on his feet, and just enough ice on to compliment his suit. The diamond cufflinks completed the ensemble. My baby looked as good as P-Diddy on his flossiest day.

I wowed in a form-fitting Roberto Cavalli mini with Christian Louboutin heels. My hair hung down my back in loose curls, while Neil Lane diamond earrings sparkled in my ears. We were hot to death. Walking the red carpet that led us inside the Sunset Room night club, Don stopped in his tracks gazing over at me. "Ma, for this to be a Saturday night it don't look like it's hittin' on nothing. The line is usually wrapped around the building," he said.

"Shit, I don't know. Maybe everybody is already inside," I said trying hard to keep a serious face.

"I don't know," he said, pulling back his sleeve and checking the time on his Rolex. "It's only 11:00. This is around the time muthafucka's start showing up."

"Did you come here to worry about other muthafucka's, or to be with yo' fine-ass woman on your birthday? Fuck the crowd, we're the life of the party."

"If you wanna get technical, I was bribed with pussy. Ma, you serious? Are we really gonna find a bitch to have a threesome with tonight? Don't be playing with my emotions."

"Yes Donnie, Dang! How many times you gonna ask me that?" I lied, and doing a good job at it. That was the only way I could get Don to go to the club for his birthday, a fuckin' threesome?

"Maliyah, let you get off-up-in-here singing a different tune, you gonna be toe-nailing it back to the crib."

"Boy please, I wish you would leave me," I shot as we approached the door, finally.

"Two, that will be forty dollars," a beautiful Brazilian-looking chick said, pretending to be a front door worker. I hired her along with some other bad chicks from a local strip club to be my pole dancers.

"Bottle Service, Ma," Don said, just like I knew he would.

"Okay follow me." As we followed behind her, I glanced down at her ass and I think she had Kayla beat. Don's thirsty-ass was looking at me and pointing at the beauty, whispering, "Ma, I think we found her." I rolled my, eyes thinking to myself. *Am I not good enough?* I regret ever having that threesome with Donnie and Kayla because I had created a monster. He wanted it all the time.

"If that's what you want, you're the birthday boy," I said nonchalantly on some whatever-you-like-type of shit. Holding Don's hand, the Brazilian chick led us through the doors, as everyone screamed. "Surprise!" In front of Don stood all of his employees, most of LA, and my girls, representing looking-good.

"Aww Ma! You got me," Don said with a big smile and a tad bit embarrassed. He couldn't believe I had pulled something like this off. Don stood in disbelief, looking around the packed club in amaze-ment. The hundreds of black and white balloons that filled the club, the gorgeous women sliding up and down poles on the stage, and all the familiar faces that were on the dance floor getting crump to the club-bangers that the DJ was spinning on the one's-and-two's. All Don kept saying was, "All this, Ma," followed by a smile.

Everyone came dressed to impress in their best get-ups that night. The groupie hoes had freshly did under hundred-dollar weaves, rocking their favorite manne-quin's outfit from the Slauson Swap meet. While the fellas came in two kinds, either on some grown-man-shit, rocking a tailored suit, or just thugged-out in some expensive jeans and button-up T's.

The lights were dimmed as the DJ played Don's favorite song, Rick Ross's *Aston Martin Music.* "Happy birthday baby. I love you," I whispered in Don's ear.

"I love you too."

I smiled at ease knowing my man was pleased with his surprise party.

"This the cut right here," Don said, bobbing his head to his jam. As he rapped along to Mr. Rozay, I signaled for the waitress to break out the bubbly and cigars.

"Happy B-Day, Dawg!" Pablo said, walking up and giving Don a pound and a hug.

"Thirty-six, nigga you getting old," Tank joked.

"What's up, boss lady?" Pablo greeted me.

"Hey y'all."

"You did yo' thing girl. This shit is crackin' like Crenshaw when the Lakers won the championship," Tank said.

"Yeah, my baby went all out," Don said, pulling me into him as he hugged me from behind.

"Happy birthday Mr. Boss." All three niggas' heads turned at the same time, as they stared, mesmerized by the beautiful waitress.

"I'm Olivia, and I'll be serving you for the remainder of the night," she said, handing Don a bottle of Ace of Spades, and his favorite Cuban cigar. Olivia then handed me a bottle of Nuvo. "I got ya', girl," she said, on top of her job.

"Damn, it's my birthday too. We're twins," Tank joked.

"She knows that's a lie," Don shot. We all laughed, including Olivia.

"Can you serve me for the remainder of the night, and possibly into the wee-hours of the morning?" Tank continued with his whack-ass game.

"B–oss," Pablo stuttered. "She got yo' face painted on her titties, nigga!"

Tank gazed in at Olivia's bangin' physique. "Damn, she sure do, nigga."

"Y'all bullshitting. So, that's not a dress your wearing with my face on it?" Don asked.

"Uh-uhh." Olivia and I shook our heads from side-to-side.

"I gotta see for myself. Can I touch it Ma?" I nodded my head giving him the okay to feel Olivia up.
"It's body paint. Hot huh?" Olivia said flirting, liking Don's touch a little too much.

"Blazin', Ma. So, then that means all of them up there is naked too?" Don said, pointing toward the stage at the pole dancers, with his hand still on Olivia's breast.

"Hmmm!" I smiled.

"Well—Damn! It's a whole lot of naked bitches lurking around here, because I see yo' face on a lot of bad bitches. Turn the lights on!" Tank said.

"Dammmmnnn! Baby, fo' real? Fo' real, you did that?"

"Hell yeah, she did!" Pablo shot, hyped.

I knew it. If niggas didn't like anything else, the naked body art was gonna seal the deal, making Donnie's party the number one topic on the streets for a while.

"Mr. Boss, let me show you and your friends to your VIP section, where a surprise awaits," Olivia said.

Don looked over at me, and I shrugged my shoulders like I didn't know a thing. "You coming Ma?"

"Nah, baby, go have you some fun with yo' boys. I'ma go find my girls."

"Yeah, come on nigga wit yo' pussy-whipped ass," Tank shot, busting Don out.

"Shut up nigga."

"Yeah Tank, respect yo' elders," Pablo shot, trying to be funny on the low. Tank and Pablo laughed.

"Y'all niggas got jokes tonight," Don laughed. "We ain't at the Laugh Factory, you clown-ass-niggas."

I watched as Don had a good time with his boys. They laughed as they followed behind Olivia to VIP for surprise lap dances. I turned my attention to the dance floor and the crowd was hype as the DJ played the New

Boys *Jerk*. It was impossible for me to spot the girls out of the bunch of muthafucka's on the dance floor jerkin'.

"What it do Andrew, you enjoying yo' self?" I said, interrupting his conversation with the chickens.

"Hell, yeah I am. You got it poppin' in this joint fo' my boy."

The coco puff looked me up and down as her homegirls stared me down through admiring eyes, jockin' my fit.

"Excuse me!" the coco puff shot, placing her hand on her hip.

"You excused."

"We were talking!"

"So, and now we're talking."

"Shawty, you outta pocket, now step!"

"Bye, bye," I smirked, waving the ho off.

She sucked her teeth and rolled her eyes as her dusty-foot homegirls followed behind her.

"My bad, I ran yo' head off for the night."

"No you helped me out, good-looking cuz, that bitch breath was hot. Plus, I got my eyes set on something better."

"Shit, it's a lot of eye candy in the building to choose from."

"You ain't never lied," Andrew said, eyeing a half-naked female who was walking past. "Ay, lil Ma'ma," he shot at the smiling half-breed.

"Let me let you do yo' thang. Have you seen Tia and Kayla?"

"Last time I seen them, they were over by the restrooms. That was right before you walked up. Mrs. Boss, I need for you to put in a good word for yo' boy. Man, I'm feelin' yo' girl. That's my something better."

"Who, Kayla?"

"Nah, Tia. When she came walking to the car tonight, I was like she's hot to death. Then her conversation is what really did it. We laughed all the way here."

"Aww Andrew, that's so cute." I smiled. *Barack! Well not really. But anything is better than Tommy,* I thought. "I got you, you got that coming. I think you'll be perfect for my girl. Now let me go find these slut buckets. Why don't you go up to VIP with Don and everyone else. It's fully-nude strippers, food, the whole nine."

"Aiight Ms. Boss, I mean Mrs. Boss." He corrected himself. "Boss made a good choice."

I smiled as I walked off toward the restrooms, killin' the last bit of Nuvo in my bottle. *What the hell he mean Boss made a good choice. I chose that nigga,* I shot to myself, talking shit. That mean't the pink stuff was kickin' in.

I was on the prowl, trying to find Kayla and Tia. Looking through faded eyes in the packed dimmed light club made it very hard. I couldn't wait to locate these bitches and let them have it. I thought it was weird that they hadn't met up with me. I saw them for a hot second at the grand entrance, then these hoes got ghost on me. When I entered the restroom I heard Tia's voice. "Here go these sluts," I said underneath my breath.

"Kayla! I'm serious. If you don't tell Maliyah, I will and that's on my momma!!"

I came around the corner walking right into the heated conversation. "Tell me what?"

They looked at me like they'd seen a ghost. Wearing the dumbest looks on their faces I asked again. "Tell me what?"

"Ask Kayla! If she's really yo' best friend she'll tell you," Tia shot, looking over at Kayla, pissed.

"Kayla, what is she talking about?" I shot, get-ting frustrated.

"Are you Mrs. Boss?" some chick asked.

"Yeah! Why?" I shot, with attitude, assuming that she was about to tell me something about Don. I stood ready to rock that ho the moment Don's name rolled off her tongue.

"They're calling you on stage."

"For what? Oh my god. Have niggas started fight-ing? We about to have to shut shit down, watch," I said, thinking the worst, already knowing how ignor-ant black folks can get with a little alcohol in their system at a pop-pin' function. The girls followed behind me as I stormed out of the restroom. When I glanced up at the stage there was an empty chair sitting in the middle of the stage, and Don holding a microphone. "Mrs. Boss please report to the stage." I walked toward the stage, as the crowd cleared the way. I glanced back at the girls, and shrugged my shoulders, clueless at what the fuck was going on. Then the spotlight shined on me and I thought. *What the fuck is about to happen?* The DJ started playing Usher's *There Goes My Baby* while Don stood on stage, watching me walk toward him. I felt so awkward, as the entire club stared at me.

Once I made it to the stage, Don told me to sit in the chair like it was my birthday. The DJ cut the volume down on the music, and Don got down on one knee. I screamed, as the crowd followed my lead. Looking Don in the eyes, I tried hard to hold back the tears. Don was just as nervous as I was. He started to speak into the microphone and his voice cracked from being so nervous.

"Baby, I wanna start off by saying you made this the best birthday I ever had. I love you Maliyah, and I wanna spend the rest of my life with you. I wasn't planning on doing this right here in front of everybody, it was supposed to be over dinner." He paused, pulling a black velvet ring box out of his pocket. I started bouncing in the chair with my hands up to my mouth.

"Maliyah, would you be my wifey?"

I screamed followed by a "Yes!" I put my hand out as Don put the 5 carat Neil Lane engagement ring on my bony finger. I jumped out of the chair and fell into Don's arms. The crowd screamed and clapped while me and Don's tongues danced in a passionate kiss. When Don came up for air, his lips was covered in my MAC Lip gloss. I smiled wiping the gloss off my man's lips.

"To everyone in the house tonight, thank you for coming to celebrate my birthday with me, and my future wife. There's plenty of champagne, lots of food, a whole lot of good music to come. We're not only celebrating my birthday, now it's our engagement party as well." Don wrapped it up, giving the DJ a signal to drop a beat and he came with the perfect song for me to floss on hoes, Beyonce's *Put A Ring On It.* I sang along to Bey while walking toward my girls with my hand up to my face revealing the 5 carat rock that sparkled on my finger.

"I's married now!"I said like Shug Avery from the movie *Color Purple,* as I approached Kayla and Tia standing and looking like question marks.

"Congratulations," Tia said nonchalantly. "Maliyah I'm not feeling good. I need to leave."

"Okay, why don't you meet Don before you leave?"

"No, some other time."

"Okay," I said, waving my hand toward Andrew, who was standing not too far from us. He came right away.

"Congratulations Mrs. Boss! I almost ruined the surprise earlier. But I really meant what I said, Boss definitely made a good choice."

"Thank you Andrew, you're so sweet," I said giving him a hug. "I need a big favor."

"What's up?"

"I need for you to take Tia home, she's not feeling well."

"Oh, that's not a favor, it's a pleasure."

"Ooooohhh!" I teased like a child. Tia smirked, then went right back to her serious face.

"You ready now?" Tia asked.

"Yeah."

"Alright Maliyah, I'll talk to you tomorrow," Tia said, then looked over at Kayla, rolling her eyes before walking off. I knew something serious had went down with Tia and Kayla by the vibe between the two. I did not entertain the bullshit because this was my night, the bitch-assness had to wait. I finally had got what I'd been waiting for, a proposal from my Boss.

"Bitch, can you believe it? He proposed to me!!" I said with excitement feeling myself getting teary eyed again.

"I'm ha–" Kayla put her hand over her mouth trying to hold back from throwing-up. She then took off toward the restroom.

"This ho done drunk too much," I said chasing behind her. "Ugh! I can't stand a sloppy drunk bitch. Excuse us." I was so embarrassed.

~~HAVE A BABY BY ME~~

CHAPTER 22
MALIYAH
Be a millionaire ...
50 Cent

"Fish!" I sat up in bed waking up out of a deep sleep of dreaming about fish. "Somebody's preg-nant!" I shot, looking over at Olivia, who was laying on the other side of Don in a peaceful sleep. Yeah, we took Olivia home with us to have a little fun. I let Don talk me into the threesome. After the proposal stunt he could have talked me into just about anything.

I can't even lie. I enjoyed the threesome with Olivia a lot more than the one with Kayla. I guess it's because Kayla is like a sister to me, it didn't feel right. Don had turned me out. I was officially bisexual. It was clear that me and Don was gonna be swingers in our marriage like Will and Jada Smith. Shit, whatever it took to keep my husband happy and our marriage full of spice.

"Olivia!" I said, awakening sleeping beauty out of a deep sleep.

"Huh? What?" I startled the poor thing. She sat up in bed, rubbing her eyes with her hair all over her head, and she still was beautiful.

"Get dressed. It's time to go," I said after using the trick for her services, just like a nigga.

I climbed out of bed grabbing my cellphone off the nightstand and headed to the bathroom. I glanced over at Don, knocked out in a nut-bustin-coma before entering the bathroom.

I dialed up Tia, and her phone went straight to voicemail. "Hey ho! Code 10. I dreamed of fish, you know the drill. CVS, we gotta go pee on the stick. Call me ASAP." I left her a message. I hung up, and called Kayla.

We made a bet on who was gonna get knocked up first. So, every time one of us dreamed of fish it usually meant someone was prego. Last time Kayla dreamed of fish, Tia was pregnant by Tommy when he came home from prison. But she had a miscarriage. For fun we continued with the bet.

"Yeah," Kayla said, instead of a hello.

"What's wrong with you? Why you sound like you been crying?"

"I'm not feeling good. I think I drunk too much last night."

"You think? Or maybe it's you that's knocked up. I dreamed of fish."

"Nah, it ain't me."

"Well it's somebody. I just called Tia and left her a message so we can hit-up CVS. You wanna meet me at the one on Crenshaw and Slauson?"

"Can we meet at the one closer to me on Florence and Market?"

"Bitch, I don't feel like driving all the way to Inglewood." Then I remembered Olivia saying that she lived in Westchester, which was close to Inglewood.

"Okay bitch give me an hour. And don't think it got shit to do with you being sick. That's what you get. I don't know why you be mixing all those different drinks!"

"I don't feel like hearing this shit, bye!" The bitch hung up in my face.

After I hit my grill and washed my face. I re-entered the bedroom to Olivia fully dressed, and Don stretching in bed.

"Good morning, Baby."

"Damn, y'all up early. Olivia you wanna eat some breakfast before you leave?"

"I–"

"No! She's straight," I cut her off, giving Don a look like shut the hell up. I got Olivia's ass up out of my house quick-fast-and-in-a-hurry. Reality had sunk in. I didn't know this bitch, and damn sure didn't trust Don. He might wanna double-back for seconds without me.

$ $ $

I stood in front of CVS, tapping my foot anxiously as Kayla's inconsiderate ass sat in her car talking on the phone. It wasn't like she didn't see me because she was looking dead at me. This bitch acted like she couldn't do two things at once, like chew bubble gum and walk.

"Come on!" I yelled, waving my hand and signaling for her to bring her ass.

She put up her finger, as she yelled, "Hold up! I'm coming!"

I gave her the finger before turning around walking through the automatic doors.

$ $ $

"How could you do this to me Don!!! Fo' real you just gonna up and marry her?" Kayla yelled into her phone.

"Kayla, don't act brand new. You know what it is between us. I love you, but I'm in love with Maliyah."

"What sense does that make!"

"You know what Kayla, you're becoming more of a headache than a good time. You stay bitchin', I can't take it! My bitch don't even do all of that. First it was I don't treat you the same, so I bought you a Lexus. Now you talking shit about me marrying Maliyah. Look I'ma say this one time, you need to get wit-it, or get lost!"

"Like that? That's how you feel Don?" Kayla asked, as she started to cry. "I'm probably about to lose my best friends because of you! Tia's definitely gonna tell Maliyah. She told me last night if I don't tell her, she will. And you know who's gonna suffer, me! Not you, me! She's too sprung over your ass to let you go!"

"Listen to me, Tia's not gonna say shit."

"How you gonna tell me about my best friend. I know her Donnie, yes she is!" Kayla cried.

"Shut up and listen! Do you trust me?"

"Yes, I guess."

"Okay then, let me take care of it."

Kayla hung up the phone an emotional wreck. Flipping down her mirror visor, she got herself together before exiting the car to meet Maliyah in the CVS.

$ $ $

Don sat in front of a plate of bacon, eggs, and grits. Slamming his phone down on the table, he shouted, "Fuck!" After hanging up from Kayla he had lost his appetite. Don grabbed the pre-rolled blunt, sticking it between his lips, and putting some fire to the perfectly rolled Swisher Sweet filled with some sour-diesel kush. He took a couple of seconds to get his thoughts together. It was something about kush that made him come up with the perfect master plan.

Don quickly grabbed his phone, dialing up Andrew. He answered on the second ring. "What up Boss, you need me to come in?" he said being Don's most reliable employee.

"Nah you straight, enjoy yo' day off man. Look, I need to ask you something."

"Aiight shoot."

"Do you remember the address where you took Mrs. Boss's friend Tia last night?"

"She stay off of Vernon on 48th and Budlong. I don't remember the actual address though Boss."

"That's good enough, thanks man," Don said before hanging up the phone. Walking into his office, Don grabbed the stacks of fraudulent paycheck stubs that he got made for his employees. Searching for Tommy's, he flipped through the stack. When he came across Tommy's he read the address off the stub, he smiled. "Yep Budlong," he said to himself.

$ $ $

Me and Kayla stood in her bathroom staring at the pregnancy test and impatiently waiting for the results. Kayla had mine, and I had hers.

"Nope, one line. You are not pregnant," Kayla said, tossing the pregnancy test in the garbage. "What mine say?"

I stood speechless, smiling from ear to ear.

"What?"

"You're pregnant!!!!"

"You lying, let me see." Kayla snatched the test out of my hand. A shocked Kayla placed her hand up to her mouth dropping the test on the floor. "I'm pregnant?"

"Yes, you're pregnant! You're the fish that I dreamed! I'm gonna be an Auntie! Let me call Tia." I went for my phone dialing up Tia to get her voicemail again. "Tia, Kayla's pregnant! Code 10 bitch. Hurry up and call back!" Kayla stood boo-hooing like a baby.

"What? You don't know who yo' baby daddy is?"

"Yes, I know who my baby daddy is," she said in between cries.

"It better be Pee Wee's. After he done bought you a Lexus. Ooooh, or is it by the mystery man that I've never met. What's his name? Um ... Donald, that's it. What kind of work does he do, just in case he don't wanna step up to the plate so child support could get his ass, because you're not gonna get a dime outta Pee Wee's drug dealing ass."

"Maliyah, will you shut up! Please!"

"I'm happy Kayla, I can't help it. You're having a baby, and I'm getting married. Gurl, 2010 is our year." I began to cry tears of joy.

~~EMERGENCY~~

CHAPTER 23
MALIYAH

"You're twelve weeks into your pregnancy," the doctor said after performing an ultra sound on Kayla. I smiled, staring at the monitor like I was the proud father-to-be.

"Twelve weeks! That can't be right. That's about three months!" Kayla shouted in denial.

"Ms. Wright, I'll get you started on prenatal care," the doctor continued, tearing the ultra sound photo off the machine and handing it to Kayla. "Here you go. Congratulations Ms. Wright. I'm sure your husband will be very happy," the doctor said flipping through Kayla's medical chart. "I knew there was something else I wanted to go over with you. I see here in your chart that you were infected with an STD not too long ago. I'll have to schedule you for a pap smear within the next day or two."

An STD! I thought, glancing over at Kayla, who had the dumbest look on her face.

"Thanks Doctor Mitchell!" Kayla shot with bass behind it, mad at the doctor for putting her business out there in front of me. I quickly put my head down and dug into my Prada purse, looking for nothing. I acted like I didn't hear a thing. I played as dumb as Kayla looked when Doctor Mitchell put her on front street.

As I dug through my purse, I couldn't help but wonder what nasty-dirty-dick nigga infected Kayla with an STD. It was too much of that nasty shit going around. Every time I heard STD it pissed me off. That was just a topic that I didn't want to get into with Kayla. Although I was now clear from the sexually transmitted disease that Jasmine passed on to me and Don, it was still a touchy topic with me.

Once the doctor exited the room, the vibe was very awkward. I switched the awkwardness to a good laugh, clownin' Kayla about her crusty-ass-pedicure-needing-feet: "Damn bitch, when was the last time you got yo' feet done? Them muthafucka's is vicious!"

"Fuck you," Kayla laughed.

"Dusty feet, hurry up and put them boots on, hide them bad boys."

We both laughed.

$ $ $

It was going on the third day that Tia hadn't answered her phone. Kayla and I were starting to get worried. I called all the local hospital emergency rooms to see if Tia was there, and to my surprise she wasn't admitted to any of the four that I called. Which told me it was something small like a black eye that she was just trying to hide until it healed.

Kayla and I drove to Tia's apartment, preparing ourselves to see a mangled Tia. It's sad, but we even tried to guess what part of Tia's body Tommy had wounded this time around. When we pulled up to Tia's apartment, I glanced over at Kayla in the passenger seat, scarfing down some Wings & Things. She smacked and sucked on the chicken wing bones like it was her first and last meal. If she wasn't pregnant I probably would have kicked the bitch out of my car.

"What?" she shot, with an attitude when she noticed me staring at her.

"Damn! You want some?"

"No, and get the crumbs from around yo' mouth."

"If you wasn't staring at me, you wouldn't see it."

"Big hungry, are you gonna bring the chicken with you, or leave it in here?"

"I gotta go?"

"Nah, you gotta go! Now come on, asking stupid-ass questions."

Walking up the walkway, I laughed looking over at Kayla. "You even got the baby momma walk now."

"What is this, observe and annoy the hell out of Kayla day?" Kayla shot.

When we approached Tia's door, Kayla and I frowned from the smell. "Ugh! What the hell is that?" Kayla said, looking around and trying to see where the smell was coming from.

"It smell like a dead dog or something," I said, positioning my hand to knock.

KNOCK! KNOCK!

"Tia open the door! It's your best friends. We already know you're in there! We're not leaving until you open this goddamn door!" I said, continuing to knock. I reached into my purse and grabbed my cellphone to call Tia's number, only to get the same result that I'd been getting for the last three days.   "Oh hell no! I can't stand here and keep smelling this shit, I'm about to throw up my Wings & Things," Kayla shot.

I then put my ear up to the door to see if I heard anything. "Eww! The smell is coming from out of there!" I began to panic, thinking the worst. I started beating on the door and trying to break the bitch down. That's when something told me to turn the door knob, and to my surprise the door was unlocked. I glanced over at Kayla and she immediately started shaking her head from side to side.

"Uh uhh Maliyah, I ain't going in there."

"Come on!" I entered with caution. The strong stench rushed me as I came through the door. I quickly covered my nose with my hand trying to block the smell. The foul odor was so strong that it seeped through. Kayla was on my heels, gagging and about to vomit.

"Tia! Tia!" I yelled at the top of my lungs. I started to cry. I've never smelled death, but I was told that it's an unbearable smell. That described the horrible stench that was lurking throughout Tia's one- bedroom apartment. When I made it to the bedroom, I screamed when my eyes laid on my best friend fully nude stretched out in a puddle of blood with her chest full of bullet holes.

"NO! NO! NO! TIA!!!!!!"

Kayla was behind me crying hysterically while throwing up. I searched my purse for my phone while crying "Noooo!!!!" Once I located my phone, I dialed the number 911 with my trembling hand.

"9ll, what's your emergency?" the operator came on the line.

"MY FRIEND! MY FRIEND! IS! DEAAAAAD!!!! HELP ME! SEND SOMEONE QUICK PLEASE!!"

"Calm down Ma'am."

"Hurry, please hurry."

"What is the address?"

"I don't know! Pleeeaaasssee hellllp!" I quickly exited the apartment and ran to the front of the building to get the address. I ran into one of the apartment tenants, who was walking her dog.

"Calm down baby. What's the matter?" The woman asked with concern.

"MY–MY FRIEND! WHAT'S THIS ADDRESS!" Not giving the women a chance to respond, I just handed over my cell phone.

"Tell them!" I said still in tears. The women did as told, giving the dispatcher Tia's address.

~~I MISS MY DAWG~~

CHAPTER 24
MALIYAH

Three months later, and I still wasn't able to get past Tia being gone. I was constantly reminded every time I appeared in court and saw the face of Tommy. I hired Dana for Tia's family to put Tommy's trifling ass under the jail.

Thanksgiving, Christmas and New Year's had rolled around and it just wasn't the same without T. I still wasn't on good terms with my parents, and Don was still on the same bullshit. He even got a little worse, staying out for days at a time.

I had a new best friend that stuck by my side during my mourning. She was good at occupying my time, and taking the pain away. Her name is White-girl. I didn't have my fiancé home to console me, and Kayla was already an emotional wreck due to the pregnancy. When me and Kayla were together we would cry the whole time, which wasn't healthy for the baby.

White-girl was with me 24/7. I filled the void of being alone with cocaine. I would snort coke, and pop X
during my mourning of my best friend's death. The first
day I was introduced to White-girl was the day of Tia's
funeral. There was no way I could have got through it.
Don came to me with a small amount of coke in his long
pinkie finger nail. He placed it up against my nostril and
told me to snort it. I did as told, and with the extra umph
that the coke gave me, I was able to get through the
homecoming celebration of my always and forever best
friend Tia. *Damn! I miss my dawg.*

~~RUDE BOY~~

CHAPTER 25
6 MONTHS LATER

"My nose is big, my neck is black, and I look like a fuckin' blimp," Kayla complained, looking at herself in the mirror.

"Girl, shut up. You're due any day now."

"I'll sure be glad when this baby decides to come out, because I'm tired of being pregnant."

"I'll be glad too!" I said rubbing Kayla's huge belly.

"Hurry up Destiny, yo' god-mommy can't wait to put you in these lil pretty Prada shoes I got for you." I knelt down, talking to Kayla's belly.

"Girl gone," Kayla pushed my head away before exiting the room. Her big round stomach led the way as she went on about her business. When the coast was clear, I pulled the small Ziploc bag out of my bra. I dug my manicured white tip pinkie nail into the bag, scooping up some of the pure-get-right, and after the toot-toot I was right. Wiping the residue from my nose, I glanced at myself one last time in the mirror, ready for my bachelorette party that Kayla was throwing for me.

$ \qquad $ \$ $ \qquad $ \$ $ \qquad $ \$

"This is too much," Kayla said to herself while rubbing on her swollen feet. The buzzing of her phone caused her to jump. "My nerves is bad. I can't wait until I can smoke a blunt," she said to herself and grabbed her phone. Kayla glanced at the caller ID and when she saw the name flashing across the screen she sucked her teeth before answering. "You are really gettin' on my nerves!" she said instead of a hello.

"You better be nice to me before your baby come out looking like me instead of Boss," Pablo shot from the other end of the phone.

"Boy, if Destiny come out looking like you, I'ma put her up for adoption as much as I can't stand yo' ass."

"So, what's up wit that Mrs. Boss situation?"

"I told you, when you're talking to me don't refer to her as Mrs. Boss. I'm the fuckin' real Mrs. Boss!!"

"You got serious problems, Loc."

"I ain't yo' fuckin' Loc! Come thru around two o'clock. Everybody should be gone by then. Now, after this I'm straight, right?"

"Fo' sho, Ma."

"I won't hear nothing about the ransom hit bull-shit that you and Tank be dangling over a bitch's head."

"That shit will be done wit, that's my word."

"Okay, I don't want no shit."

"Kay, one more thing."

"Now, what!"

"Where's Boss?"

"He's at my house, where he will be for the rest of the night. He knows about the bachelorette party, so he won't be returning."

"Aiight Fok."

"I ain't yo' damn fok'. Now bye!" Kayla shot into the phone before disconnecting the call.

Hmmm! I got something fo yo' ass too, nigga, Kayla shot with a devilish grin.

Walking the short distance over to the couch, Kayla grabbed the walkie-talkie to page Maria.

"Maria."

"Yes, Ma'am."

"Is everything good to go?"

"The food is set up, the alcohol and cups is already to go, the strippers just called and said they'll be here at eleven o'clock, and your guests are arriving as we speak."

"Okay, thank you Maria. You're good to leave."

Kayla took the walkie-talkie away from her mouth as she thought, *I can't believe I'm throwing this tramp a bachelorette party so she can marry my man. Who does that?*

$ $ $

I don't know how Kayla talked Don into letting her have me a bachelorette party at our estate. Don did not play when it came to bringing a bunch of muthafucka's to where he rested his head. So many of Don's employees and close homeboys would try to talk him into letting them throw functions at the mansion. One that I've been hearing them ask him a lot lately was pool parties since it was summer time, but it never failed. Every time they asked Don, he gave them the ultimate Hell—No.

The pool house was full to capacity with a bunch of hoes I didn't care too much for. It looked like Kayla had went on my Facebook and MySpace pages and invited all my web friends.

Waka Flocka Flame's *No Hands* was blasting out of the Bose speakers as one of the strippers popped his dick in my face. Horny hoes was screaming and throwing dollas. Kayla had shut the Right Track down for business this night, because every last G-string-dolla-chasin-nigga that was shaking dick and balls was from the popular hood hole-in-the-wall strip club that had some half decent looking brotha's and I can't forget the homo-thugs strippin' in the joint. If you was a bitch into paying niggas that rock G-strings up their ass, The Right Track was the go-to spot in LA.

Me personally, I've never been one to like strippers. That's why I was sitting here with this look on my face like get the hell away from me.

"Maliyah smile!" Kayla yelled from across the room to get my attention as she took a picture. I rolled my eyes then gave her ass the finger. Kayla laughed, standing beside my hairdresser, Rhonda. Them bitches were rollin' because they knew I was irritated by this bald head, hot karate, cheap cologne-wearing muthafucka that was standing in front of me doing it with *No Hands*.

$ $ $

"Let me go get her another drink," Kayla said in between laughs.

"Yeah, that's a good idea, get her ass drunk so she can loosen up," Rhonda replied never taking her eyes off the stripper that was dancing in front of her. Kayla made her way to the bar area. She checked her surroundings to see everyone's attention focused on the dick-swinging strippers. Once Kayla saw that the coast was clear, she dug into her pocket and pulled out a Ziploc bag that contained five X pills. With the bottom of the glass that she was about to use to make Maliyah's drink in, she crushed the pills in tiny pieces, and dumped it into the Hennessy with no chaser. Heading back over to Maliyah, Kayla wore a devilish grin with the glass of concoction in her hand.

$ $ $

Kayla glanced over at the clock that read 1:45 a.m., then back at Maliyah passed out in bed.

"Drunk bitch!" Kayla shot staring Maliyah down with envy in her eyes. The bride-to-be was high as a kite. The cocaine that she was snorting on the low, and the X pills that Kayla mixed in her drink got the best of her. The party ended with Maliyah throwing up and Kayla getting a stripper to carry the comatose bride up to her bed.

Bzzt ... Bzzt. Kayla glanced down at her phone, vibrating in her hand. "Right on time." She smiled when she saw Pablo's number flashing on the caller ID screen. She walked the short distance over to the entertainment center where a video recorder hid perfectly between the Blu-Ray player. She quickly pressed the record button on the video recorder before exiting the room.

Kayla came down the stairs to run into Pablo. "You must don't get no pussy," Kayla chuckled, passing Pablo coming up the stairs.

"Shut yo' big stomach ass up," Pablo shot back.

"Just hurry yo' minute-man ass up. I'm tired and my feet is swollen."

"That ain't the only thing that's swollen."

"Yeah, yo' balls for never getting no pussy," Kayla shot, then flickin' him off from the bottom of the stairs.

When Pablo entered Maliyah's room, he walked over to the bed. "I've been waiting a long time for this moment," he said, as he traced her body with his eyes. He then unzipped his True's, pulling out his already stiff dick. He stood over Maliyah, stroking his long, skinny pencil dick and getting off just by the sight of the woman that he'd been wanting ever since he first laid eyes on her that night at the club. "Give me this pussy!" he said, pulling Maliyah down to the foot of the bed. He shoved his dick inside of her, wearing no protection.

"Ooooh! It's good just like I knew it would be," he moaned, staring at Maliyah passed out in a wasted coma. He was so lost in the moment that he never no-ticed the video camera that was facing the bed in record mode.

"Oooooh! Now I see why Boss wanna wife you," he said going in deeper and deeper and feeling himself about to bust.

"Ahhhhh!!" Pablo screamed in complete bliss, shooting thick cum inside of his Boss's soon-to-be wife on candid camera. After busting the hellafied nut, he grabbed Maliyah by the face as his tongue danced in a passionate kiss with a woman that thought she was kiss-ing her husband.

"I–Baby–Love Youuuu," Maliyah mumbled in her sleep.

~~REAL TALK~~

CHAPTER 26

Listen to the wise. They lived it, and learned from it. It will make sense once it's too late. "Only if I would have listened," is what you will say.

"Rise and shine party animal. There's a lot that has to be done today," Maria said, pulling the curtains back and awakening me with the bright California sun shining through the window. "Here comes the bride ... Here comes the bride."

"Maria please! The wedding isn't until tomorrow. Now get out, I have a bad headache." I shot, throwing the blanket over my head.

"I came prepared. I have something just for that hangover. I don't need the bride getting cranky on me. Take these Tylenols and drink this hot tea."

I peeked my head from under the blanket. "You just not gonna leave are you?"

"Uh-uhh," she said, standing over me holding the tea and pills.

"Lord! What am I gonna do with you." I grabbed the cup of tea and pills, poppin' them bitches immediately.

"Ahh–hot!!" I burned my damn tongue with the scorching tea."

"Mommie, I told you it was hot."

"Yeah hot, but not scorching, damn," I shot with a sizzling tongue.

"I'm sorry Mommie," she apologized, trying to hold back a laugh.

"Mmm-hmm, whatevea. Where's Don? Did he leave?"

"When I came in at five o'clock this morning he wasn't here."

"This makes the second day that he's been out doing God knows what."

"Mommie, I don't know what to tell you. We have had this same talk on numerous occasions. After tomorrow there's no turning back."

I had my head down listening to Maria, and my thong on the floor beside the bed caught my attention. *Wait, he was here,* I thought. "Maria, are you sure Donnie wasn't here?"

"Yes, I'm sure."

Maybe I was dreaming. It got to the point where I'd make love with Don more in my dreams than in real life. The dreams were getting more and more intense because I could have sworn Don was kissing me last night like he used to when we first met.

"Mommie, listen to me."

OH MY GOD. I DONE GOT HER STARTED.

"God has blessed us women with womanly intuition. Whatever your gut feeling is telling you, nine times out of ten it's right. Sometimes it takes for us to have to see it with our own eyes. I was just like that when I was your age, couldn't nobody tell me nothing. Friends and family would tell me all the time that they've seen my husband with other women. I'd listen but somehow we fool ourselves to think; they're lying, they just don't wanna see me happy. What y'all young kids say now, they're haters. And sometimes that can be the case, but you have to consider the source. Look Mommie, I have told you all that I can tell you. It's time for you to open up those beautiful eyes and see for yourself. Dig a little deeper, so you can know exactly what you're getting yourself into. Follow your man, check his phone, double back home, pay more attention to the bank accounts, and one last thing and this is the most important of them all— put you some money off to the side for a rainy day, instead of buying all those expensive pocket books."

"Pocket books," I smiled. "My mom calls purses pocketbooks."

"Have you talked to your parents?"

"Maria, every time I call they don't answer."

"So, they don't know about the wedding?"

"No."

Maria sighed, shaking her head from side to side. "There's no love like the love from your parents. Mommie, you're a smart girl, you know what you have to do. Get yourself a savings account because ain't nothing a for-sure thing, including marriage. I just don't wanna see you make the same mistake that I've made. Look at me, I thought I had a for-sure thing, and now I'm a maid. So, like I said before. After tomorrow there's no turning back. Mommie, please make sure this is what you want."

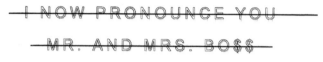

CHAPTER 27

July 6, 2010

"You look amazing" is all I kept repeating to myself as I stood looking in the mirror. I was stunning in my ivory-white Vera Wang gown draped in Neil Lane diamonds with an up-do of loose curls.

The day had finally come. The nervousness outweighed the happiness. Everyone was running around like crazy as I stood in anticipation with so much on my mind: the talk with Maria, Don—the selfish bastard that I'd be spending the rest of my life with—and the hoes that I knew he was pushing dick in on the side.

For the past couple of nights, Don had been staying out all night. It had to be someone else. That womanly intuition shit that Maria was spittin' made a lot of sense. But when I called Don out on it, he came with some bullshit like always. I was trippin'. It was just my insecurity getting the best of me. Let him tell it, he wanted to give me my space before the wedding. What sense does that make? That was the best he could come up with.

I scanned the room looking at all the expensive bottles of champagne from DP to Ace of Spades, the bling that I was glitzing in, and the pack of excited purple-dress-wearing bridesmaids to see no Kayla.

"Rhonda!" I called for my hair stylist. She came right away in her purple bridesmaid dress with a comb in her hand.

"Aww, you look so pretty." She smiled with tears in her eyes, and went straight to my head, making sure a curl wasn't out of place.

"Stop Rhonda, look me in the eyes," I said raising one eyebrow with my hand on my hip. I knew if I wanted to get the truth out of Rhonda I had to give her eye contact.

"What Maliyah? Why you looking at me like that?"

"What's going on? Why is the wedding planner walking around looking like a question mark, and you better tell me."

"Nothing, I don't know what you're talking about," Rhonda said, going right back to picking at my curls. I backed away looking her in the face, and her left eye started twitching, which meant she was lying.

"Rhonda! You better start talking."

"Maliyah, don't panic. They told me not to tell you that Kayla is a no-show. I was supposed to do her hair like an hour ago. They're stalling the ceremony for a little while longer to see if she shows up."

"What! And nobody told me! This is supposed to be the happiest day of my life!" I burst into tears.

"Calm down Liyah."

"Fuck that! Give me the phone so I can call this bitch!" I yelled.

The wedding planner, Cynthia, came walking toward us. "Debra! Come touch up the bride's makeup," Cynthia said then looking over at Rhonda. "Why did you tell her?"

"Because she needed to know. Shit, if this was your wedding would you wanna be left in the dark?" Rhonda said, reminding Cynthia why she didn't like to work with black folks because of the ignorance.

Cynthia gave Rhonda a dirty look, then turned her attention back to the bride. "Calm down, Mrs. Boss. I'll try calling her. Just sit down and get your makeup touched up, remember this is your day."

"No! I'ma call her!" I picked up the bottom of my Vera Wang gown and stormed over to my phone. Dialing Kayla's number, her phone went straight to voicemail. Tapping my Jimmy Choo, I waited for the beep to leave her a message, as tears ran down my cheeks.

"Kayla! I know good-goddamn-well you're not pulling no bullshit. Get your fuckin' ass over here now!" I ended the call, slamming the phone on the table. "I can't believe this shit! She was complaining yesterday at dress rehearsal about how big she looked in her dress, but I didn't think nothing of it. How could Kayla do this to me?" I cried.

"Aww, look at my daughter in-law. She looks so gorgeous," Don's mother, Sonia, entered the room to see me in tears. "Wait a minute, who told her?" the diva questioned with her hand on her hip. Everyone in the room pointed at Rhonda.

"Aww, y'all scandalous, just throw me up under the bus. Sonia," she asked, "what was I supposed to do?"

"Shut yo' mouth like I told you to do. You know what, the damage is already done. Everybody get out! Give me a minute with my daughter in-law," Sonia shot with attitude.

Sonia was a plastic-surgery mess. I met her once a few months back, around the time Tia had passed. Her high-maintenance diva attitude was very intimidating. But once I got to know her, she was alright. Sonia helped out a lot with the wedding. She worked hand-and-hand with the wedding planner like she was the one getting married. She was more excited than I was. I watched as the woman that was still stuck in her prime locked the door behind everyone that she just kicked out of the room.

Don's father had fucked this lady's head up. Through all the plastic surgery and expensive trinkets she was a miserable mess. I looked at Sonia as she walked back my way and I saw me in the next twenty years.

"Maliyah, we need to have a woman-to-woman talk. My son loves you. Yeah, the little hoodrat didn't show, but at least now you know who your real friends are. But don't let this ruin your day. You have 250 guests out there waiting to see a beautiful bride walk down the aisle. Now stop that crying."

"Mama Sonia, if your son really loves me, why is he sleeping with other women?"

"Baby listen, you're sitting in this gorgeous wedding dress worrying about some lil hoodrat that would die to be in your shoes right now. You have a man out there willing to give up everything for you. Do you know I went through the same thing with Donnie's father? All the other women, staying out all night, but I never let them other women come between what I had going on. Your husband is rich and handsome. What woman in her right mind wouldn't want him?" Sonia sat in front of me trying to talk me into the same miserable life that she lived with Donnie's father.

I pondered for a second, thinking about all the bitches that was waiting in line to take my spot and shine. *He won't never floss on me with the next bitch.* I fell for the okey-doke. I passed on being happy for worrying about the next bitch.

"So, you ready to go marry yo' man?"

I nodded my head, wearing a Kool-Aid smile.

"Okay, let all the haters back in there wish they were you," Sonia said, opening the door.

Cynthia led the pack of purple dress brides-maids. She looked over at me, and gave me the thumbs, up waiting for a sign. I shot her a thumbs-up and nodded my head. Cynthia sighed in relief, clapping her hands together. "Okay, everyone. Places. We're having a wedding." Cynthia snapped her fingers at Debra, signaling for her to touch up my makeup. Debra came pronto, dolled up in a purple bridesmaid dress, with her MAC make-up case in tow.

$ $ $

After all the chaos, Don and I were married in a Marina Del Ray venue that looked like a castle with a moat. I walked down the aisle as Charlie Wilson serenaded the lyrics of his song *You Are.* With my sweaty palms I carried a purple calla lily bouquet that coordinated with the boutonnière pinned to Don's Prada tux. Don blew me a kiss and a tear escaped from my eye as I awaited the privilege of becoming Mrs. Boss.

Two hundred fifty tearful guests watched as Donnie and I recited our vows in a purple-and-white themed celebration. From the wedding to a lavish reception, the DJ spinned hip-hop and R&B, as Don and I danced our first dance as a married couple to Beyoncé's *Dangerously In Love.* Don held on to me as we stared into each other's eyes. I felt as if no one else was in the room.

"I love you Mrs. Boss," Don whispered in my ear.

"I love you, too, Mr. Boss."

"Wifey, I'ma put a baby in you tonight. I wanna start on our family," Don said wiping the tears of joy from my eye and then planting a kiss on my lips. As Don's lips touched mine, I took this time to say a quick prayer to God, asking him to transform Don's mind and heart. I hoped Sonia was right about Don's willingness to give up everything for me, because this man that looked me in the eyes was the Boss that I wanted to spend the rest of my life with.

~~FULL MOON~~

CHAPTER 28
DON/ MR BO$$

Don glanced over at Maliyah lying beside him in bed, snoring with her mouth wide open. The loud snoring let him know that she was in a deep sleep. He eased out of bed, grabbed his cell phone and headed downstairs to his office.

Don sat in his leather chair and turned the TV on ESPN Sports Center. Firing up a cigar, he powered on his phone that been off since the day before. *A nigga straight married,* Don laughed to himself at the thought. He glanced down at his iPhone sitting on his desk. It displayed ten voicemail messages. He checked the messages. "You have ten urgent voicemail messages." Don's ear was put to the phone. *Urgent?* he said to himself. His first message was from Kayla. When he heard her screaming, he knew it was serious.

"Ahhh! Donnie you fuckin' bastard! Answer the phone! I'm in labor having our fuckin' baby! Ahhhh! This shit hurts! While you're jumping the broom with that bitch

I'm here in pain! I hope both of you mutha-fucka's trip and fall! Get your fuckin' ass up to this hospital now!" Don ended the call without listening to the other messages. He grabbed his car keys and stormed out of his office to run into Maria.

"Boss, you guys bags are all packed."

"Okay tell Mrs. Boss I'll be right back. I had to go handle some important business," he said, running out of the front door in a hurry.

$ $ $
MALIYAH/ MRS. BOSS

"Maria, he didn't mention where he was going?" I asked, furious.

"No, he just said something about going to handle some business."

"I knew it! This muthafucka will never change!" I barked, storming over to the bar, grabbing a bottle of Patron and taking it to the head. I paced back and forth, blowing up Don's phone to get no answer. Our flight to Costa Rica for our honeymoon was for two o'clock. I glanced at the time displayed on my phone screen and it was now twelve o'clock.

"Mommie, maybe something important really did come up," Maria said, trying to calm me down, but wasn't doing nothing but making matters worse.

"More important than our honeymoon! And if that's the case, why not answer and tell me some-thing!"

Maria shrugged her shoulders. She didn't know whether to say something or just stand there and listen. "Boss does a lot of things that I don't agree with. Now, I'm not taking no sides, but I just don't see him not com-ing back for you guys' honeymoon."

"Maria, are we talking about the same selfish bas-tard? I'm glad to know you got faith in the sonof-abitch!"

Less than ten minutes later, my phone was ringing with the name Hubby flashing across the screen. I couldn't answer the sonofabitch fast enough. "Where the hell are you!" I answered, instead of a hello at my boiling point.

"Ma, calm down. Listen, something very import-ant has come up. It's life or death. We're gonna have to leave tomorrow or the following day. I'll get Maria to han-dle the travel plans."

"Donnie! This is our fuckin' honeymoon!"

"Maliyah, stop acting like an inconsiderate bitch! I run a business here, and my money comes first! Go take a look in the mirror. All that fly-ass expensive shit you're wearing is bought with money, my money! And that shit don't grow on trees!"

"An inconsiderate bitch! Fuck yo' money, and fuck you! I regret ever marrying yo' triflin ass. Go to hell Don!" I barked into the phone before hanging up in his face.

"Oh, you just don't see him not coming back for our honeymoon? Well see it, and believe it. Be-cause the muthafucka is trying to reschedule our honeymoon," I said to Maria, standing in front of me in disbelief.

$ $ $

Later that night, I sat on the couch with a box of Kleenex crying my heart out. Melanie Fiona's *It Kills Me* was on repeat. I was in a daze sitting in front of an 8-ball of White-Girl. Something had to give. I'd be damned if I continued to live like this. Did God hear my supplication to transform Don's mind and heart? The day after our wedding and he went right back to his same ol' routine of staying out all night.

I sat in front of the fireplace racking my brain, try-ing to figure out what I'd done wrong to make my hus-band wanna leave me home alone on our honeymoon night. It was time for me to take Maria's advice and dig a little bit deeper. I grabbed my cell phone dialing up En-terprise Rental Car.

I should have listened to the wise, is all I thought, but it was better late than never.

$ $ $

Dig a little bit deeper, so you can know exactly what you're getting yourself into. Follow your man. Maria's voice was on repeat in my head. I couldn't sleep until I found out who the bitch was that Don was staying out with. She had to be a very important bitch with that VIP "VERY IRRESISTIBLE PUSSY" to make this nigga put our honeymoon off.

When Don came strolling in the house the next morning, I killed that sonofabitch with kindness. I even gave him some pussy. He hopped in the shower, got dressed and went on his way. I sat on the balcony waving him off. As soon as he got into his Benz, I ran down the stairs, getting the rental car keys from Maria.

"It's a white Camry parked down the hill."

"What are you talking about? You coming with me. You have to drive my car back. Now bring ya' ass." I snatched the car keys out of Maria's hand.

"Oh, okay." My road dawg followed behind me. We hopped in my whip, driving to the rental car that was parked down the road. I exited the car in a hurry, so I wouldn't lose Don.

"Be careful Mommie, and remember to drive at a far enough distance so he won't see you," Maria yelled out the window. I reached in the backseat, grabbing the fitted cap, and putting it on top of my slicked pony. I was incognito, following behind Don with my heart beating out of my chest.

"Please don't let it be another woman," I said to myself driving in silence. I was so nervous I didn't even turn on the radio. Don pushed it to the limit on the 405 freeway. I kept up with his ass in the piece of shit Toyota.

Don finally pulled up to a house in Culver City. I parked down the street, slouched down in the seat. Bzzt ... Bzzt ... The vibration of my cell phone startled the shit out of me. When I glanced down at the screen, Kayla's picture flashed across the screen indicating that she was calling. "This bitch!" I shot. I'd been avoiding her call all day. That shit she pulled with my wedding wasn't cool, and now she wanted to call like nothing never happened. Fuck her.

What are you waiting for? Get out the car nigga, I said to myself, staring out the window at Don sitting in his car in the driveway of this unknown house.

Bzzt ... Kayla was starting to get on my damn nerves calling back-to-back. "What? Lose my num-ber!" I screamed into the phone. As I was about to hang up, I heard her say. "I had Destiny!"

"What?" I put the phone back to my ear.

"I had Destiny the day of your wedding. That's why I didn't show up. Maliyah, you already know, I wouldn't have missed your wedding for nothing. But them labor pains kicked in, and gurrrl it was a wrap. I was discharged out the hospital early this morning. I've been trying to call you to tell you, you a god-mommy. Did you get my messages?"

She had the baby! Why the hell didn't I think of that? I'm such a selfish bitch.

"No, I haven't checked them. Kay, I wanna see her. Who does she look like? I hope she don't look like Pee Wee."

"She looks like her fine-ass momma."

"Oh my god, poor baby," I said looking out the window in stalker-mode, with my eyes glued to Don. He finally exited the car, walking up to the door. He shocked the hell out of me when he opened the door with a key. My heart started beating as tears formed in my eyes. A key wasn't a good sign.

"Maliyah, let me call you right back!" Kayla said trying to rush me off the phone.

"Make sure you do. I wanna see the baby," I said.

"O–kay," Kayla stuttered. "Where's my baby?" a familiar voice questioned from the other end of the phone. I could be trippin' but that sounded just like Don.

"Kay ..." I said into the phone but it was too late because she had already hung up.

$ $ $

For the next hour, I sat stalking this unknown house. I was determined to find out who lived in this house that my husband had a key to. I was beginning to get restless, but damn sure wasn't leaving until I got the information that I came for.

When the door opened, I sat up in the seat. It was like everything was moving in slow motion. Staring out the window without blinking once, scared that I might miss something. My eyes laid on Don exiting the house carrying an infant seat as Kayla followed behind him. I blinked to make sure my eyes weren't playing tricks on me. *I can't believe this shit!* My body had frozen as tears ran down my red cheeks. As much as I wanted to move, my body was in a state of shock. *This bitch! So Kayla, you're the bitch on the side!* I shot to myself, waiting for Aston Kutcher to jump the fuck out, because I just knew that I was being Punk'd. I ain't never been to jail, but I was going today because I was about to pull a fuckin' nutty.

I started the ignition, following behind Don. I couldn't stop crying. I gripped the steering wheel with my trembling hands. If the baby wouldn't have been in the car I would have rammed the rental right in the back of Don's Benz.

Don pulled into a nearby CVS. My blood was boiling as I watched Kayla exit the car and sashay into the store. I tried to get a good look at what she was carrying. It looked like film. Not giving a fuck if my cover was blown, I parked and exited the car. Once I made it in the drug store, I looked over at the photo center and I was right. It was film because the home wrecking bitch was at the photo center talking to the sales clerk. I waited until Kayla exited the store and made my way over to the photo center.

"How may I help you? Are you okay?" the nosy gay guy asked, poppin' on some bubble gum all up in my business. I could imagine my face was probably red as hell from crying, which was a dead give-a-way because I knew the faggot wasn't no physic. The hurt was written all over my face.

"I'm fine. My friend Kayla just left."

"Oh yeah, with the cute shoes. Let me see your shoes." The he-she peeked over the counter. "Oh yeah, y'all are friends. Gurl, yo' shoes are cute too, YSL right?"

"Hmmm." *Damn he's a true fag.*

"I have her film right here. Let me guess, she decided to get the pics back in an hour instead of tomorrow, huh?"

"As a matter of fact she did. How did you know?" I played along.

"Because who wouldn't want their baby shower pictures back ASAP? I told her. Us women are so indecisive at times."

"Oh, before I forget, she said to get doubles too."

"Okay, that's gonna up the price a little. It's gonna be $18.00."

"Run it. I'm gonna wait." This was the longest hour ever, waiting for the film to get developed. I could not shake the vision of Don, Kayla and the baby. I sat by the pharmacy tapping my YSL pump anxiously. I glanced down at my heart shaped diamond face Jojo Rodeo, and it had been 59 minutes exactly. I got up, and did it moving toward the photo center. I figured it should take me a minute to get over there.

"Hey doll face. You're right on time," the sales clerk said, switching harder than me over to the cash register. I paid for the pics and got on. Walking back to the car, I prepared myself for the worst. Once I made it to the car, I took a deep breath then opened the envelope of pictures. The first picture I laid eyes on was of Don hugging Kayla from behind with his hands on her pregnant stomach. My heart dropped. I began to cry uncontrollably as I thumbed through the rest of the photos that was of a secret baby shower. It damn sure wasn't the one I had thrown for Kayla because Don wasn't in attendance. The cheating bastard was in every last picture of this baby shower. I was crying so hard, I started to get nauseated.

"My husband! This Bitch! A baby!" I shouted, hitting the steering wheel. This was all too much to grasp. *Don is the father!* It hit me. It was time to get stupid, but first stop at the bank, ching ching.

$ $ $

I had to make a pit stop at the gas station. When the signal started flashing on the dashboard and making this annoying-ass buzzing sound indicating that the car was low on fuel, I pulled up to the pump.

"Hey beautiful," some asshole said, pumping his gas.

"Fuck off!" I shot, hurt beyond words, taking it out on buddy in male-bashing mode. I went into the gas station, trying to hold in tears long enough to get gas, and get back in the car to continue to let it all out.

"Fill up on pump seven," I said, paying for the gas. I looked to the left and saw a big red gas can. I smiled with an evil thought. "I want this too," I said with a devilish grin.

On the way out I got a few hand claps as I passed. Niggas tooted their horns, and yelled perverted shit out the window, but I ignored them clowns. Toting the bright red gas can, I was on a mission with one thing on my mind, fucking Kayla and Don up. I tried hard to keep it G, but the betrayal of a friend, and being played by a man that I truly loved got the best of me. Tears started to flow down my cheeks as I put the nozzle in the gas tank. I sat in the car trying to locate some Kleenex in my Chloe tote.

"I thought that was you. Long time no see."

When I glanced up, it was Terry. "Are you okay? Why are you crying?" he asked with concern in his voice.

"I'm fine," I said a little bit embarrassed, wiping my tears with my hand.

"It doesn't look like it."

"Really, I'm okay!" I shot, getting a little defensive. I caught Terry looking at the pictures in the passenger seat. I quickly flipped them over, and sat my purse on the seat.

"Why you never called me?"

"Terry, I just recently got married." I raised my hand flashing my rock.

"Are you happy?"

"What do you mean am I happy?"

"You just don't have that newlywed glow to you. To tell the truth, you look miserable."

The pump clicked right on time. I stood to remove the nozzle, and Terry walked around to the other side of the car. "I got it," he said being a gentleman.

"Wait, I have to fill this up," I said, unscrewing the top off the gas can. Terry looked at me, then at the gas can, confused.

"What you need? Never mind." He asked no questions, instead he filled the can with gasoline. "I don't know if you're trying to egg me on with the "I'm- married" story. But this has to mean something. This makes the third time that we ran into each other. Maybe God is trying to tell us something, or show us something. Maliyah, if you're not gonna call me just keep it one hundred percent with yo' boy. So, I can stop running women off, telling them I already met the woman of my dreams."

Sounds good. Niggas make me sick. "Terry, to tell you the truth, I don't think I'll be the same after today. I'm through with love, dating, the whole nine. With that said, I have to go. I need to catch the bank before it closes."

"Okay, I respect that. But can I leave you with something to think about?"

"Go head."

"All men aren't the same. For every heartless man that breaks your heart, God is just taking you on a journey, preparing you to know a good man when he comes along. And with that said Maliyah, you're too beautiful to settle for less, or to be alone. Now, where do you want me to put this. In the front or back seat?"

"The back is good." I unlocked the back door for Terry to put the gas can full of gasoline on the floor.

"Think about what I told you."

"Okay." *Hmmm. Now get the hell away from my car with that bullshit.*

$ $ $

Terry watched as Maliyah pulled off. He grabbed his Nextel out of his pocket. With the phone to his ear, he anxiously waited to hear the person come to the line.

Once he heard a hello, he said into the phone. "We can't wait until the morning. It has to happen now."

~~HIT'EM UP STYLE~~

CHAPTER 29
MALIYAH

I handed the withdrawal slip to the bank teller along with my ID and Don's credit card.

"How would you like your cash?" the teller asked.

"Big faces please," the young girl smiled.

"Ma'am for this amount I have to get my supervisor to approve the transaction."

"That's fine," I said. I stood patiently, waiting with Maria's voice programmed in my head. *One last thing, and this is the most important of them all. Put some money off to the side for a rainy day. Get a savings account.*

"Mrs. Boss, you're withdrawing sixty thousand dollars out of this account ending in 1718?" the bank supervisor asked, interrupting my train of thought.

"Yes."

"Okay, step to the side while we get this ready for you. Would you like someone to walk you to your car?"

"Yes please." After about ten minutes, the teller was calling me over to her window and handing me a money bag full of cash.

"Tony will be walking with you."

I looked over at Tony the security guard's frail behind. *Who was he supposed to protect? I could kick his ass,* I thought.

Exiting the Washington Mutual Bank, Tony followed behind me. Once we made it to the car he looked over at me wearing no dentures, just all gums and said, "It must be a good feeling to have all that money."

"Not at all, a lot of pain came along with this," I said, getting into the car and pulling off. God always seems to find a way to remind you that it's always someone that has it a lot worse than you do. I sat at a standstill as a funeral passed by. It was a big one too. I thought about Tia, and the pain I felt on the day of her funeral. I felt the family's pain, losing a loved one is the worse pain a person can experience.

The last car of the funeral went by, and it looked just like my Aunt Carla's Nissan. It wasn't the car itself that stood out, it was the two Laker flags she kept on each side of the car.

Bzzt ... Bzzt ... I glanced at my phone screen in disgust to see Kayla's picture. I was past the feeling-sorry-for-myself stage. I was ready to get even and make them two scandalous individuals feel the same pain that I was feeling.

"Hello." I answered the phone like I knew nothing.

"Hey, god-mommy. Where you at?"

"Leaving Target," I lied.

"What new CD came out today? Because I already know that's what you went for."

I had to think quick. "I went to go get another Trina CD, *Hot Commodity* kept skipping. I can't have that, you know that's the one that bang the hardest on the CD."

"When you going home?"

"I should be there in an hour or so."

"Okay, I'ma bring the baby so you can see her. Call Alice from the Brady Bunch and tell her that you're expecting me," she laughed.

But I didn't find shit funny, and she won't either once she gets to my house.

$ $ $

"Just calm down Mommie! Please talk to me!" Maria followed behind a mad black woman. I had all of Don's expensive clothing, loafers and sneakers in my Jacuzzi style tub soaked in bleach.

"I got something for this muthafucka! He got a real bitch fucked up!" I barked, out of breath, but it didn't slow me down. I was in full-blown beast mode. Maria was on my heels like dead skin. "Mommie! What happened? Just please think this through before you do something that you will regret!" Maria stopped me in my tracks trying to talk some sense into me.

"Maria, I like you, but if you get in my way, you can get it too! I'm gonna ask you one last time to get out of my way! You don't wanna get caught in the cross fire! This ain't got shit to do with you!!"

Maria seen the rage and fury in my eyes. She took my advice to get the fuck outta my way. She threw her hands up and stepped to the side. I stormed down the stairs to Don's office. *OUT OF BOUNDS MY ASS MUTHAFUCKA!* I made my way to his desk. I threw papers everywhere, when I stumbled over a Lexus dealership invoice, that didn't do shit but add fuel to the fire. *SO, HE BOUGHT THE BITCH THE FUCKIN' LEXUS!* I opened the top drawer to spot a nine millimeter and what I was looking for. "Bingo!" I shot when my eyes laid on Don's ring of car keys. I grabbed the keys and put the pistol on my waistline feeling like a true gangsta bitch. Maria came to the door.

"Mommie, Kayla's here."

"Right on time. Let that bitch in!"

I waited until I heard Kayla enter the house. I removed the pistol from my waistline and exited Don's office.

"Hey god-mommy. Come see our beautiful little girl. Don't she look like me?" Kayla said, being a proud parent. Maria stood over Kayla looking at the baby. The look that was displayed on Maria's face told it all. I made my way over to Kayla and the baby.

"Are you on your period?" Kayla asked.

I sucked my teeth before saying, "No!"

Kayla handed Destiny to me. I took the beautiful bundle of joy into my arms. When I looked at her, all I seen was Don. She was his twin. Staring down at the precious baby that didn't ask to be brought here in this fucked up situation, I cried, as my whole body started to shake.

"You're such a cry baby," Kayla shot.

"Hold her." I handed Destiny over to Maria. Then with no warning I came with a left hook knocking the dog-shit out of Kayla.

"What the fuck is wrong with you?" she asked, holding her face.

"You scandalous bitch!" I balled my fist, striking her with a mighty blow to the face.

"Ahhhh!" she screamed, as blood slung from her mouth. She lost her balance falling to the ground, and that's when I lost it. I blacked-the-fuck-out, get-ting on top of her, and repeatedly slammed her head to the ground.

"You fucked Don behind my back! And had a baby by the nigga! I thought we were better than that! I trusted you!" I barked, furious.

Kayla was trying to fight back, but she didn't stand a chance to the beast in me. Maria held the baby, and still tried to stop me. "Mommie, that's enough! Get off of her! You're gonna kill the girl!!"

"Good! Fuck this dirty bitch!"

"Please–Please," Kayla pleaded. "Maliyah, get off of me–Please!"

Maria sat Destiny in her infant seat and dragged me off of Kayla. I kept breaking loose from Maria, running right back to Kayla, and stomping that ho to the ground. Maria used all her might to hold me back. "Kayla, get the baby and leave!"

Kayla stood staggering with a bloody face. "I–got you!" she shot.

"Kayla shut up! Get the baby and leave, before I let her loose."

Kayla made her way to the door with the car seat and diaper bag in tow. Stopping in her tracks, she glanced over at me with her bloody face. "Don't get mad at me because yo' man chose me! Evidently you wasn't doing something right! Don't hate me, hate the game and the nigga!" she shot before exiting the house.

"Let me go Maria! Let me get this bitch!!"

"Mommie, just let her go, you got her good!"

I couldn't even get mad at Maria, because if she wouldn't have stopped me, I probably would've killed the bitch.

$ $ $

DON/ MR. BO$$

On the other side of town at Millennium Barber Shop, a plushed-out Laker-themed hang-out spot, and resource to everything illegal, Don sat in the barber chair getting lined up while talking shit.

"That bitch got a fat ass!" Tank shot, drooling over Nicki Minaj in her new video on BET's 106 & Park.

"Nigga, that shit is fake," Pablo added, staring at the plasma screen mounted on the wall.

"Hell yeah, fake as that pinkie ring homie got on right there!" Don shot a lug at a nigga that was shooting dice in the packed barber shop.

"I don't give a fuck. She's still bad, and she goes both ways. Perfect bitch to have on yo' team, a straight freak. I'll knock her down."

"Nigga you'll fuck anything," Mink chimed in, with his eyes glued to the dice.

"I wouldn't fuck yo' baby momma," Tank shot back, and everybody in the shop burst in laughter.

$ $ $

Outside of the barber shop, Kayla pulled up to a pack of niggas posted-up on a smoke break. She reached in the glove compartment grabbing a DVD.

"Ay, I got some fire porno's fo' y'all. West Coast freaky bitches gone wild."

"Word, how much?" one of the horn-dawg niggas asked, hyped.

"It's a promotion free-bee. I'm trying to pro-mote and make it hot."

"You brought it to the right place Shawty." The nigga walked up to the car, grabbing the DVD from Kayla.

"I told that bitch I got something fo' her ass! She fucked with the wrong bitch!" Kayla said to herself as she pulled off.

$ $ $

"Ain't no kids up in here?" The barber shop owner looked around the shop. "Aight, I got some-thing for y'all fellas," he said with a huge smile. "West Coast freaky bitches gone wild."

"Hell yeah!" the niggas shot in excitement. Every-one's eyes were glued to the 52-inch plasma on the wall.

"Nigga, dis better not be no bullshit," Mink shot.

"Hell naw, look he fuckin' the shit out of ole girl," the owner added.

"It looks like he's fuckin' a corpse," a customer shot.

"Hold up, nigga that looks like you!" the owner shot, looking over at Pablo, who was standing looking up at the TV in shock.

Don stood to his feet, walking toward the TV to make sure his eyes weren't seeing things.

"Ooooh! It's good just like I knew it would be ... Ooooh! Now I see why Boss wanna wife you."

Everyone in the shop looked at Don, then back at Pablo.

"I– Baby–Love Youuu," came from the TV.

"You muthafucka!" Don barked, heated.

"Boss, it's not what you think," Pablo stuttered, scared to death.

Don walked over to Tank, who was standing in disbelief. "Give me your burner!"

"What?"

"Nigga, give me your goddamn burner!!"

Tank did as told, handing Don his pistol off of his hip. Don struck Pablo in the head with the butt of the gun. He fell to the ground with blood oozing from his dome.

"B–oss," Pablo stuttered. "Man I'm sorry, it's not what you think. Please don't kill me," he pleaded. As Don aimed the gun to his head. "You fucked my wife nigga!"

"Don, calm down. Give me the gun," the shop owner tried to talk some sense into a deranged Don, who was foaming at the mouth.

"Tank, get the gun from him," Mink said.

"Nigga you crazy, you get it. That nigga won't kill me."

"You fucked my wife! You bitch-ass-nigga!! You won't fuck another piece of pussy again!" Don barked before pulling the trigger and shooting Pablo in the dick.

"Ahhhhh!" Pablo screamed from the pain.

"That feels good nigga! Huh?" Don pulled the trigger again blowing Pablo's brains out, killing him in the packed barber shop. Leaving Pablo stretched out with his brains splattered on the ground, Don exited the barber shop in a hurry as Tank and Mink followed behind him.

$ $ $

MALIYAH/ MRS. BO$$

I sat on the balcony looking down at Don's Ferrari in flames; and the Cadillac and Beemer that was parked not too far from the burning vehicle with "YOU ARE THE FATHER" carved in the exterior. I also busted the windows out with a crow bar, adding a little extra touch. I never understood why women fucked up niggas' rides. Now I know. It's a wonderful feeling and the sight afterwards is even better.

When I seen Don's Benz driving toward the house in full speed, I rushed down the stairs toting the nine millimeter, ready for war. Standing in my Charlie's Angels pose, I aimed the pistol to the door, ready to empty the clip on my husband. Don entered the house to a gun aimed at his head. Our eyes locked and I immediately burst into tears looking in the face of a man that vowed to love me as his wife as long as he shall live.

"What the fuck!" he jumped, startled.   "Congratulations on the baby, Daddy. Why Don? Why? I thought you loved me. How could you fuck my best friend?"

"Boss!" Maria ran toward us out of breath. The poor lady gave up on me a long time ago when she realized she couldn't tame the beast in me. "I tried to stop her Boss from burning your cars. The fire department is on the way!" Maria said, then gazed over at me. "Mommie, please put the gun down! You guys can talk about this. This is what married people do, talk out their problems," Maria continued, playing referee with the hood Mr. and Mrs. Smith.

"It's all good Maria, fuck the cars! This bitch knows I'm rich!" He walked toward me with bloodshot eyes. "We got bigger shit to deal with. Like you fucking Pablo in our bed you nasty bitch!!!" he said through clenched teeth. I cocked back.

"Muthafucka, play wit-it! You better stay put if you wanna live!" I said, holding the gun with my trembling hand. I couldn't believe this nigga. He tried to accuse me of the same thing that he was guilty of. Now, the naive

Mrs. Boss would have went for that turning the tables bullshit, but Maliyah was too smart for that shit.

"The fire department is here!" Maria said, running out the front door when she heard the sound of sirens.

"Shoot me bitch! Shoot the nigga that made you! You ain't shit without me. The name Mrs. Boss made you who you are!!"

A voice in my head was saying, *Shoot the bastard,* but my heart wouldn't let me do it.

"Bitch, you ain't got the heart!" Don shot, giving me that famous back hand and causing me to drop the pistol. Instead of seeing stars from the slap to the face, I seen every type of law enforcement there was, rushing into the house.

"Get down on the goddamn ground now!" Every bit of fifty alphabet boys shouted wearing windbreakers and bullet proof vest that said FBI, ATF, DEA, and LAPD. Me and Don did as told, getting on the ground. My heart was beating out of my chest.

"Put your hands up!!!!" they yelled, with pistols drawn out on us. "Cuff 'em!" an officer said with authority. A lady cop came pronto, putting my new Tiffany & Co. bracelets on my small wrist.

"That hurts! They too tight! What am I going to jail for?" I shot to the rough lady cop.

"Johnson, not so tight. You can loosen them a little," a familiar voice said. I turned to see who it was, and I couldn't believe what my eyes was seeing. It was Terry, wearing an FBI bullet-proof vest.

"Terry! You sonofabitch!" I yelled.

"Baby, you know this pig? Don't say nothing. Remember what I told you, Dana," Don said winking his eye.

"Oh, now I'm baby. Just a second ago I was bitch. Fuck you Don!!"

"Oooh she's mad at you," Detective Daniels said, walking through the crowd of flat foots. "I've finally got you Mr. Donnie Boss," he said with a smile. Then, looking over at me, "Hey tough cookie. I told you that I'll be seeing you again."

I rolled my eyes at the fat-fuck.

"Donnie, you are going down for the murder of Jasmine Coley, Tia Cooper, and your childhood friend, Pablo, who you just gunned down over at the Barber Shop on Crenshaw."

"What! You killed Tia!"

"Baby, don't believe that shit! These punk-ass pigs are just trying to turn you against me, that's what they do. Tommy is already locked up for that."

"Mr. Boss, you did murder Ms. Cooper, and we have evidence, we're the Feds," Terry declared. "With that said, Mr. and Mrs. Boss I have a Federal warrant for your arrests," Terry continued, going straight to the blah-blah-blah bullshit that went in one ear and out the other:

"You have the right to remain silent. Anything you say can be used against you in a court of law. You have the right to an attorney. If you cannot afford legal counsel, one will be appointed to you. Have you understood your rights as they've been explained?" Terry looked at Don.

"Don't ask me shit! Ask my attorney mutha-fucka!"

Terry then looked over at me, waiting for my response. I nodded my head, as a tear fell down my cheek. "Why am I going to jail? Can you please tell me! I didn't do anything!!" *The trip overseas,* I thought, answering my own question. I began to cry uncontrollably.

"I'll help you, but you have to help yourself first. Think about Maliyah," Terry said, then glanced back over at Don. "Mr. Boss, you know all about getting the small fish to get to the big fish. I'm pretty sure your father, Goldie, schooled you on the game. I got a whole lot of guppies, you going down muthafucka!" Terry shot, looking at the federal agent who held Don by the arm. "Take his ass to the van."

"Baby! Don't fall for it. They're gonna try to talk you into snitchin'! Don't do it! Remember what I told you!" Don shouted as two federal agents escorted him to the van.

"You told me you loved me," I said, in between cries.

"I do."

"You said that, too. Don't drop the soap, Boo."

Triple Crown Publications presents ... MR AND MRS BO$$

~~EPILOGUE~~

SIX MONTHS LATER
MALIYAH

I thought about self alright. I testified against the man that made my life a living hell, Donnie Boss. He had that coming. The federal indictment was huge. Everybody went down. From all of Don's employees, to his nickel-and-dime hustlers that he fronted dope. All I gotta say about that is *WATCH WHAT YOU SAY ON THEM FUCKIN' PHONES*. The Feds even indicted Maria, but she later got off on probation. It's a few niggas that's still on the run, but the Feds will catch them, that's a fact.

MINK, TANK, And SHANE all got sentenced to 15 years.

DON got the big "L," exactly what his ass deserved.

KAYLA got four years for conspiracy, that wasn't nothing but Karma.

TOMMY was released after the charges were dropped for the murder of Tia, but the Feds picked his ass up. He also got 15 years.

HEATHER and HALLEY, the twin dummies, were both sentenced to 6 years.

TIFFANY, the informant who worked with the Feds, still ended up doing a year and a day. Don later discovered in court documents that Tiffany aka Tif, Pablo, and his right-hand man, Tank, staged the robbery in Atlanta. They were tired of being Don's yes-men. They had plans to take Don out, with his dumb-ass. So maybe it's good that the feds got his ass before his own men did.

The only good that came out of this was lil Destiny, and the lesson of the true meaning of LOVE. Terry was my blessing in disguise. God took me through all the havoc to bring me to the happiness. Remember the funeral I ran into coming out the bank? That was my mother's funeral. She died from breast cancer. Sometimes I think God took me through all of this so he could make me stronger as a young woman. He knew I wouldn't be able to handle my mother's death, so he took me away to prepare me for the pain ahead.

I stepped up to the plate and got custody of Destiny. I couldn't let her go to a foster home while her parents were in prison. She's so beautiful and looks just like Don.

"Hi, Pretty. Say god-mama," I said, holding her in my lap as I sat at my mother's grave.

Once I found out about my mother passing, I've never missed a day of going to drop off flowers at her grave. I glanced at my watch and seen it was time to meet Terry at his favorite soul food restaurant M & M's for lunch. I made sure Destiny's car seat was secure and pulled out of the Inglewood Cemetery. When I arrived at the restaurant there was my man, my blessing, my Boo. "Hey baby," he leaned in the window and kissed me.

"Hi, my other baby." He walked around to the other side of the car talking to Destiny. She just smiled. Every time she seen Terry, she would just light up. "I'm gonna go in and get us a seat."

"Okay."

I walked around to get Destiny out the back seat, and that's when I heard "Ay!"

I turned around to look in the face of the same little young gang bangin' nigga that the Feds showed me a picture of, he was supposedly some kin to Craze. The two cousins been on the run ever since. I was now standing looking in the face of America's Most Wanted Goon. He took a gun from behind his back, aiming it at my head.

"Please don't kill me! Here's my purse, take it!"

"I don't want your money! I want my homie back! You got him killed you triflin' bitch!"

"No I didn't! I don't know what you're talking about!" I said in between cries.

"You know what the fuck I'm talking about! You fucked my homie, and my cousin Craze partna Pablo on tape. Don seen it and killed him. Now I gotta stick to the G-code and kill you!"

"Please don't!" I screamed, but it was too late because the little nigga that went by the name Tiny Mac pulled the trigger, shooting me. My life flashed before my eyes the moment my body hit the pave-ment ... *Welcome to McDonald's, how may I help you? ... I found my dream man ...I'm grown ... You fucked my best friend! ... All men aren't the same ... I do ... I now pronounce you Mr. and Mrs. Boss ...*

My eyes closed.

MY DEDICATIONS

First and foremost, I would like to thank the creator. Without God nothing is possible. I will forever praise your holly name.

My mother, Michelle Collins Thank you for always being there. Through it ALL you had my back and I can't say thank you enough. I Love you Mommy Aka Oprah ☺

My Stepfather Terry Hall Aka Papa. I will always love you for being a wonderful Papa to the girls in my absence. Thank You

My Bros, Kerry "BIGG" Hall, Corry Hall, and Terry "So Cali" Hall, this is our year MPR Baby☺ I Love you guys.

To my beautiful Daughters, Kyla and Malia Carroll: Everything I do, I do it for the both of you. Mommy loves you.

To my wonderful grandmothers, Mary "Nonna" Twitty and Dorothy "Granny" Butler, Thank you for always supporting me in everything I do. I love you guys.

To all my family and friends, Anita "Fuzzi" Chamber, Carlos "Duke" Collins, Nelson Collins, Frieda Carson my #1 Facebook Fan, Fredrick Collins, Aja Chambers, Ferrari Collins, Lolita "Bossy Leo" Jennings, Kierra Collins, Nelson "Too-Too" Collins , Jodari Collins, Tamari Collins, Sean Morris, Candis Williams, Landis Hall, Dominique

Epps, Michlay, Donnie "Don Dizzle", Cornelia Brent, Alicia Collins, Carlos "CeCe" Collins, Cameronn Carson, Carla Davison, Kevin Butler, Sharon Collins, Maple Vargas, Robert Sims, Cynthia Sims, Sandra Aka Bear, Kevin Morton, Janette White, My God baby Kayla Gooden, Keithan " T-man" Gooden , Auntie Jill Butler, Jerry Butler, Michael Butler, John Bethune, Auntie Cheryl, Tara Gatlin, Allen Boyd, Brian B-Dogg Freeland, Monique Bates, Melvin Finner, Patrick Henry, Yung Walt, Rhonda, Brandon, Brian, Piggy, Monica Wright, Rodney Wright, The Ford Family, Keithan Gooden SR, Pat, Toy Jenkins, Fatty Jenkins, Valarie Jenkins, Uncle Tony, Daymeon Aka Superman, Sophie Robinson, Michelle Barker, Manual Drought, Bo, Santana Aka Crazy legs, Alejandra Castillo, LucyLu, Dino, Dream, Patrice Eubanks Canada where you at, Christina Jackson, my girl Bay from the D, Creighton Douglas, Necie Davis, Krystal Hart, Linda Kao, Travon Collins, and Reina Salgado I love you all. Anyone that I've forgot I love you all as well.

Vickie Stringer and the TCP staff, thank you for believing in me. Vickie, you have inspired me to give my all and be the best. Can't say thank you enough. Demetrius Duncan, Jim Wiggins, Esq & Jason Harrell, Thank you for being patient, and working so hard on this project. Let's get it Vickie!

To all my peeps on Lockdown, I never knew you could meet such good people in such a terrible place. Debra

Brown, my human daily bread, I love you, and you will never be forgotten. Linda Finch, You are such a good person and funny as hell, Monica Brumfield Aka Sexy Chocolate, I told you that I would not forget about your mean butt, New Orleans stand up! Uniqueka Cunningham Aka Miami's Finest, Keep yo head up and don't forget about our King of Diamonds trip, Ms. Margret, Thank you for all your kind words Powerful woman, Shannon Jones, Lakeisha Williamson, Evil Twin, Stacy Watkins, KT, Joanne Prosper, and anyone I've forgot at the FCI Tallahassee women's prison and MDC LA, keep your head up and remember this too shall pass, just have faith. The staff that never treated me like an eight digit number but still did your job, C. Rabon food service, Mr. Carter, Mr. Williams DAP, C Dawkins, S Wilson, and Ms. Henderson DAP, thank you for treating me like an human being despite my bad decisions that I've made in the past.

The Carroll Family, my BD Ryan Carroll, Sharon Walker, Tina Walker, Phillip aka Bang, Bill, and Norman Aka Chub I love you all.
All my love ones that couldn't be here, Jerry "Blue" Hall there's not a day that goes by that I don't think about all the wonderful memories on 10th Avenue, Rest in Peace

Uncle. Rochelle Coo Coo Ford, We miss you and will never forget the good times at the Pink apartments. Bo Dean, I know your looking from up above and saying that damn Kee-kee, you are truly missed, Mr. and Mrs. Anderson, Mike aka Monster, Marcel, Mr. and Mrs. Hall, I love you all R.I.P

Last but not least, hi haters you see it! BO$$

Much Love,
Lakiesha Butler

Please send all comments to:
Mrandmrsbossthenovel@gmail.com